Carma

CHAOS

OTHER BOOKS AND AUDIO BOOKS
BY JEFF DOWNS:

Heaven's Shadow

Rewind

Standoff

CHAOS

A NOVEL

Jeff Downs

Covenant Communications, Inc.

Cover image by Simon Osborne © Digital Vision/Getty Images, Inc.
Cover design by Jessica A. Warner © 2007 Covenant Communications, Inc.

Published by Covenant Communications, Inc.
American Fork, Utah

Copyright © 2007 by Jeff Downs
All rights reserved. No part of this book may be reproduced in any format or in any medium without the written permission of the publisher, Covenant Communications, Inc., P.O. Box 416, American Fork, UT 84003. This work is not an official publication of The Church of Jesus Christ of Latter-day Saints. The views expressed within this work are the sole responsibility of the author and do not necessarily reflect the position of The Church of Jesus Christ of Latter-day Saints, Covenant Communications, Inc., or any other entity.

This is a work of fiction. The characters, names, incidents, places, and dialogue are products of the author's imagination, and are not to be construed as real.

Printed in Canada
First Printing: June 2007

14 13 12 11 10 09 08 07   10 9 8 7 6 5 4 3 2 1

ISBN 978-1-59811-158-3

*This book is dedicated to all of my students—
both past and present.*

*Each one of you has been
both a student and a teacher to me;
it's what I believe education is all about.*

PROLOGUE

The young blonde reporter, dressed in a no-nonsense blue-gray business ensemble, sat up a little straighter behind the news counter, her expression more dour than before. "In other news tonight, Officer Jake Wellington, a fourteen-year veteran of the Denver Police Department, was shot dead last night in Montebello while investigating what an anonymous caller had referred to as a 'drug house.'"

Footage of that drug house now replaced the reporter's image as she continued with the story.

"There have been complaints about the abandoned apartment building before. Homeless transients have occasionally used the condemned five-story building for shelter."

Quick interior shots of clothing and garbage strewn around haphazardly were shown next—clear signs of someone having once lived there.

"When an anonymous caller reported having witnessed the selling of drugs, officers were sent to investigate."

The blonde reporter's image returned, the head shot of a police officer filling the upper right-hand corner of the screen. "Officer Jake Wellington, the father of two, was surprised by a gunman hiding behind a door on the second floor."

The officer's portrait was suddenly replaced by the image of a police squad car with a set of blood-red cross hairs superimposed on top of it.

"Officer Wellington is the fourth officer to die in the line of duty in the last two months, and an intense hunt is now on for his killer . . ."

CHAPTER 1

It was the end of the day—Wednesday. I had begun the day teaching eighth graders the wonders of intransitive verbs, tried to teach a group of seventh graders in pre-algebra—again—the difference between a rational and irrational number, and had rounded out the day with a computer class followed by two classes in wood shop.

When the day had finally come to an end, I immediately rolled up my long sleeves, loosened my loud tie, and made my way to the teachers' workroom. I had a couple of worksheets I needed to copy for one of tomorrow's classes, and I knew if I didn't get there quickly I'd find myself standing in a line of similar-intentioned teachers waiting to use the copier.

I rounded the door of the workroom and quickly discovered that I was too late. Again. Mr. Henderson, our history and geography teacher, appeared well-entrenched in a copying project that I could see would take some time. The man never ceased to amaze me. I'm convinced he alone has contributed substantially to the destruction of the rain forest—40 percent, maybe even 50 percent.

Hoping I was wrong about how long he'd be glued to the copier, I walked over to the water cooler instead. As I downed my first cup of water, I noticed him fiddling with the automatic stapler on the machine. That was it. I knew I wouldn't get to the copier until morning. I refilled my cup.

I had just tossed the paper cup into the garbage can when my eye caught my mail slot on the opposite wall. I pulled the pile from the box labeled Mr. Harrington and began leafing through each unsolicited book order, office supply catalog, and workshop invitation, tossing them appropriately into the nearby trash can or paper recycling box next to it. Within the stack of junk mail and ads were two envelopes, one large and bright yellow, the other white and shorter.

The yellow envelope contained a receipt from a local building supply store for the plywood I'd ordered for shop class a week ago.

On the second envelope, in sloppy writing, was my name, and then the name of the school: Jason Harrington, Wilcox Middle School, Golden, Colorado. I ran a finger through the top of the envelope and withdrew a greeting card. On the outside was a simple cartoon drawing of a friendly looking duck shaking hands with what looked to be a sick turtle.

Underneath the cartoon were the words, "Since you're stuck in your shell I thought I'd drop in for a visit . . ."

The turtle had a look of dismay on his face, and I could guess what was coming next. I opened the card to discover I was right. On the right-hand side, the card's message was completed: ". . . whether you wanted me to or not."

I chuckled for a second or two before my eyes were drawn to the left-hand side of the card. On it was the same sloppy printing that had appeared on the card's envelope.

At the time I had no way of knowing the significance of those two simple sentences.

CHAPTER 2

I read the words a third time: *I found you, Musor. Now you will die.*

I had no idea who this Musor person was, but it certainly wasn't me. If this was a new marketing tactic, it was one of the strangest ones I'd ever seen. A practical joke, perhaps? I looked around the workroom for anyone who might be trying to gauge my reaction to what had to be one sick practical joke. Except for me and Mr. Henderson, who was still married to the copy machine and oblivious to everything else, the room was empty. I quickly poked my head out the workroom door to see if anyone was in the hallway.

No one.

The message made absolutely no sense to me, and I quickly dismissed it as being irrelevant. My name wasn't Musor, I didn't know a Musor, and the envelope being addressed to me had to be a fluke. It was then I made the first biggest mistake of my life: I tossed the strange greeting card into the garbage, turned, and left.

As I passed the school's office, I saw, through the large office windows, the secretary still at her desk so I stepped inside. "Hey, Ann."

She was deeply involved in her Quicken program, but managed, as usual, to do two things at once. "Hi, Jason. What's new?"

"Oh, nothing. Say, I got a small greeting card in my box. You wouldn't happen to remember who delivered it, would you?"

Ann's fingers stopped typing, and she looked in the mirror she kept by the side of her computer monitor—a mirror that allowed her to address whoever was behind her without having to turn her head. It took me some getting used to. "You're serious?"

I threw up my hands in a conciliatory gesture at the expression on her face and began backing up from her reflection. I had temporarily forgotten that she handled hundreds of pieces of mail every day. "All right. Easy. Easy there. I was just asking."

We threw each other a friendly grin, and I fished out of my pocket the receipt I'd slipped there minutes earlier. "Here. We'll stay on safe ground, what do you say?" I wrote my name on the receipt for my shop supplies, reached over, dropped it in the correct wire bin next to her computer, and left. Ann's fingers had resumed their tapping before I'd even stepped out the office door.

"That I can handle," she called out as I waved good-bye.

I was in the process of shutting down my three classroom computers when I suddenly remembered I'd come in twenty minutes early that morning so I could have a shot at the copier. That obviously hadn't worked out, and, the way things were looking this afternoon, it appeared I'd be doing the same thing tomorrow. I walked over to the door and hit the button that signaled I wanted to talk with the office over the intercom.

"Yes?" Ann replied.

"Hey, I came in early this morning. I'll be coming in early again tomorrow. Permission to skip out a half hour early today?"

"Just a minute."

I knew she was wheeling her office chair back three feet and delivering my request to our principal, Mr. Bell. He was a reasonable man, so I'd already hit the lights and had my key in the door when the expected answer arrived.

"His eminence says yes, Jason. See you tomorrow."

And that was that.

I shut the door. The day was over and Mr. Harrington was just Jason again.

It felt great!

I lived only five minutes from the school in a small two-bedroom apartment. Two years with mission companions and a slew of roommates in college after that convinced me that when I finally graduated, I wanted to come home from work to someplace quiet—someplace I could relax and just put my feet up. Of course, that didn't rule out my desire for female companionship. But the truth was I'd been so busy trying to get my feet under me in education that I really wasn't doing the kind of socializing I wanted to. Singles ward or no, the fact was that after a long day of students I was pretty well shot both mentally and physically. Besides, only one of the four door handles of my '89 Dodge Omni worked, and that was on the driver's side. The red, sun-faded hunk-of-junk wasn't exactly what I would call a chick magnet.

Of course, I might not be giving the little car the credit it deserves. Because a couple days earlier, while filling the gas tank of said hunk-of-junk, I was surprised to run into Kelly Nicholls—a girl I'd dated in college—coming out of the convenience store. She was passing through Golden on her way to Boulder but seemed genuinely pleased to see me. And, to be honest, I was pleased to see her too. It was obvious we'd both changed over the past few years, but there was something in her eyes that hinted a touch of magic might still be there between us. Unfortunately she was running late and I had a few cars behind me wanting my place at the pump, but I asked her out for dinner Thursday night—an odd choice, I know, but it just worked out that way—exchanged phone numbers, and was really looking forward to getting together again and catching up. Tonight I needed to call her up and make the arrangements for tomorrow. It would take some careful planning, since she said she lived a couple hours away.

By the time I'd pulled into my parking stall, aside from making that phone call, I had my entire evening planned—one thick steak on the grill, a garden salad, a bowl of Fruity Pebbles to wash it all down, and just me in my recliner watching college basketball.

I was a bit surprised when the apartment manager, a man in his late fifties who was always busy with something around the complex and always wore a faded blue jumpsuit, approached me just as I was getting out of my car.

"Jason. How were the kids today?"

I grinned, shutting the car door and straightening. "Well, they're all still alive. I'd guess you'd say it was a good day."

He continued standing there.

"Is there something I can do for you, Jim?"

The man ran a hand through his thinning silver hair and pursed his lips a few times.

I slapped my hand against my forehead. "I'm late again, aren't I?" I removed my tie and threw it through the open driver's side window. "So help me, Jim. I'm sorry. All the days just seem to run together this time of year. I'll get you the rent right away."

The man nodded a few times and grinned. "That's fine, Jason. If I'm not in my apartment, just slip it under the door. I've got to get the checks off to the landlord by tomorrow morning."

I gave him a quick salute and, to show I was sincere, began jogging toward my unit. Five squat, two-story buildings made up our complex, with my particular unit seemingly built as an afterthought. It was turned at an odd angle to the others, which was good in the sense that my bedroom window on the first floor never had headlights slashing past it during the night.

I rounded the far end of the building and had just about reached my front door when I stopped short.

Everyone in my building worked, and all the others wouldn't start arriving home for another hour at the very least. Consequently, the building, as expected, was silent. What was not anticipated, however, was my open door. At first I thought maybe Jim had been fixing something. But then I realized he would have told me if he was going to go into my apartment.

When my eyes first noticed the deadbolt fully extended, the doorjamb splintered, and pieces of door molding littering the linoleum entry, I was stunned.

Seconds later, however, I was downright angry.

Here I was, working hard for the few things I had, and someone decided to break into my place and steal them from me.

Without thinking, I pushed open the door and walked across the wood splinters and into my apartment's small kitchen.

I couldn't believe what I was seeing. This wasn't a theft; it was vandalism. My second most favorite possession in the world, my microwave, was lying on its side against the kitchen cabinets, its acrylic door cracked, its metal casing askew. Cabinet doors were either broken open or kicked in, and what few dishes I had were shattered on the floor.

I took only a few steps and was in the living room. My olive green couch—a Deseret Industries treasure if there ever was one—was slashed open in several spots, its cushions, also slashed, lying at the opposite end of the room. My black leather La-Z-Boy recliner, my most favorite possession, had also been slashed in several places. The entertainment center leaned on one of the recliner's arms. My DVD player, stereo, and CDs were scattered all over the floor.

I was seething.

Why in the world would someone do something like this? I thought.

I walked down the hallway and glanced into the bathroom. The mirror was shattered, and the top of the toilet tank lay in several large pieces on the floor.

The bedroom next to it wasn't any better. My bookcase and computer were melded into a single unit, crumpled together on the floor. My office chair had been slashed and thrown on top of everything like chocolate sauce on a massive ice cream sundae.

When I finally entered my bedroom, I was ready to put my fist through the wall.

But I checked my anger the moment I saw a kitchen knife sticking out of my simple wooden headboard. No doubt it was the very knife that had been used on the couch and chairs and was just about where my head would be if I were to suddenly feel the desire to lie down.

It was seeing that knife sticking into the headboard that changed everything. At that very moment, my apartment took on a completely different feeling. Rather than the cozy refuge I'd always considered it to be, it suddenly had become vast and open, offering me no protection whatsoever.

My skin was crawling, and the hairs on the back of my neck standing up when I realized what I'd inadvertently done. Yes, my place had been trashed, but I'd just barged right into the middle of it. *Is the robber still here? Have I just backed myself into a corner? What if he's armed?*

Every corner and every closet door in each bedroom and the hallway suddenly seemed the perfect hiding place. The best thing for me to do, I decided, was to back out and call the police right away. I could be as angry as I wanted, but I knew full well that anger wouldn't offer much protection against a lead bullet.

Of course, if the intruder was unarmed, then stand back. Two years of football, three years with the wrestling team, and growing up with three brothers had to count for something. But I forced such thoughts from my head; false bravado wasn't what I needed right now.

I was turning to leave when something struck me as odd. I looked at my room once more.

There wasn't anything on my bed.

Well, not exactly. The bed had been stripped of the normal sheets and blankets, but in the center of the queen-size mattress sat my telephone. When I took a few steps forward to take a closer look, I noticed a couple of open pill bottles amid the floral design of the bare mattress. Scattered atop the mattress were small blue and white pills. I picked up the first bottle and then the second. One was for a prescription for something I couldn't even pronounce. The second bottle was empty and contained no markings whatsoever.

The phone rang.

In that single instant I think my life span was reduced by three years.

After taking a few deep breaths, I was finally able to reach down and pick up the receiver, stopping the ringing that seemed much louder than I ever remembered it being.

"Hello?" I said, dropping the empty pill bottles back onto the mattress and then pinching the bridge of my nose with my thumb and index finger.

"Ah, Musor! So good to finally put voice with picture."

Musor? *There's that name again.* "I think you've got the wrong number. Who is this?"

"My apologies for what I do to apartment. But was necessary."

The voice had an accent of some kind. A strange, thick accent. Russian? I was very confused. "Look . . . I . . . Who is this?"

"I told you. I am one who destroyed your place and, when time is right, I will be one who kills you."

I stood there shaken, not knowing what to say. I had to be talking to some kind of nut. But then, apparently it was the same nut who'd put a knife in my headboard.

"Look, I don't know—"

"Calm, *Musor*. You knew this was coming. It was only matter of time before I found you. And, soon, you worry about nothing. I am almost ready now. Oh, yes, feel free to call police as I know you want to. I give you warning. They believe nothing you say. You have nowhere to run or hide . . . cop killer."

The line went dead.

Stunned, then frustrated, I slammed the phone back on its base, cracking it in the process. *What in the world is he talking about? Kill me? Cop killer? And why does he keep calling me Musor?* I suddenly regretted throwing the strange greeting card away earlier. Maybe it could have helped the police figure out this mess.

I lost another three years of my life when the phone rang again. I grabbed it and growled, "Look, you idiot—"

"Jason?"

I knew that voice. It was a familiar one. When it suddenly dawned on me who it was I'd just started yelling at—my principal—I stood straight and cleared my throat quickly. "Mr. Bell. I'm sorry. I've been getting . . . some calls lately—"

"Jason, the police were just here. Several of them. They were asking where you were. They looked very serious, Jason. Are you all right? Is there some kind of problem that . . . ?"

I didn't hear anything else my principal said as my hand slowly fell away from my ear. I was seeing everything around me for the first time. My trashed apartment, the call threatening my life, the strange voice on the other end of the line accusing me of being a cop killer. And then, of course, there was the odd greeting card I'd received at work.

I suddenly remembered hearing something on the news about an officer getting killed a few days earlier.

Somehow my stunned mind put all of these seemingly disjointed pieces together. I wanted to talk to the police, to straighten all this out, but I had the strongest impression that I needed to get out of there. And quickly!

I sprang for the door and happened to notice a small red daypack on the floor behind a kicked-in closet door. I grabbed it and my jacket and bolted out the front door. I was about to head for my car when I caught a glimpse of my mountain bike in the bike rack near the laundry room.

They'd be looking for my car. And with over 309,000 miles on it, it wasn't exactly something I could rely on to get me very far fast.

It took several seconds longer than usual for my shaking hands to get the key in the bike's padlock, but after that it was only a few seconds before the chain was pulled free. I slipped on my thin jacket and threaded my arms into the straps of the daypack. Mounting the bike in a single move, I headed toward the large, worn cedar fence that lined the back of the complex. Pulling aside two loose boards, I slipped my bike through a space perhaps only I—and every kid in the apartment complex—knew about. I had just replaced the two loose boards when I could clearly hear the screaming of police sirens in the distance. I stood behind the fence long enough to see three squad cars pulling abruptly into the mostly vacant parking stalls. Several officers poured out of them and raced toward my apartment, weapons drawn.

I turned, mounted the bike once more, and quietly made for the safety of the warren of narrow streets that made up my neighborhood.

My only thought was to get as much distance between them and me as I could. I headed northwest—without ever looking back—until I eventually ran into Ford Street. Adjusting the gears, I willed my burning legs on, as I'd done in football years ago, imagining them as two large pistons in an engine that only I could control. I headed north for a while until finally turning right on the first cross street I encountered. I had biked into Mesa Meadows Park, a fairly large subdivision that lay at the base of North Table Mountain.

At the nearest corner, I came to a stop and proceeded to get my breathing back under control. My heart was pounding in my chest, and I could feel the sweat flowing down the sides of my face, my jugular vein pulsing in my neck with a strong and unnervingly determined rhythm. I had only ridden a little over a mile according to the small odometer on my handlebars, but with all the turning and braking, it felt like ten.

Paranoia came next. There were many homes in this neighborhood, and for all I knew, several pairs of eyes could be watching me. The last thing I wanted was to draw attention to myself, and I suddenly felt the need to alter my appearance in some way. Trying to look as casual as possible, I removed the daypack, slipped off my jacket, and tied it around my waist as I took a moment to stretch my legs and cautiously look all about me—for what, I didn't know. After all, I was new to this fugitive business.

There was no mistaking what had just happened. The police had only moments ago pulled into the complex to arrest me. *Right?*

Cop killer?

But how could they suddenly suspect me of doing something so heinous? Surely when they saw the apartment they'd . . .

I wiped the sweat from my face with the rolled-up sleeves of my shirt and concentrated on lowering my heart rate before I started hyperventilating.

As I turned around, slipping the daypack onto my shoulders, my eyes locked onto a blue pickup as it made its way around a corner nearby. The color of the truck was an instant reminder.

The blue and white pills. *They'll find the pills!* I realized. *Maybe they'll think I overdosed or . . .*

But they aren't mine! There's no way!

My mind was spinning, along with everything around me, and I had to close my eyes and focus for a minute only on my breathing. Seconds later, wishing I had the water bottle I usually clipped to my bike frame whenever I went biking, I felt my rattling train of thought come to a sudden, screeching halt.

That was when I realized my mistake—a very *big* mistake.

I'd picked up the pill bottles. I'd touched them.

Why wouldn't they believe they're mine? I realized, feeling slightly nauseated. *My fingerprints are all over them!*

CHAPTER 3

I stood there straddling my mountain bike, sweat dripping steadily from the bottom of my chin, my shirt damp and clinging to my body, my mind in a state of absolute confusion. *What in the world is going on here?* I thought. *One minute I'm looking over my junk mail, the next I'm running from the police!*

Common sense was screaming at me just to return to the apartment, turn myself in, and try to explain everything that had happened to me. After all, it was clear I was being set up for something. The death threat, the destruction of my apartment, the pills, the phone call, the ludicrous suspicion that I, a second-year junior high teacher who loved my job, was a cop killer. It was absurd!

This is what common sense was telling me. I even went so far as to turn my bike around when I found myself asking some vitally important questions: *What if they don't believe me? What if I can't prove myself innocent? What if this setup goes deeper than just a trashed apartment and a phony drug prescription? And once the police have me, am I really going to be able to contact anyone for help? I don't know any lawyers or cops. Who am I going to call?*

Call me paranoid, but I'd seen enough television and movies to make me a bit skeptical about just how I would be treated once the police got hold of me. Killing a police officer was tantamount to slapping all of law enforcement in the face, wasn't it? What had started out as fear was now bordering on terror. Whoever was behind all of this knew what they were doing. The single most logical place I could turn to for help had just been eliminated.

Unconsciously, I turned my mountain bike in the opposite direction of my now-distant apartment and began pedaling, trying to clear my head, trying to figure out what in the world I should do next.

I found myself scrunching up my shoulders in a weak attempt at hiding my face. I also tried to control my breathing, all the while fighting the incessant urge to look over my shoulder. Leaning over my handlebars in a racing posture helped some, but I was also fighting for control over my feet as they would occasionally slip off the pedals.

After another half mile of pedaling, my mind kept returning to the strange phone call I'd received. *Is that the person responsible for all this? And if so, who is he? Why is he after me?* I think I owed a late fee for a video, but other than that, I was just your plain vanilla citizen. I went about my own business, paid my bills and taxes, went to church on Sunday, and did my part for society by educating its youth.

I stopped the bike abruptly and looked behind me once more. I wanted so badly just to talk to those police officers that I knew had to be poring over my apartment that very minute. After all, if everything that was going on seemed this ridiculous to me, then surely . . .

As I began pedaling again, a few cars passed by me, making me feel very exposed, and I was again having trouble controlling my feet. They were beginning to feel like concrete blocks. My erratic breathing had finally caught up with me, and I was certain I was either going to black out or vomit if I didn't find someplace to collect myself. I pedaled behind a small convenience store I saw ahead of me.

The back of the store showed signs of recently painted-over graffiti, and the smell of rotting garbage from a battered dumpster made me gag. But I wheeled myself in behind the dumpster anyway. I needed a place to stop and collect my thoughts, a place where I could be less conspicuous than I was on the street.

I felt stupid. I felt like a grown-up playing a bizarre game of hide-and-seek. Only in my case, no one had told me that the game had started or had even bothered to explain the rules.

At that moment, as I struggled to get control over my breathing, I made up my mind to stop reacting so quickly to what was going on around me. Sure, my world was being turned inside out, but I'd already made a few foolish mistakes that only seemed to have tightened the invisible noose strung around my neck.

For one thing, I should have kept that stupid greeting card I'd received. Where had it come from? The postal mark on the outside would have at least told me that. Did it even have a postal mark? If nothing else, I could have used it to try to convince the police *I* was the one being threatened.

I briefly thought about returning to the school before the janitors emptied the garbage cans.

I glanced at my watch. They would have emptied them by now. Besides, I couldn't exactly go digging around in the dumpster without attracting attention from the houses that surrounded the school.

What about the prescription? Had it actually been my name printed on the label? I couldn't remember! Was it a phony label? Because if it wasn't and it could be traced to an actual doctor, that would only tighten the noose.

Why hadn't I grabbed a few of the pills so I could try to find out what they were? Why had I picked up the pill bottles with my bare hands, leaving a clear set of prints for the police to pull?

The answer to all of these questions was obvious. I wasn't qualified for anything like this. I wasn't some super spy with years of training and zillions of dollars worth of equipment at my disposal. For crying out loud, I was a school teacher who was lucky to get to the copy machine each day! I simply wasn't prepared to take in this kind of information or to look beyond what I saw directly in front of me.

Something was going on and somehow I was in the middle of it. I didn't know why. Nor did I know who was responsible for it. All I knew for certain was that I had to start thinking differently. I had to try to anticipate the results of each move I made from this point on. Someone wanted to kill me. I had to think before I reacted or I wasn't going to last very long.

I closed my eyes, forcing myself to ignore the stench from the dumpster, and offered up a quick prayer. I might not know what I was supposed to do next. But at least I knew who I should ask.

When I opened my eyes, a small piece of me had expected everything to be normal. But I was still wearing the clothes I'd put on that morning, and I was still straddling my mountain bike with a bright red daypack slung over my shoulders.

Right now I need distance, I thought. Distance between both the cops and whoever was obviously setting me up.

Feeling the need to alter my appearance once more, I removed the daypack, wrapped it in the jacket I'd tied around my waist and then, using the sleeves of the jacket, tied it securely to the front of my bike.

Casually, I began working my way south, passing the Coors Brewery—a popular stop with tourists, surpassed only by Heritage Square on the west end of town and the Buffalo Bill museum to the southwest atop Lookout Mountain. I wound my way through the various streets, stopping occasionally to readjust the daypack that would shift on my handlebars, all the while struggling to accept what was taking place.

I'd biked another two and a half miles before I realized the sky had an orange tint to it. Evening was approaching and I had nowhere to go. I thought of various friends and family, but then the thought of the knife sticking out of my headboard made me promptly dismiss that idea. I didn't want anyone else hurt because of what had to be one colossal misunderstanding.

Besides, most of my family lived on the east end of Denver, almost thirty miles away, or in Boulder, twenty miles to the north. Straddling my mountain bike there in the middle of Golden, I felt that both places might have been on the other side of the globe.

I loved living in Golden. It is where mountain and city living come together. With a population around 18,000, most now consider Golden a suburb of Denver, overlooking the fact it had at one time been Colorado's territorial capital. It was the birthplace of the Jolly Rancher and where Buffalo Bill Cody was buried and, thanks to the Colorado School of Mines—one of the world's foremost engineering schools—is a primary contributor to our nation's mineral industry. For me, though, Golden is simply a great place to fish, camp, and ride some of the best mountain biking trails around.

I was the one who wanted to be closer to the great outdoors. Now here I was, nestled in the foothills of the Rocky Mountains with nowhere to turn. Where Golden had once been instrumental in the opening of the West to settlement, for me it was looking more and more like a dead end.

To the east, toward the base of South Table Mountain, the glow of a sign caught my eye. I biked a few blocks until I was finally able to make out that it was a motel.

The thought of a quiet room, someplace where I wasn't out in the open, seemed very appealing. *If I can hide away someplace where I can think this through and rest a bit,* I thought, *then maybe I'll do a better job of untangling myself from this mess.*

Before my foot hit the pedal to cross the busy street, my mind threw up a few of the mystery and espionage movies I had seen throughout my life.

Cash. I need cash!

I had only a few dollars in my wallet. I knew that the moment I used a credit card to pay for the room, law-enforcement authorities would be all over me. At least that's how it was in movies or on television. But to get any cash, I'd have to either cash a check or use my ATM card, and all of the banks had been closed for nearly an hour.

After rolling the predicament over in my mind, I finally settled on the only solution I had left.

Feeling the chill of the evening, I slipped into my jacket, readjusted the daypack, pulled the bike around, and began heading north toward an ATM machine back near the Coors Brewery. I knew the police could find out I'd used the ATM, but at least it would only tell them where I'd been, not where I was staying.

It was dark by the time I reached the ATM. Housed in a small metal-and-glass room, it was well-lit within. While biking I had thought through how I was to proceed next.

I knew most ATMs took your picture as you made your transaction. The last thing I wanted was a photograph of me revealing exactly what I was wearing. Before entering the large glass cubicle, I removed my jacket, untucked my shirt, and carefully parked my bike well away from the machine. When I was certain no one was heading anywhere near the cubicle, I slipped inside and quickly fed the ATM my bank card. I was sure a million eyes were on me, and I ended up having to enter my PIN twice. I breathed a sigh of relief when I finally saw the familiar menu of options displayed.

From this particular machine I could withdraw only three hundred dollars. I anxiously snatched up the cash, my card, and the receipt as quickly as they slid through the stainless steel door at the bottom of the machine. Then I bolted for my mountain bike.

In minutes I was pedaling at top speed down darkened streets. I had little doubt someone, somewhere, had somehow noticed the withdrawal, and I knew the farther I was from that machine, the better.

For a moment, as I rounded a corner and began to head south again, I considered stopping at another nearby ATM machine. It was sponsored by a different company, and I could pull another three hundred dollars. But I nixed the idea. Two points of withdrawal, or even attempted withdrawal, would only serve in my mind as an arrow pointing in the direction I was headed. Oh, I knew I could zigzag around, but I decided not to press my luck. Instead, I continued pedaling in a roundabout way back to the motel I'd spied earlier at the south end of town.

Ten minutes of riding felt more like an hour as I concentrated on the road in front of me. It was quite dark by then. And even though I had a small headlight on the front of the bike, I wasn't about to use it for fear of attracting attention—any kind of attention—from the light traffic and the occasional passerby. I had by this time given up on trying to camouflage myself, relying on darkness and shadow for protection.

Finally, I spied the red neon sign belonging to what had to have been one of the oldest motels in Golden. It was a cheap motel, but I needed a quiet, out-of-the-way place to hide and collect my thoughts, appearance notwithstanding. The Mine Motel fit that bill perfectly.

I left my bike behind one of the buildings and walked to the manager's office. A young man, likely an engineering student from the School of Mines in town, was deeply involved in a book entitled *Mineral Science* when the door chime announced my arrival. By now I was becoming more or less accustomed to inspecting my whereabouts, noticing details. The wood-paneled walls of the tiny office were covered with faded art prints. A stand of pamphlets and postcards filled a wire rack just to the side of a battered counter. Completing the decor were two dead plants and a couple of worn chairs from the seventies lined up under the front windows. The desk manager had hardly given me a glance before lapsing into a routine he obviously knew very well.

"Room?"

"Yes," I answered.

"Smoking or nonsmoking?"

"Non."

"Just one night?"

"Yes."

"Cash, credit, or check?"

I hesitated at the thought of writing a check, but decided it would be unwise. "Cash."

"All right." He took the cash and handed me back the change. He then plucked a key from a rack somewhere just beyond my field of vision and handed it to me. "Checkout's at eleven. Return the key or leave it on the table in your room before you leave. Sign here please."

It was a registry of some kind asking for my name, phone number, and license plate. As soon as I gripped the pen, I realized I couldn't use any real information, and neither could I hesitate for fear the clerk would notice and become suspicious. I accepted the pen and immediately wrote Donald Ashbee, a distant relative, if I remembered right. I then casually wrote out a phony telephone and license plate number. I was initially worried about what might happen if the clerk noticed I wasn't driving a car, but the way his eyes kept returning to his book let me know that I was probably in the clear.

As I accepted my key, the young man, using a few well-choreographed gestures, told me how to get to my room.

The motel consisted of two single-story buildings facing each other. Each room had its own parking stall directly in front of its door. From what I could see, several of the rooms were dark and perhaps empty. I retrieved my bike and, moving quickly past the clerk's office, pulled it through the open door of my room, leaving the interior dark.

With the lights off and no car in the parking stall, I was hoping anyone driving by would assume the room was vacant.

The moment I'd entered the room, the smell of Lysol and bleach assaulted my senses. Even in the dark I could tell the room probably wasn't on anyone's five-star list. Half a star? Maybe.

I didn't care. It was shelter and there was a bed. And if the odor was any indication, it was very, very clean. I pulled the bedspread off the top of the bed, pulled the cheap room-darkening curtains closed above the room's heater/air-conditioner, slipped out of my jacket, and collapsed. The bed was surprisingly comfortable, as long as I remained in its center. In moments I found myself beginning to drift to sleep.

Just a few minutes of rest, I thought.

Seconds later I was fast asleep.

CHAPTER 4

The stocky man standing before me had a friendly face. From the way he was dressed, I could tell he was a firefighter. No, not by the heavy clothing and boots associated with firefighting. Nor an ax or even a fireman's helmet. I knew he was a fireman because of the logo on the black T-shirt he wore and because I was standing inside one of those fire-preparedness trailers you find at most state fairs.

Tendrils of artificial smoke curled heavenward from beneath the door just behind the firefighter, who was in the process of explaining to me the importance of feeling a door for heat before attempting to open it. I just stood there, watching him.

Unexpectedly, the firefighter's head turned with a jerk. He looked directly into my eyes. "Sir! Stop, drop, and roll."

I could hear his words, but they weren't making any sense.

"Stop, drop, and roll, sir!"

I looked about me. We were standing in the middle of what was essentially a fifth-wheel trailer. With the couch and the table where they were, it would have been impossible to do what he was asking me to do.

He took a few steps forward and began shouting even louder. "Stop, drop, and roll!"

Again, I looked all about me. I was totally confused.

The firefighter's nose was nearly touching mine when he yelled once more, "STOP, DROP, AND ROLL!"

I dropped and attempted to roll and . . .

. . . fell out of bed. Waking from the dream I'd been having, I landed soundly on the carpeted floor of my motel room. It was dark, and I'd barely managed to remember where I was when the motel window exploded under a sudden barrage of gunfire.

The curtains jerked and writhed as a hailstorm of bullets riddled them. I'd awoken from one nightmare only to find myself smack-dab in the middle of another!

I snaked my way toward the wall, under the window, away from bullets that were mercilessly peppering the mattress, wall, and nightstand. I curled up into a ball and threw my hands protectively over my head. An occasional round would hit the metal housing of the air conditioner beside me, and I would wince, fully expecting to be hit at any moment.

After an eternity of terror, the heavy curtains abruptly stopped moving. I heard the sound of tires screeching—a vehicle peeling out. Without the glass in place, the noise was loud, and I could smell the burning rubber the driver had left behind.

I lay there, hearing only the pounding of my heart and the sound of my breathing as I struggled for the air I'd unconsciously withheld from my lungs since the start of the attack. When I did move, it was slowly.

My hands came away from my head. I had several small cuts on the back of them, undoubtedly from some of the glass that had exploded inward. My knees were also cut from small bits of glass that had ground into them through my Dockers when I'd unceremoniously inched my way to the heater/air-conditioner.

I got on my knees, ignoring the stinging pain, sat up, and slowly parted the tattered remnants of curtains. A few doors on the opposite side of the motel were beginning to open, lights were turning on, curtains hesitantly being pulled aside as curious occupants worked up the courage to look into the frighteningly silent parking lot.

In only minutes, someone would begin asking questions, inquiring about my well-being. And the truth was, I could have used that. But with that concern would come calls for help. Police would be notified and perhaps an ambulance dispatched. Obviously, I just couldn't deal with those right then.

I had to get moving.

In two steps I reached my mountain bike. A few rounds had nicked it in places, but the tires appeared undamaged. I reached down, grabbed the red daypack, and flung it over my shoulder. I yanked open the door and awkwardly pulled my bike through the doorway.

Two men—one I recognized as the student who'd checked me in—had reluctantly been walking toward my door and seemed both startled and relieved to see me emerge in one piece. Wasting no time, I hopped on the bike and headed toward them. They instinctively parted to let me by, as I'd hoped they would, and I quickly rode off toward the street adjacent to the motel.

It was still quite dark and the traffic was light. Not wanting to take any chances, I immediately steered into a subdivision and began winding my way through it, away from the motel, away from the busier street.

After nearly ten minutes, I stopped behind a large grocery store. There were a few scattered security lights back there, but it was definitely darker than the well-lit sides or front of the building. There were a few dumpsters in the area, as well as a rather large and conspicuous trash compactor. I pedaled the bike so as to be out of sight between the compactor and building.

It was a chilly night—in the forties—and I longed for the jacket I'd inadvertently left at the motel. My hands were red and slightly swollen from the cold, and I held them to my mouth, cupping them, blowing into them, trying to warm them.

A loud *thunk* from inside the compactor nearly sent me to the ground. But the longer I stood there, the more I was convinced it was one of the grocery store's employees on the night shift throwing something away. My shallow breathing nearly choked me, and I struggled once more to regain control of my heart rate.

Only after tending to my hands for a minute or two did I finally have the presence of mind to check my watch. It was just after three in the morning. Only a few minutes past three and here I was out in the open again. Was it only twelve hours ago when my life had ceased being mine? Surely eternity couldn't be any longer than the past half-day had felt.

Still straddling the bike, I rolled down the sleeves of my shirt and buttoned them at the wrists. Then I folded my arms across my chest. That was when I noticed my body beginning to shake. I couldn't stop.

Shock? I wondered. *Are my mind and body suddenly realizing just how close I've come to death and only now reacting to the fear?*

I continued holding my arms close to my body, forcing myself to continue taking deep breaths as I willed myself to calm down, to get control of my body's natural reflexes. Two or three minutes later, my heart was beating at a steadier rate, and my breathing was no longer ragged and forced.

Of course my body had been in shock! I had just dodged what had to have been the emptying of a complete magazine from some kind of automatic weapon!

Whoever was firing into the room clearly wanted to make sure they didn't miss.

At this thought, my eyes slammed shut. *If I hadn't rolled . . . if I hadn't rolled when I did . . . I'd be dead right now!* This thought seemed to reverberate throughout my head like some lonely voice bouncing off the cold hard walls of a vast and empty canyon.

I slowly got off my bike, lowered the kickstand, and stumbled a few feet until my back was against the store's painted cinderblock wall. I began to lower myself to a sitting position. There, on the cold, solid pavement with my hands and arms encircling my legs and pulling them into my body, I tried feebly to get warm.

I could see spots of blood where glass shards had cut my knees. *I should be dead*, I thought.

I must have sat there for quite some time before I finally realized just what I was doing. If anybody accused me of overreacting before, what I'd just dodged now validated—even to myself—my actions from the very beginning.

I was running, but from what, I didn't know.

I remembered the card, the pills, the knife in the headboard. I then remembered something the mysterious caller had said over the phone hours earlier. It was something about almost being "ready."

Was that it? Was the attack at the motel supposed to be the moment I was to have been killed? But then who knew I was headed there?

My mind refrained from interrogating itself any further. One thing was pure and simple: I was being hunted, and not just by the police. At that moment it didn't matter why. Not with me being exposed as I was. I thought I'd been safe using a phony name, paying cash, and going someplace I normally wouldn't have gone. But in spite of my mediocre precautions, I'd been tracked. And apparently without much effort.

I raised my head and looked around me, beyond the dim security lights of the building. To either side were the bright lights of the parking lot. I was sitting behind a twenty-four-hour grocery store. One I'd frequented a few times, in fact. The store was only a mile or so from my apartment.

I stood, dug my hands into my pants pockets, and slowly began walking past the trash compactor and the two bay doors used by semis for unloading freight, expecting any minute for someone to round the corner of the building. I stopped short of the end of the building by a few feet and looked off into the distance, scanning the dark horizon to the north and northwest.

I needed a safe place to hide, someplace where I could put my thoughts together and figure out my next move. I needed a place where I knew for certain I wouldn't be disturbed or discovered.

Although my eyes couldn't discern anything on the horizon in that inky-black darkness, beyond the light traffic, beyond the streetlights and buildings, I could see in my mind's eye the foothills. At the top of one of those mounds was a large capital M marking the home of the Colorado School of Mines. Near the top, west of the M, was a place I'd gone mountain biking before. Perhaps I could get there without being noticed.

The irony of where I was headed didn't escape me and, in fact, drew a nervous and unexpected grin. I was heading for the protective safety of Mount Zion.

Whoever had shot at me probably assumed I was dead. I had no doubt the shooting would make the local news by morning, and by then I'd have just enough time to get to Mount Zion before my hunter caught wind of my fortunate escape.

No one should have survived that barrage of . . .

I pulled my mind away from the thought and tried to focus on what my mind's eye was not only seeing quite clearly, but also desperately longing for in the distant foothills.

I turned and began walking toward my bike and the red pack. I knew where I was headed next, but I also knew I couldn't go there unprepared.

Pedaling a block to a small convenience store with an outside telephone kiosk, I hurriedly checked the phonebook for the address of a store I'd seen on a television commercial. Satisfied, I slowly began pedaling south.

The store wouldn't open for several more hours, but moving in the dark seemed the logical next step. Not only would the movement help to keep me warm, but I would get there in plenty of time to find a good hiding place for my pack and mountain bike.

When the store did open, I hoped I would get the chance to try to free myself from the knot I was inadvertently tied up in.

CHAPTER 5

"Whoa, you look like you've been through a war already, pal."

The burly, middle-aged man at the checkout counter was a bit heavyset but pleasant. Dressed in a well-worn, olive green T-shirt and jeans, he appeared very much in his element.

Trying not to miss a beat, I went with the story I'd formulated while waiting for the Army surplus store to open. "I've been through my entire garage and I can't for the life of me find my tent and sleeping bag. I could have sworn I'd stored them in the attic. Nothing. I've been on my hands and knees cleaning out the garage and still nothing. I'm supposed to help our community Scoutmaster. We've got a campout tomorrow. Can you help me out?"

The man grinned at the mention of Scouts. "Oh sure. If we don't have it, you don't need it. Down this way. What size tent you looking for?"

I chose this store for two reasons. First, I knew from past experience with my own father that if you wanted rugged, quality gear, an army surplus store was the place to go. The new merchandise that filled the front aisles, plus the hodgepodge of used and unique military items I could see at the back of the store seemed to confirm that. Second, I knew it wouldn't have nearly the kind of security and surveillance equipment I'd find in a Wal-Mart, Target, or any other major retail outlet. I hoped I could slip in and out that morning without leaving any trace of having been there.

Halfway into the store, the clerk pointed down a couple of aisles. "New tents on the left. Used on the right. Sleeping bags are just one aisle down from here."

"Thank you very much. I should have come here in the first place."

The man nodded politely and left me to explore the aisles at my leisure. I could have found them on my own, I knew, but I felt I had to come up with some excuse for why I looked as bad as I did. I'd added some ground-in dirt to my knees to help hide the blood, but I certainly didn't look like the typical shopper.

I found a tent set up on top of one of the shorter shelving units that caught my eye immediately. According to the sign next to it, it was a Dutch Ground Troop tent. Made of heavy-duty, camouflage-print cotton canvas, it had a sturdy, waterproof PVE floor. I had no clue what PVE was, but from the feel of it, I couldn't imagine anything coming up through that floor. The tent was about eight-and-a-half feet long (important when you're just over six feet tall like me), forty-three inches wide, and at the center, just over four feet high. Taller at the head, it tapered down to where the feet presumably would be. It would work perfectly.

Making sure that the rolled-up tent I'd selected came with its own poles and stakes, I tucked it under my arm. For forty dollars I wasn't going to find anything better.

For another forty-five dollars, I found a mummy bag that promised to keep me warm in temperatures as low as five degrees. When rolled up, it was extremely small and lightweight. I tucked one of those under my other arm.

I was sorely tempted to buy a used army coat from a nearby rack. I decided against it, however, not wanting it to appear that I was running for the hills. I could buy one later from someplace else, I figured, without drawing nearly as much attention to myself.

Instead, I hooked a metal canteen with my finger and took my purchases back to my helpful friend at the cash register. It would be an awkward bundle to carry on a bike, but I couldn't see any other solution. The tent I figured I could probably strap with my belt somehow to the rack that sat just behind my seat. The red daypack I'd snatched from my apartment I could wear on my back, the canteen over my shoulder. The sleeping bag would fit under the handlebars or could be wedged under the extra length of brake cable looping from the front of my bike.

I'd make it work.

I paid the cashier, thanking him for his help.

After successfully securing the tent to the rack behind the seat and wedging the sleeping bag beneath my handlebars, I mounted my bike and began weaving my way to my second target.

It was early in the morning and the sky was gray and overcast. Most of the morning traffic was confined to the outlying highways and interstate. Hoping I wasn't attracting a lot of attention, I took a path up the center of Golden, near the eastern edge of the School of Mines. Near the school was a small convenience store that I was sure had an ATM machine inside.

Twenty minutes later I spotted the store up ahead. A woman stood at the gas pumps, fueling a worn Dodge Neon, and I saw only a handful of shoppers inside the store. I left my bike by the side of the store, the red daypack jammed between it and the building, and quickly went inside. I was a mess and was still worried about drawing attention to myself. But then I thought, *How many people really take a close look at anyone they run into at the gas station?*

According to my watch, it was close to nine o'clock in the morning. Normally, I'd be right in the middle of my first-hour English class, and as I opened the door of the convenience store, I couldn't help wondering what my students would do today. Of course, Ann would bring in a substitute. But did the teachers or students know anything about what was taking place? What was the talk in the faculty lounge?

The ATM machine was near the door. I figured I should get some more money before leaving the area. If I could pull another three hundred dollars out, then perhaps I'd have a better chance at surviving while I tried to figure things out.

Feeling as though a thousand eyes were on me, I pulled the ATM card from my wallet, slipped it into the appropriate slot, and readied my finger for the PIN request. Accepting my card, the machine proceeded to make a sound I'd never heard an ATM make before. Instead of displaying the normal menu of options, a simple text message appeared, informing me that my card had just been taken and that I was to contact the bank immediately.

I looked around. No one seemed to have noticed I was even standing there. I abruptly turned and walked toward the door.

Just because no one around me seemed to be reacting to what had just taken place didn't necessarily mean it had gone completely unnoticed. The bank, the police, whoever had done this to my account, had surely been made aware of my attempted withdrawal. I had to move—fast.

As I left the convenience store, however, I hesitated as I passed the national and local newspaper machines. "Police Slaying: The Work of a Teacher?" It wasn't the local paper's main headline, but it filled a prominent portion of the paper's right-hand side and had caught my eye immediately. I tossed two quarters into the machine, snatched up a copy, and jammed it into my daypack when I reached my mountain bike.

In seconds I was heading west toward the foothills.

I decided on a more straightforward route and, passing Brooks Field and a large baseball diamond, I found the dirt path that ran alongside Highway 6 north of I-70. I followed it to the so-called single-track trail that led right into Chimney Gulch, just south of Mount Zion.

Had this been a weekend, I might have encountered quite a few bikers and hikers, but thus far I hadn't spotted a soul, so I hit the trail hard and fast. The first mile was the toughest, and the steep, pea-gravel switchbacks forced me off my bike a few times. Several times I had to stop and readjust the tent and sleeping bag to keep them from falling off. But once I crossed Lariat Loop Road, the trail improved, and after two and a half miles of tree cover, I eventually reached the summit. I followed a faint trail into a large gulch filled with tall pines and littered with rocks and boulders.

At the far end of the dry gulch were several particularly large boulders. It was behind those boulders, beneath a tall stand of pines, that I'd finally come to rest.

The moment I got off my bike, I dropped to the ground, exhausted. Sitting up, resting my hands on my knees, I struggled for air, taking in large gulps of it that I finally felt free enough to enjoy.

After ten minutes of catching my breath and listening for the slightest sounds of anyone who might have followed me, I began clearing the ground beneath me. I tossed aside large rocks and fallen branches until I had a relatively smooth area. The tent I struggled with for a bit. I'd never set up a ground troop tent before, but with a rock as my hammer, and after tying a handful of half and clove hitches, my camouflaged retreat was ready.

I rolled the bike out of sight between the boulders and crawled inside the tent. There was just enough room for me to spread out my sleeping bag. It didn't take me long to shed my shirt and Dockers and slip into the clean, new bag. The cool morning and the shade of the trees had cooled my sweat-drenched body quickly, and the instant warmth I experienced slipping into the bag was a welcome change from the morning chill I'd been fighting for hours.

I was hungry—really hungry—but my greatest craving was sleep. I needed some rest.

A light breeze moved the heavy canvas, but only slightly, and I could hear the wind gently blowing through the pine needles above. These were fleeting impressions, however. It wasn't too much later that I was lost in sleep.

CHAPTER 6

When I awoke, my sleeping bag was unzipped and I was again saturated in sweat. I raised my wrist to glance at my watch. In a moment of panic, I realized it was three o'clock in the afternoon. Though my tent was shaded by pine trees and well camouflaged by the print of the heavy fabric, my recent experience reminded me that I was totally vulnerable to any type of attack.

Easy, man. Calm down, I told myself.

I moved, slowly. My body ached. Was it from sleeping on the hard ground, or had I strained some muscles from what I'd been through earlier that morning? I decided it had to be a combination of the two. I relaxed every muscle and lay still, feeling a measure of peace in the humid silence.

Another five minutes passed before I finally sat up. I'd noticed two small straps on the sides of the front entry. I turned my head and found similar straps on the rear entry. I unzipped both the front and rear entrance and rolled each door up, tying them off with their respective straps. The cross draft I had created began to consume the sweat on both my face and arms.

After opening my sweat-damp sleeping bag to let it dry, I was about to slip my clothes back on when I noticed my knees still covered in dirt and dry blood. They'd been cut in numerous spots and I thought I could see bits of glass in the wounds. I reached down toward the foot of my tent and retrieved the red daypack.

It was a 72-hour kit I'd been given two years ago for Christmas by my parents. My sister and three other brothers had also been given identical ones. Never in my wildest imagination had I thought I'd be clinging to it as I was now.

I removed the newspaper I'd crammed in there at the convenience store and set it aside for later. Inside the pack were nine small, thin cardboard boxes—MREs, Meals Ready-to-Eat. Military rations. Also included were several small pouches of water.

I had been hungry the night before. Now I was famished. I selected the best-sounding entree for my meal: BEEFSTEAK, CHOPPED AND FORMED, GRILLED WITH MUSHROOM GRAVY. The olive green bag within the box didn't look all that appetizing. However, considering I was hungry enough to eat the cardboard box itself, I wasn't about to complain. I tore off the top of the plastic pouch and was pleasantly surprised to find mushrooms that looked like mushrooms—in gravy that actually looked like gravy. It was delicious, even straight-from-the-package cold. I ate every bite of "beefsteak" and slurped up every drop of gravy—squeezing it toothpaste-like from the pouch. I then washed it down with a pouch of water.

My most immediate need satisfied, I took stock of my remaining possessions. A disposable 100-hour emergency candle, a foil-like emergency blanket, toilet paper, hand and body warmers, matches, light sticks, and other survival odds and ends. And, on the very bottom of the pack, a pocket-size first-aid kit. These were my possessions. My world had suddenly been reduced to a tent and the so-called emergency essentials in front of me.

I grabbed the first-aid kit, which was my main reason for examining the pack in the first place, and opened it. Using those meager supplies, I quickly cleaned up my knees, removing as much dirt and glass as I could find. Then I tackled the concentration of dirt and sweat on my neck, hands, face, and elbows.

After I got dressed, I sat once more, again staring at my "worldly possessions."

The food and water, I determined, giving little attention to any rationale for the decision, would remain at the foot of the tent. Perhaps I just wanted to keep an eye on it, considering it was all the food I had. All of the other items I slipped back into the daypack.

Since I'd finally had some food and rest, I felt like I had the strength to read the newspaper. The article beneath the title that had caught my attention earlier was incisive. The newspaper had received an anonymous tip that a school teacher might in fact be responsible for the shooting and killing of not one but *four* police officers over the last two months. The unnamed source also suggested that new evidence would soon be surfacing that would, "without question," tie said suspect to all four of the killings. Authorities declined comment, neither confirming nor denying the validity of the tip, and school superintendents all over the state were refusing to comment as well. The article then briefly summarized each of the murders and ended with a phone number police had long ago established as a confidential tip line.

I must have read the tiny article fifteen times before finally putting the paper down. It was insane. Was I really being hunted like a common criminal for the killing of *four* police officers?

I spent the rest of the afternoon rereading the article countless times. When I'd finally moved on to a few of the related articles, I discovered on page three a short blurb about what appeared to be a gang-style shooting that had taken place at a local motel early that morning. The incident was obviously still under investigation, and the article had no further information other than the fact that no one had been killed. It was a tiny piece of information that spoke volumes to me and was bound to catch the interest of whoever had pulled the trigger earlier that morning—my hunter.

It was just after five o'clock when I finally set the paper aside and exited the tent. Dusk was rapidly approaching, and the drop in temperature was especially noticeable on the mountain. Until that point I hadn't wanted to leave the tent at all. Making any observable movements outside was the last thing I wanted to do, but I had to stretch my legs and back. I couldn't hide in the tent forever.

I stayed near the tent, never wandering more than ten or twelve feet from it, and tried to keep the boulders between me and the upper edge of the gulch. When the visible horizon had turned a bright orange and purple, I sat on a smaller rock and watched the sunset. Soon after, the temperature dropped even more.

A fire? I relished the thought, but I didn't want to chance it. I thought about lighting my 100-hour candle, but the truth was I didn't dare even do that. I didn't want to draw any attention whatsoever to my position, and if that meant spending hours in the dark, then so be it.

When I could barely see my hand in front of my face, I decided to call it a night. There was nothing I could do at that moment anyway. To wander around in the dark was only begging for more trouble—something I seemed to have in abundance. A twisted ankle was the last thing I needed. The tiniest smile crossed my lips when I glanced over at my tent, its faint silhouette still visible in between the tall pines and the large immovable boulders. My English background latched onto the perfect idiom. I was literally stuck between a rock and a hard place.

I crawled inside the tent, zipped both the front and rear entries closed, slipped out of my clothes, and crawled into my bag. I was warm in no time.

Aside from the sounds of the outdoors, it was quiet and still. I was alone.

I was genuinely alone . . . and that, I realized, was the problem. I needed help!

Who was I fooling, for crying out loud? I'd sorted my food as if somehow it would last me for weeks. I figured I could probably stretch it out a week, but then what? Begin wearing a loincloth and living off the land?

And yet, as I lay there watching the canvas move ever so slightly from a sudden gust of wind, I didn't know what else to do. Yes, I needed help. But who was I going to run to for that help? *Perhaps I should turn myself in,* I thought. *At least I'd have solid walls surrounding me.*

And then there was that foreign-sounding man on the phone. He appeared dead set on killing me and had to be the anonymous tipster the newspaper had been referring to. If I did turn myself in, could authorities really protect me against someone like that? An image of Lee Harvey Oswald taking a round in the gut sprang to mind.

I couldn't run to family or friends. What would happen if he found out whom I was with? The way he'd shot up my motel room made me think he could care little for anyone that happened to get in the way. I couldn't take that risk.

I shut my eyes and muttered a prayer. I prayed for help, for understanding, for guidance. What was I to do? Where was I supposed to go? Who could help me? And, more importantly, how was I supposed to survive?

When I'd ended my prayer, the warmth of the bag, the smell of the outdoors, and the solitude of my surroundings began to take hold of me. I could feel myself drifting to sleep—to a place where I wouldn't have to think about my problems for at least a while.

I was nearly asleep when a name announced itself inside my head. *Kelly Nicholls.*

My eyes shot open.

That's when I realized it was Thursday night—the night I said I'd take Kelly out to dinner to "catch up." I'd stood her up, and now something inside was telling me she was someone who could help me.

I shook my head. I was tired and emotionally spent. Given everything that had happened so far, my mind was clearly all mixed up. I'd call her only when everything was settled, I decided, and try and make it up to her. I rolled over onto my side and tried to force all thoughts from my mind. I concentrated on my breathing, counted to a hundred several times, then started counting backward from a hundred. But my mind refused to let her name go.

When I said the name aloud, my chest began to burn. It was then that I rolled onto my back and with great resignation looked up into the darkness of my tent. "All right. All right," I whispered. "I'll call her. I just need one more day of rest. Please, can I have that?"

Seconds later I was drowsy and very much at peace. I'd received an answer to my prayer.

I had no idea what the phone call would lead to, but only after agreeing to do something with the prompting was I allowed to sleep.

Somehow I'd sneak into town and place the call. I had nowhere else to turn.

I'd call her. The question was, what would she say?

CHAPTER 7

"Her name is Kelly Nicholls."

"Could you spell the last name please?" asked the operator.

"N-I-C-H-O-L-L-S."

"Thank you. City?"

This is where it could get sticky, I thought to myself. We'd attended Colorado State University together in Fort Collins, but later, when she changed her major, I remembered her mentioning the fact that she liked the flexibility of the university's many extension sites. She could have been anywhere from Fort Collins to Denver. All she mentioned at the gas station was that she lived a few hours away.

I swallowed, hoping I'd reached an operator with some patience. "I'm not really sure. Could you check the state for me? There can't be that many."

"Sure."

From the sound of her voice, she seemed patient enough. I just hoped the number wasn't unlisted.

"I show five. How does she spell her first name?"

"K-E-L-L-Y"

"All right. That narrows it down to three. Of course, the last names are spelled the same. I do have one with a middle initial—"

"L. Her middle name is Lyndon." I remembered this because we shared the same middle initial.

"Well, then I think we've narrowed it down to the right person."

She told me a Kelly L. Nicholls lived in Pueblo—a two-hour drive at best—and asked for my name. I gave it, wincing, praying that I hadn't just made a huge mistake. My paranoia was working overtime: was my name already out there on some kind of watch list?

After only a few seconds, though, she told me to hold while she tried the number.

I could hear the phone ringing, and I held my breath, hoping this was the right Kelly, that I hadn't called too early or too late, and that she wasn't upset about last night. The sun hadn't been on the horizon long, but I didn't dare call any later for fear she'd leave for work or whatever it was she did now.

"Hello?"

It was her voice.

"I have a collect call from Jason L. Harrington. Will you accept the charges?"

"Who?"

"Jason L. Harrington," repeated the operator with the same patience she'd shown me.

I could hear a small laugh on the other end of the line. "That's who I thought you said. Of course I'll accept the charges."

"Thank you," replied the operator. And with an almost imperceptible click she was gone.

"Kelly?" I began with some reticence.

"Jason! Long time no hear. So how are you this fine *Friday* morning?"

I could hear the touch of tension in her voice. "Kelly, I'm sorry for calling you collect. I'm also very sorry about not call—"

"Hey, that's okay. It's been awhile and we just happened to bump into each other is all. I under—"

"No, Kelly. You don't understand. I . . ."

When I didn't continue my sentence, her voice suddenly took on an air of concern. "Is everything all right?"

I hesitated. I didn't want to discuss my situation over the phone, but if I wanted her help I knew I had to throw her something. "Look . . . I really do want to get together."

"Jason, it's seven thirty in the morning."

"I know. I . . ."

"Are you sure you're alright?"

There was a long silence as I struggled to come up with the right words.

"Jason?"

"I . . . need your help, Kelly. I can't really get into it right this minute. Is there any way you could maybe make a drive up here? To Golden, I mean. I would come to you, but . . . my car's . . . not available."

"Jason, what's wrong? You sound super stressed."

I glanced down at my dirty shirt and pants and caught a faint reflection of my scruffy self in the marred Plexiglas shielding the sides of the pay phone I was using near Prospect Park. I'd tried to pick an out-of-the-way phone. So far, no one had walked by me. I ran a hand through my hair. It felt greasy.

"Kelly, I . . . I need some help. As crazy as it sounds, you're the only one who came to mind. I know it's been awhile, but I really could use a hand right now."

"Jason, I'd love to help. But I'm at the end of my master's program here. I've got a presentation coming up and . . . maybe in a few days—Monday—I could—"

"Have you been watching the news lately?"

"I haven't. That's just it. That day we ran into each other was the first time I've been away from the university or my apartment in weeks. I can barely find time to eat, I'm—"

"Go to the library, the Internet. Check out the front page of the *Journal* here—day before yesterday." I knew it wouldn't be difficult for her to find a copy of the newspaper somewhere. Research was what Kelly was best at. "Read the front page and page three. Please. I need your help, Kelly."

"Jason, I just can't dr—"

"Please. I . . . I have no one else to turn to. Read it. Stay on Highway 6 until you reach 19th Street. Exit and head west. Stay on 19 for about a half mile. The road makes a hairpin turn and becomes Lookout Mountain Road. There's a place to pull off the road just after the turn. I'll meet you there at seven tomorrow morning. I'll be on a blue mountain bike."

"Jason! I don't think you're hearing me!" The tone in her voice had definitely changed—she was becoming frustrated. "I can't—"

"You're all I've got, Kelly."

"But you don't know what you're asking, Jason. I can't just—"

"Kelly. Please. I . . . I wouldn't be calling if this wasn't critical."

"Then tell me what it is. I'm sure we can wor—"

"I can't, Kelly. Not over the phone. Besides, Golden's starting to wake up. I really shouldn't be standing here."

"Are you on some kind of medication, Jason?"

"No. Why?"

"Because you sound awfully paranoid. How about your folks?"

"Kelly . . ." I just didn't know what more I could say.

"I just don't think you're being fair here, Jason. You call me up first thing in the morning, after standing me up, and right out of the blue ask me—"

"I know," I interrupted. "Just find the paper, read it, and be here tomorrow morning. Please!" I plowed on before she had a chance to respond. "It's a matter of life or death, Kelly. Please?"

I hung up the phone before she could respond and stared at it for some time. I didn't blame her for being upset. Here I was, a man she hadn't really seen in over two years, coming out of nowhere, asking her for help she was under no obligation to give. And to really make matters worse, I had inadvertently stood her up when we finally did run into each other again.

I exited the booth and looked up into a chilly, gray-clouded sky. It looked as though it might rain, and I really didn't want to get stuck in the middle of it. I got on my bike and headed once more for the foothills—thinking about Kelly the entire time.

We'd first met in a methods class at the university. We'd been assigned to the same study group and, though I must admit it was her beautiful hazel eyes that first attracted me to her, it was her bright, energetic personality that finally motivated me to ask her out.

We dated often and I really enjoyed being around her. She was smart and fun to talk to. And at the time the fact that she wasn't a member of the Church hadn't bothered me in the least. I'd only been home from my mission a year and a half, and so I suppose I felt I could teach anyone about the gospel—and that everyone would listen. But as our relationship became more and more serious, I could see that her own religious convictions ran deep. After six months it was clear to both of us that our theological differences were becoming a larger stumbling block than we'd originally expected.

But I'm not convinced this alone was the reason our relationship faded out. Our interests and social circles eventually got in the way, too.

Kelly had a tendency to be analytical about things. She would study something from all angles and then act fairly and decisively. It was a personality trait that in my mind separated her from other women I'd dated, a trait I generally admired. Eventually, however, this strong personality trait bled into her choice of major.

Kelly had gone into teaching because it was what her older sister had done and really enjoyed. But the year our practicums began—five months into our relationship—it didn't take long for the unpredictability of students to get to Kelly, and she knew she'd have a tough road ahead if she continued in a program her heart wasn't into any longer. "Too many variables," she'd said at the time. She decided to go into business administration instead.

It was shortly after she switched majors that our social circles naturally began to change. Because of this we rarely bumped into each other anymore. The simple lack of contact, coupled with our religious differences, slowly began to drive us apart. Occasionally we would bump into each other, but it was always awkward. Soon thereafter it became easier just to avoid each other. It pained me inside, but a temple marriage, a family raised in the Church, meant a great deal to me. I never realized how much until the day I made up my mind to finally let Kelly go.

And now here we are two years later, I thought to myself, shifting gears as I prepared to tackle the steep grade of the bike trail. *Me, running from the law, and Kelly . . . What was she doing these days?* She'd mentioned the university and a master's degree.

A master's degree in what? I wondered.

She wasn't married—that was clear. And she probably wouldn't have agreed to go out with me at all if she was engaged or, at the very least, seeing someone.

When raindrops began to fall, I was only halfway up the bike trail. If it decided to suddenly start pouring, I would be soaked clear to the skin before I ever reached the tent.

I shifted gears again and forced myself to pedal faster, digging into the steep trail toward my pitiful shelter.

I needed someone's help. The coming rain made that perfectly clear.

But why Kelly? I wondered, my breathing now labored, the muscles in my legs screaming at me for rest.

When I'd finally reached the summit and was positive I was hidden from view, I stopped and rested—heavy raindrops pattering all around me. Several minutes passed before I could finally breathe again.

I was about to pedal toward camp when I suddenly stopped short. The feeling I'd had when I'd muttered Kelly's name in the dark the night before returned momentarily.

The Lord seemed to know I needed her help, and I could definitely use it. But what if Kelly didn't feel the same way? *Will she show up tomorrow? Or will she just write me off as a loon?*

What would I do if she didn't show?

I had absolutely no idea.

The rain began to pour from the heavy gray clouds overhead.

Hurriedly I pedaled toward my tent.

CHAPTER 8

To say I felt self-conscious standing there the following morning, looking the way I did, would be a gross understatement. There I was, about to meet a girl I had barely seen in over two years, and I didn't even have a comb to run through my hair. At least when I ran into her at the gas station I had on a tie and a pair of slacks. *What kind of car had she been driving anyway?* I wondered.

I reached my hand up to scratch my cheek; the three-day's growth on my face was rough and itchy. I couldn't help wondering what she'd say when she came. *If she came,* I thought. *She may not come at all.*

With my left hand on the handlebars of the mountain bike, I looked down at the wet dirt and gravel at my feet along the side of Lookout Mountain Road and shook my head. Who was I kidding? A guy out of her past calls her one morning—out of the blue—and begs her to drop everything and come running. Why would she?

I was asking way too much from Kelly.

My mind stopped berating itself when I raised my head and noticed a navy blue Lexus making its way slowly around the bend of the hairpin turn I'd described to Kelly on the phone.

It's her! I thought. *Kelly. It has to be.*

She spotted me and pulled over into the turnoff—her car well off the paved road—not more than twenty yards away.

When the car had come to a complete stop, the driver's side window smoothly disappeared into the door. Her auburn hair caught my eye immediately, just as it had at the gas station. It used to fall to her shoulders, but now it was cut short, in a carefree style. Her expression, however, was far from carefree. She just sat there with the window rolled down, engine running, looking at me. It was then that I *really* felt self-conscious. Even at twenty yards I knew I had to be a sight.

I did the first thing that came to mind. I raised my hand and, after some hesitation, waved.

She remained seated in her car for nearly a full minute before she finally rolled up the window and shut off the engine.

Traffic at this time in the morning was practically nil, and, with only a cursory glance for oncoming cars, she proceeded to cross the street toward me, keeping an eye on me the entire time. She was dressed in jeans and her hands were shoved into the pockets of a beige coat. Soon she was standing in front of me and, being four or five inches shorter than me, was looking up at me.

The look of suspicion in her hazel eyes gradually softened to one of concern. It then switched to something else as a wry grin slowly began to emerge. "I'd like to tell you that you haven't changed a bit . . ."

I knew she was nervous. She liked to hide behind a dry sense of humor, which I'd learned long ago was simply her way of dealing with stress. She was also as beautiful as ever, and I could see that her short hair only served to accentuate her features.

I stirred the wet dirt and gravel with the toe of my shoe. "Yeah. I admit I've seen better days." I turned and began walking my mountain bike toward the side of the road and toward a cluster of pine trees, motioning for her to follow. "Come on, we'll have a little more privacy in here. Walking in silence, I led her along a path I'd made only a few minutes earlier. I didn't know what to say, and I was sure Kelly's feelings were becoming more and more mixed the longer we walked.

It had rained nearly all of the previous day and throughout the early part of the night. The air smelled clean and fresh because of the rain, but clear skies made for a chilly morning. Had I not biked to our meeting place, putting my major muscle groups to work, I knew I'd be shivering from the cold. Walking kept me warm, though even with my sleeves buttoned at the wrist, I knew it wouldn't be long before I felt the biting chill creeping into my flesh, especially since my clothes were still damp from yesterday.

After we'd walked for some fifty yards, I leaned my bike against one of the taller pines and disappeared into a stand of younger, smaller pines. With some obvious reluctance, Kelly followed. She had withdrawn her hands from her coat pockets for balance as she carefully made her way through the tall, wet grass and over tree roots and snags.

Soon we came upon a clearing. Here, an old fallen tree would give us a place to sit.

I walked over and sat on a section of damp bark with my hands sunk deep into the pockets of my filthy Dockers. "Please, have a seat."

"Why, thank you. I can't believe what you've done with the place."

We both smiled at her light—though somewhat forced—comment. Seconds later, her expression turned serious. "What's this all about, Jason? What's going on?"

I tried to smother a sigh before it escaped my lips, but couldn't. Instead I just shook my head. My right hand slid from my pocket and I began picking nervously at the dead tree bark beside me. "Kelly, I honestly wish I knew." I glanced up at her inquisitive eyes. "Did you read the paper?"

"Yes. The police shootings and the gang drive-by shooting. I take it those were the articles you were hinting at on the phone?"

I nodded, not knowing what to say next. "Kelly, I . . . I had nothing to do with those killings, and I have no idea what kind of evidence they're referring to. I . . ."

Kelly's hand reached over and touched mine. "Don't be ridiculous, Jason. I know you didn't do it. You don't have to try to convince me."

Out of nowhere tears began filling my eyes, but I swiped at them with my hands. "It all started when I checked my mail slot at school. I teach now—junior high."

"I'm not surprised. You had a knack for it."

I nodded, not really hearing her compliment, and then told her all about receiving the strange card, dismissing it as nothing more than a prank, and pitching it in the garbage without another thought. I told her about the ransacking of my apartment, the drugs on the bed, the knife in the headboard, and the mysterious phone call that let me know I had nowhere to run for help.

"Jason, I'm sure if you talk to the police and tell them your side of the story they'd—"

"Kelly," I interrupted more sharply than I had planned, "I don't know *what* they'd believe! Yes, in my mind, I'm sure I've got an alibi for whenever those killings took place. But remember what happened to my apartment? If this guy who's obviously setting me up was able to do all that with the apartment and the prescription drugs, how do I know he hasn't planted more stuff out there to contradict whatever I might say? The article in the paper pretty much tells me he's ready to do just that."

"But when the police look into it, surely—"

"Kelly, I don't know what they'll find. I sure as heck have no idea how they'll react. I'm accused of killing four of their own! You don't think they're going to be out for blood on this one?"

Kelly didn't answer. She just sat there and slid her hands back into the pockets of her coat.

I suddenly became aware of my lip quivering from the morning chill that was finally penetrating my skin. I hopped off the tree and began to pace, trying to generate a little more body heat by moving.

"Kelly, I've given this a lot of thought over the last few days, believe me. The moment I turn myself in, if I don't have a pile of physical evidence waiting to collapse on top of me, you can be sure there will be enough circumstantial evidence to accomplish the same thing. Whoever this guy is that's out there trailing me for whatever reason is not only good, he's a professional. Who is he? I haven't a clue. But it's clear he's experienced at what he does and . . ." I threw up my hands in desperation. "I don't know *what* to do!"

"You've been up in these hills for two days?"

"Going on three. After getting shot at in that motel room, I needed someplace I could collect my thoughts . . . get my feet back under me . . . try to figure out what my next step should be."

I could see her glance all around me, and from the expression on her face I think she was beginning to understand my reasoning for picking the foothills as my place of retreat.

"You've been sleeping out in the open?"

I couldn't help chuckling. I was relieved at her temporary acceptance of my situation and her apparent desire to learn more. "No—though I know I look it. I've got a tent just west of the M over there. I've been living out of a 72-hour kit my parents gave me a few years back for Christmas."

She nodded, accepting that.

I approached her cautiously. "Kelly, I'm so sorry I called you like this. And I'm really sorry for standing you up. I had no intention of doing that. I . . . I didn't know where else to turn. Your name came to me out here on this mountain my second night on the run. I was seeking guidance from the only source I could rely on. You know what I mean? Whoever's doing this has got to be watching my parents and maybe even my friends. And if he isn't, I'm sure the police are."

When she remained silent, I added, "I'd understand completely if you want to walk away from here. It's been awhile since we . . . since we were together. I guess I didn't think he'd know about . . . you." I swallowed hard, feeling extremely awkward. "If you'd rather leave, I'll understand completely."

Kelly sat there the entire time, just looking at me. It was a strange look—a mixture of both happiness and sorrow. "I'd . . ." Her eyes closed and a tear escaped her eye, rolling over her cheek. "I'd never do that, Jason. You know that."

I felt incredibly guilty at that moment and was about to press her about what had prompted her obviously painful feelings. But she, too, hopped off the log, her face struggling to look resolute and determined. "I . . . I came to help. And that's exactly what I plan to do." She wiped at her eyes.

I stood there not knowing what to say. Kelly was holding something back. I knew she was. Before I could press her, however, she walked toward me and gently put her arms around me in a hug. It felt just like I remembered.

"I'm here for you," she whispered.

As we held each other, her warmth and the faint scent of her perfume brought me comfort similar to what I'd felt when her name came to me two nights earlier.

When Kelly finally released me, she stood back, her eyes still moist, and seemed to study me anew. I felt self-conscious once again. I was a mess, and I smelled worse than the boys' locker room at my school.

"The rugged look . . ." She laughed and cleared her throat, pulling up her dry-wit shield once again. "The rugged look just isn't you, Jason." I noticed her voice was a bit stronger and more determined. It was as if she had finally made up her mind. "The first thing we need to do," Kelly continued, "is get you out of these hills. Come on. We'll find someplace where you can clean up."

She started to pull my hand toward the path we'd followed minutes earlier, but I hesitated.

"You're sure about this, Kelly? It could be dangerous."

For nearly a minute we had a stare-down. Then she bit at her lower lip and nodded. "I am. Just promise me you won't ask me that question again."

I thought it an odd request and was about to say as much when she placed her index finger lightly on my lips. "I'm here to help you, Jason. Let me, okay?"

I nodded, but when she started walking I made no attempt to follow her. "What's wrong?" she asked.

"I wasn't sure you'd say yes," I said, feeling sheepish. "Let me grab my bike and go back and break camp. I don't want someone stumbling over my stuff by mistake. And I don't want to lose it either. I'll be back in thirty minutes or so. Wait in the car, okay?"

Kelly nodded and continued toward her car. I retrieved my mountain bike from the pine tree and began pedaling toward camp the moment I reached the paved road.

As I pumped the pedals, I looked heavenward. "Thank you," I whispered. "Thank you so much!"

CHAPTER 9

There is nothing—absolutely nothing—in this world as refreshing as a hot shower! There is also nothing like soap and shampoo, even the cheap ones furnished by a nondescript hotel, especially when you haven't used either one for several days.

After I'd broken camp earlier that morning, I stashed the tent, daypack, and sleeping bag in three separate spots—crevices in the rock and brush where I knew they'd not only remain hidden but somewhat protected as well. The mountain bike I stashed in the clearing behind the fallen tree Kelly and I had sat on earlier that morning. I covered it with fallen branches, thinking it was doubtful anyone would run across it unless they knew what they were looking for. I decided I'd retrieve all of my gear when I finally cleared up the mess I was in. For the time being, though, it was nice to know the stuff was out there.

After I met Kelly at her car, I hunched down in the passenger seat for the next half hour before we pulled into a hotel neither of us had ever used before. It was just a short distance outside of Denver. Kelly paid for the room while I remained hidden in the car. Just as we'd discussed on the way over, she requested a room as far away from the street as possible. She told the clerk that she'd been traveling all night and didn't want to be disturbed. The truth was we wanted a room far enough away from the front desk that there would be less of a chance of anyone who worked for the hotel noticing me slipping in and out of the building—let alone the room. We had considered two rooms, but I didn't want to attract any undue attention to Kelly. As far as the hotel was concerned, a woman by the name of Kelly Nicholls was staying the night. And with only one room, I could think of no possible way anyone could link the two of us together.

With a slight shudder, I pulled the room-darkening curtains closed before hitting the light switch near the door. Two lamps on either end of a simple dresser threw weak light into the middle of the room, leaving the corners in the shadows.

Before I stepped into the shower, I opened the bathroom door a crack and tossed out my filthy clothing. Kelly then took everything I was wearing to a Laundromat she'd spotted on the way over. Dropping my clothes off, she swung by a store and picked up a few toiletries for me. I was embarrassed having her buy my toothpaste and deodorant, but I knew I couldn't risk drawing attention to myself looking the way that I did.

Rinsing the last of the shampoo from my hair, I lathered up once more with the soap and began my final rinse. At that moment my worldly possessions consisted of my watch, my wallet, and a pair of shoes. I felt very literally naked and vulnerable.

I shut off the water and reached around the shower curtain for a large white towel that was tucked into a chrome rack above the toilet. Once I was dry, I wrapped the towel around my waist and pulled aside the wet shower curtain.

I grabbed a smaller towel from the towel rack and ran it over my head as I walked into the main part of the hotel room. I snatched up the television remote from a nightstand, pressing the power button at the same time I sat on the queen-size bed.

Although my channel surfing found nothing that I really wanted to watch, I enjoyed hearing the sounds coming from the stereo speakers. Even commercials were a welcome change from the silence I'd endured in the hills.

I looked around at the standard, no-frills hotel room. It was definitely an improvement over the exploding motel. And it felt good to again be able to walk on carpet with bare feet and have the freedom to move around without bumping into canvas walls. I was beginning to feel human again.

A cheap digital clock on the nightstand confirmed that it was eight thirty in the morning.

Dad might be at work, but Mom would be home. My older sister and brother, who also lived on their own, usually worked on Saturday. Trevor, who'd just returned home from his mission, would probably already be out and about, and my youngest brother Chad was probably out with his friends doing who knew what. I wanted to pick up the phone and dial any one of them. The longer I sat there, the worse the temptation became. But I couldn't risk it. I was someplace safe—someplace civilized—and I wanted to enjoy it for a while.

I pulled my eyes away from the phone and glanced at the television instead. I was shocked to find a picture of myself above the shoulder of a well-dressed female news anchor. I jumped up, nearly losing my towel in the process, grabbed for the remote, and punched up the volume as quickly as I could.

". . . continue to mount against this man, Jason Harrington, a local junior high school teacher wanted by authorities in connection with the slaying of four police officers. If you have any information regarding him or his location, you are encouraged to contact police immediately. He is reported to be armed and dangerous."

Armed and dangerous? Me? Jason Harrington?

My picture faded away and was replaced almost immediately with a moving clip of a group of people sitting at a table, outside what looked like a park of some kind. It appeared to be a press conference. I struggled to understand the reporter as my eyes and mind suddenly recognized my parents and siblings seated at a table littered with microphones.

"... family continues to insist there has been some kind of mistake and yesterday held a news conference to share with the public their thoughts on what they continue to call a 'witch hunt.'"

The reporter was replaced with a head shot of my graying father at the microphone. He looked stressed and his words sounded forced and terse. "We are urging the police to show restraint. My son has no record of any kind. He is being pursued as if he were the only possible suspect."

"What about DNA linking him to each location?" asked a media reporter from somewhere out of camera range.

"I don't know that there has been such evidence found," responded my father, tersely. "From what I understand, that is a rumor—nothing more."

The reporter at the anchor desk filled the screen once more. "Jason's family is urging their son, wherever he might be, to turn himself in to authorities. They are vowing their love and support with what they perceive as a huge misunderstanding on the part of police."

The graphic over her shoulder was replaced with several green dollar signs. "In other news, local business proprietors blame the construction of a new overpass for a tremendous drop in sal—"

I shut off the television, dropped the remote onto the bedspread, and, for several minutes, could do nothing but stare at the black screen of the television in front of me. When I finally did look away, my eyes locked once more on the old beige phone.

I wanted to call Mom and Dad—talk to each of my siblings—tell them I was all right. But paranoia stopped me. How did I know authorities wouldn't be listening in, just waiting for a chance to trace the phone call?

It appeared I'd been right from the start. Local law enforcement was acting—reacting—like a pack of hunting dogs that had suddenly caught the scent of the fox. And, if I wasn't careful, they'd tree me in nothing flat. I couldn't call. Not yet, anyway.

I briefly entertained the idea of having Kelly place a phone call for me, but I dismissed the thought right away. Kelly was doing enough for me as it was. I didn't want anyone to know she was with me. Everyone thought I was running alone. Of course, up until a few hours ago that was true. But I had to watch out for Kelly, and the police having a recording of her voice they could use against her later was the last thing I wanted.

The sliding of a plastic key in the electronic lock of the door caught me completely by surprise. The door opened a crack. "You decent?" called Kelly.

I started to answer, realized I wasn't decent, and tightened the towel around my waist as I dashed for the bathroom. Once I was there I closed the door behind me, leaving it open a crack. "Okay!" I shouted. "Come on in."

I heard the door open. "I'm putting your clothes on the floor in front of the bathroom door. I picked up a few new ones for you. I hope you don't mind."

Her voice was louder, the door being the only thing separating us. "You didn't have to do that, Kelly."

"I know I didn't." The volume of her voice faded as she walked away.

When I was sure she was gone, I opened the door and found my clothes laundered and sitting atop a few plain-colored T-shirts and two pairs of blue jeans. She'd obviously pulled my sizes from the clothes I'd been wearing. I shut the bathroom door and quickly dressed.

The jeans were a little big on me, but the denim, so much stronger than the flimsy cotton I'd been wearing for the past three days, made me feel invincible—for maybe five seconds.

As I slipped on a light blue T-shirt, I glanced at myself in the bathroom mirror. It was definitely an improvement.

Satisfied, I reached around and yanked off the sales tags, noting the prices before pitching them into a small trash can beneath the sink. Kelly had refused to take any of my money this morning, insisting that I might need what little cash I had. I assured her that I would pay her back for everything. She'd nodded and considered the matter closed, but I was determined not to let even a single item go unaccounted for. *When all of this is over,* I thought stubbornly, *she's going to get back every cent she's given me.*

When I opened the bathroom door, Kelly was seated at the head of the bed, waiting for me.

"Now you're starting to look like your old self." She reached into a plastic sack next to her and held out a comb. "Care for one of these?"

I grinned. "I've wanted one of those for the past three days." I quickly ran it through my hair.

"And now you look too much like your old self," she laughed. "Here, maybe you'd better add these to today's attire." She handed me a pair of sunglasses, a pair of low-power reading glasses, and a Colorado Rockies baseball cap. I took them from Kelly and then stopped when I suddenly recognized a very familiar smell.

From behind her back, Kelly produced a few more paper sacks.

"Two sausage Egg McMuffins and some orange juice," she announced with a smile. "I thought you could probably use some real food. Well, maybe not 'real,' but at least a fast imitation."

One sip of the juice and my taste buds exploded with the flavor. I had been grateful for the MREs. Had it not been for them I would have been starving, but the smell of a simple, warm Egg McMuffin was paradise. I consumed it in under a minute.

Kelly smiled the whole time, laughing lightly at my eagerness. "Feeling civilized and American again?" she asked as she took a bite of her own breakfast.

"Yes," I said, finding a paper napkin in one of the bags and wiping my mouth. "As a matter of fact, I am. Thank you, Kelly. Thanks so much."

She nodded, a touch of sadness still in her face, and reached for her own orange juice. She took a short sip and continued eating her breakfast sandwich in silence.

"Did you catch the news this morning?" I asked, sitting on the end of the bed after she had finished eating

"No, I didn't. I did pick up a paper though." There was something in her eyes that made me feel a bit uneasy.

"What did it say?"

She hesitated before pulling from her coat pocket what had to have been the article she'd torn from the newspaper. I took it and unfolded it: "DNA Evidence Found."

It was nearly double the length of the first article I'd read a few days earlier and more or less contained everything I'd heard in the news snippet I'd caught minutes before. There were no specifics on just what kind of DNA evidence had been discovered. Just that it had. The printed article, however, did reveal one thing the anchorwoman on television had failed to point out—the fact that anyone knew my name and identity was solely the result of a leak to the press.

Of course, I had a pretty good idea who'd been responsible for the leak. I might be busy running from the law, but it was clear that whoever was hunting me wasn't just going to sit on his hands until I decided to surface again. No, whoever this person was, he was busy making sure the noose around my neck remained good and tight.

I looked up from the article to find Kelly studying my face.

"They showed my picture on television. It was a picture from last year's school yearbook."

She nodded silently.

"Kelly, I'm telling you, I have nothing to do with these murders. Whoever—"

She placed her hand on my leg, silencing me. "I believe you, Jason. Relax. I believe you."

A companionable silence followed.

I cleared my throat. "This is like some incredible nightmare." I stood, tossing the newspaper article on the table. "DNA evidence? How am I supposed to counter something like that?"

Pacing, I eventually came to rest on the corner of the dresser directly in front of Kelly. When I'd finally stopped moving, Kelly reached over to the table and plucked up the article, presumably to read through it once more.

"It's pure chaos, is what it is." She skimmed the article once more with her eyes.

Her word choice jolted me. "What did you say?"

"I said everything's chaos. None of this makes any sense. If you really did—"

"Chaos," I muttered.

Kelly fell silent, giving me time to work through my obvious confusion.

"Chaos!" I grinned, slowly, and for the first time in days I felt as though a ray of sunlight was finally beginning to shine down on me.

"What did I say, Jason? What is it?"

I sat there on the edge of the dresser, lost in my thoughts. My mind began reaching back—remembering the quotes . . . the information a bit of research on the subject had given me several years back.

"Jason?"

Chaos? Why hadn't I made the connection sooner?

"Jason?"

I looked up, snapping back into reality at the sight of the puzzled expression on Kelly's face.

"Oh, it's just . . ." I stopped, took a few seconds to collect my thoughts, and began again. "When I was a missionary, I had a companion that loved chaos."

"You lost me."

I grinned. "Well, missionaries sometimes tend to latch onto . . . pet themes during scripture study—dinosaurs, the lost tribes of Israel, stuff like that. In fact, sometimes the topics were downright ridiculous. Did Adam have a belly button? Which *did* come first, the chicken or the egg? You know, goofy stuff that isn't critical to your salvation, but somewhat intriguing when you're looking for something new and different to study at six o'clock in the morning."

Kelly grinned. "And missionaries waste time on these themes?"

"Well, we're not really encouraged to, if that's what you mean."

From the look on her face, I got the impression she wasn't buying it. "Hey, some take these subjects very seriously."

"Dinosaurs in the Bible?" she added with a chuckle.

"Did you know there's a painting of a brontosaurus and a pterodactyl in one of our temples? The Manti Temple in Utah."

Her smile slowly disappeared. "Really?"

"Yup. I'm told if you go there you can't miss them. There are goofy subjects a lot of members of my church fiddle with at some point in their life. It creeps in."

"But how does this relate to—?"

"Chaos?"

She nodded.

"Well, one of my companions was a fanatic about something called Chaos Theory. Of course, he was also a fanatic over something he called the Complex Theory, but—"

"Whoa. Slow down, Jason. One thing at a time. Let's stick with Chaos Theory. I've heard about it, and even heard about some business applications for it, but it's been awhile. What can you tell me about it?"

"When I returned home from my mission I ran across a book on the subject in the university library and so I read it. I'm still certainly no expert on the subject, but I do cover it briefly with my pre-algebra students each year when we hit our unit on probability."

Kelly still looked confused, so I continued.

"The mathematician Euclid invented a geometry that has, for the last two millennia, been based on planes, lines, triangles, cubes, spheres, and cones. Of course, the problem with his method is that in the real world mountains aren't perfect cones, and it's tough to find a perfect sphere in nature. The universe, and everything within it, is pitted, warped, and misshapen."

"Okay. I'm with you so far."

"Well, Chaos Theory helps us make sense of what on the outside looks rough, random, and accidental."

"You lost me again."

I grinned. "It's a relatively new science that's teaching us that randomness is in fact structured and stable. We've just never looked for anything like it before."

"You're saying there's order in randomness?"

I nodded. "That's why I discuss it with my students when we get into probability. Probability studies randomness but says the outcome is determined strictly by chance. In other words, you can't know the outcome of a random event before it occurs. But if there actually *is* order in randomness—"

"Then an outcome can be figured before the event happens," finished Kelly.

"Yeah," I replied. "Assuming you understood all of the laws surrounding it."

"Interesting," Kelly said, nodding her head.

"'I shall never believe that God plays dice with the world.' Einstein said that."

"But what does all of that have to do with what's going on with you right now?" asked Kelly.

"I've been looking at everything that's been happening to me as if there is no pattern at all. I'm reacting without trying to determine a pattern first. It's there. I just need to discover what it is."

"And if there is a pattern?"

"Let's just say that in my mind, this entire mistake would become a bit more manageable. The harum-scarumness of it begins to disappear and . . . I can start sorting things out rationally, rather than just reacting blindly."

We both remained silent for some time. It was Kelly who spoke up first.

"Maybe you need some help to even find the pattern."

"What do you mean?"

"Well, you won't go to the authorities, but you have to admit there's only so much you and I can do from this hotel room. We need help, Jason."

"But how?"

"How about hiring a private investigator?" Kelly suggested.

"A PI? Seriously?"

"Of course I'm serious. They're trained in how to dig up information. We could get a private investigator to act as our go-between for us. My masters was in public relations, Jason. And, to get anything done, you have to network—establish connections."

I ran my hand through my hair. All I could visualize was a lantern-jawed man in a trench coat, lurking in dark alleys. "Well . . . they are licensed, right?"

Kelly winced slightly. "Actually, in Colorado there is no licensing." The skepticism on my face must have been glaringly obvious because she quickly added, "The state's working on changing that though."

I looked at her, trying to figure out just how serious she was about all of this. She looked serious.

I then ran a hand over my stubbled chin, which reminded me of something else I'd asked her to pick up for me. "You didn't happen to find a razor did you?"

She pulled a pack of disposable razors and a can of shaving cream from a plastic bag near her feet. "I did. But, you know,

I've been thinking about it. Are you sure you want to get rid of it? In another week, I'll bet it'll change your appearance quite a bit. Maybe even more than the glasses and cap."

"I've thought about that. No, I wasn't going to shave it completely, but I want to trim it up a bit—make it look a bit more intentional on my part." My fingers scrambled through my thick hair. "Oh, by the way, remember that haircut you gave me back in college? You up for a little clipping?"

A shared smile passed between the two of us. It happened on our fourth or fifth date and had taken a lot of convincing from Kelly, as well as her roommates, for me to work up the courage to let her cut my hair for the first time. It turned out she had a knack for it.

She pulled from the bag a gleaming pair of barber scissors. "I'm way ahead of you. Let's head for the sink."

I got up from the bed and started for the bathroom when I noticed Kelly wasn't following me. Instead, she'd pulled the phonebook from the nightstand and was flipping through it with her thumb and index finger. "What are you doing?" I asked.

After a few seconds, when she'd found the section she'd been looking for, she laid it open on the bed. It read, INVESTIGATOR. "When we're through shearing you, we'll find us an investigator to give us a hand."

"Do you know someone?"

"Nope. But there are three pages of people we can choose from."

Then, before I could respond, she held up an index finger. "You were the one who was telling me how randomness can be a good thing."

There was no sense in arguing. Kelly had me there.

CHAPTER 10

A few hours later Kelly and I were driving through Littleton, a suburb ten or so miles south of Denver that looks nothing like the city proper. Gone is Denver's high-rise skyline, replaced instead by a community that feels manageable—something not so overwhelming. I know some people are exhilarated by a big-city environment, but I'm not one of them.

We had just exited Highway 85 and were heading east on West Main Street. On both sides of the tree-lined street were two-story brick buildings, easily over a hundred years old, sandwiched next to each other. Each business tried to distinguish itself from the others with store fronts as varied as the businesses they represented.

Though we saw almost no one around, what little parking the narrow street offered was completely full, so we ended up parking nearly a block from the building we'd been looking for.

Even with my nominal disguise, I felt very uncomfortable out in the open. Driving and walking around in broad daylight seemed abnormal after having just spent three days in the hills. But I tried my best to act conventional. With my hair cut shorter, my growing beard neatly trimmed, and my new clothes, ball cap, and sunglasses, I didn't think I was likely to draw much attention.

Just blend in, I told myself.

The private investigator we'd settled on had an office on the second floor of a brick-and-stucco building that was also home to an antique store. It wasn't hard to spot the antique store—a large, working traffic light sat in the corner of the window, its slow advancement from green to yellow to red a definite eye-catcher.

Above the store on the second floor were two large windows. The one on the right was painted with a black and white yin-yang symbol and letters that seemed to promote some kind of martial arts school. The window on the left contained only a closed set of blinds, offering no indication that another business existed, or, for that matter, that anyone was even there.

An old blue wood-and-glass door complemented the feel of the antique store perfectly. But you had to go beyond the door and into the narrow stairwell immediately to your left to realize that there was more to the building than simply a collection of used and dusty antiques.

We climbed the wooden steps to the second floor and soon found ourselves standing in the middle of a moderately large landing. To our right were pictures and trophies one would expect to see outside a martial arts school. A door led to what was definitely their workout space. Peering through the narrow glass window in the door, we could see kids and adults lining up and beginning a series of kicks and punches.

To our left were two doors. One was marked as the karate instructor's office. The other bore a small brass plaque that read simply, MARINO INVESTIGATIONS.

The door was closed, and there was no sign that the man Kelly had spoken with over the phone was in his office. I said as much to Kelly as I was switching out my sunglasses for my reading glasses.

"He said he'd meet us at one," she responded. After glancing at her watch, she approached the door and was about to knock when I gently grabbed her wrist.

I looked around carefully and said, "You're sure about this? This guy doesn't appear to be advertising himself at all. How do we know he isn't some washed-up, wannabe cop?"

Kelly bit at her lower lip, a habit she found useful when giving something serious consideration. It didn't take her long to come up with an answer. "We don't," she whispered. "And we won't ever find out if we don't knock. Besides, this was the only guy I called whose fee seemed reasonable, and . . ."

"And what?" I prompted.

"He seemed the most polite."

I simply looked at her. Hiring someone who sounded polite was the last thing I would have looked for in an investigator. But I trusted Kelly's instincts. She'd made more calls than I could count before finally settling on this particular individual. Besides, she was right. There was no way to know what the guy was like until he opened the door. I let go of her wrist.

"All right. Let's give him a shot."

She nodded and knocked on the door

"It's open!" shouted a deep, gruff voice from the other side of the door. "Come in!"

I looked at Kelly. "That's polite?"

She ignored me, her jaw set as she opened the investigator's door and stepped inside.

I'm not exactly sure what I'd been expecting. Perhaps a beat-up wooden desk with an old-fashioned desk lamp as the only source of light in the room, a ceiling fan slowly spinning overhead. Behind that desk I'd probably imagined finding a Sam Spade–looking character smoking a cigarette, glancing at us from under a fedora of some kind. I couldn't have been further off.

The man seated behind the cluttered glass-and-steel desk looked like a character right out of a gangster movie. Reclining in his black leather office chair, he motioned us to enter and have a seat while at the same time talking into the telephone receiver wedged between his thick neck and fleshy head.

I threw a glance in Kelly's direction. The man, who was probably in his early fifties, looked like he belonged behind a meat counter, not an office desk. He wore a white shirt rolled up to the elbows, his thick arms, hands, and even knuckles covered with coarse, black hair. He had a five o'clock shadow that I doubted ever went away completely. And the insides of his collar, which he could probably never button even if he wanted to, were rough and worn from rubbing against the stubble of his double chin and neck. He also had on a faded brown polka dot tie that hung loosely around his neck.

Everything about the man seemed big except his height. He didn't look to be all that tall, but his fingers, hands, lips, and nose were thicker than average. His bushy eyebrows accentuated his mostly bald head. What little hair he did have was graying, clipped short, and went from one side of his head and back to the other, like the bottom half of a headband. His skin was a few shades darker than mine.

"I told ya. Don't worry about it. I've got it covered. So, relax." His voice was gravelly. From the full ashtray on the corner of his desk, it wasn't hard to figure out why. His eastern accent identified him as someone who wasn't from the area—perhaps Boston or Philadelphia.

"Yeah, I know. But, ya gotta understand . . ."

My eyes began drifting around his cluttered office as he continued talking on the phone. A neat freak this investigator wasn't.

I looked over at Kelly, who was also surveying the office, wondering if she still wanted to do business with a character like this.

At last he hung up the phone by slamming it back on its cradle. "Sorry, kids. My ex-wife called to wish me a . . . good afternoon." He stood to introduce himself. "The name's Lou Marino. Nice ta meet ya."

Both of us stood automatically, each of us shaking his thick hand in turn, an act that seemed amusing to him, though I couldn't imagine why. He couldn't have stood more than a shade over five feet, though his smiling hazel eyes and booming voice made up for his lack in height. He was noticeably more friendly with us than he had been with his ex-wife on the phone.

"Please, have a seat. I take it ya've seen my handiwork." Gesturing to the picture-covered wall, he winked. "Now, ya take your auto body shops. They're going ta have before and after shots all over their walls. Plastic surgeons, well, they do the same thing. I figure it's the easiest way ta show yous what I can get." He pointed toward the wall. It was covered in photographs—salacious photographs showing couples in various acts of passion. "Take that underwater shot in the upper right. I was in the pool for two hours before I finally got it." He held up his hands. "My fingers were prunes for days, I'll tell ya."

Kelly gave the picture a polite glance, though I could tell she was embarrassed by what was in it. Even though he'd drawn thick black lines over the eyes of each person in the photographs, that only helped to conceal their identities, not their behavior.

I saw the investigator take note of Kelly's reaction. "Hey, I'm sorry, sweetie. It's an ugly world out there. I don't mean ta offend ya, but it's what I run into."

She smiled slightly and cleared her throat. "I called you earlier. My name is—"

"Wait! Don't tell me!" The investigator began looking about his desk. "Ah, here it is." He picked up a take-out menu from a local Chinese restaurant. Something was scribbled on the back of it. "Your name is Kelly . . . Nicholls, and ya said ya had somethin' very important ta discuss with me."

Kelly and I both looked at each other. I, for one, was surprised at how rapidly he'd found the note. His desk was tornado territory.

The investigator's eyes fell on me next. "And you . . . you must be *Jason Harrington*."

My body stiffened and I suddenly felt as if a trapdoor had opened under me while I was suspended on the hangman's platform. I could scarcely breathe. I was sure Kelly wouldn't have given out my name over the phone. From the genuine look of shock on her face, I knew she hadn't.

"Relax, kid. Relax. You're face is all over out there."

"But how—?"

"Would ya want ta hire me if I wasn't able ta pick ya out? Relax. Now, what can I do for ya?"

I was still digesting the fact that he'd recognized me despite my cosmetic changes—the haircut, beard, and glasses—when Kelly spoke up.

"He's innocent, Mr. Marino."

"Whoa! Hold on there. It's Lou. Call me Lou, okay, sweetie?"

"Fine. Lou. The reason I called you is because we need some help. We need some way of proving that Jason's innocent."

"I see." He glanced at me again. "And are ya, kid?"

"Am I what?"

"Innocent."

"Of course I am. If I wasn't do you think I'd be coming to you?"

The man slouched in his chair, chin number two becoming more pronounced than chin number one. "Hey, in this business I get all kinds of people looking for help."

I nodded. "I'm sure you do. Sorry about that. Yes, I am innocent. I have no idea what triggered all of this, but I promise you I had nothing to do with the killing of those police officers." I then took a deep breath and started from the beginning. I described the card I'd received at school and how my apartment had been trashed. I also told him all about the strange phone call I'd received.

"And what was it ya said he called ya?"

"Musor? I don't know. I could be remembering the card wrong, but I think that's what the guy on the phone said too. Though he was a little hard to understand. He had some kind of an accent—German, maybe Russian." I finished by describing the motel shooting I'd survived and how I'd been hiding out in the hills ever since.

"And yous two want me ta give ya an alibi?"

"I'm not asking for you to *give* me anything. I'm here because I'm innocent and I want to clear my name. Mr. Mar— Lou," I corrected myself, "I'm telling you the truth. I had nothing to do with the deaths of any police officers. I'm being set up. Someone's after me."

"Why?"

"I don't know!" I shouted in frustration. Both he and Kelly remained silent as I struggled to control my emotions. When I finally felt as though I could speak, I asked him, "Can you help me?"

The older man just sat there with his fingers steepled, resting on his large middle. "And ya want me ta clear your name and discover who's been doin' all the killin'?"

I had to admit, when he put it into those words, it did sound like a very tall order.

His office was silent for some time as Lou peered into our eyes in turn. He finally glanced at one of his lewd photos on the wall. "Well, what you're asking me ta do isn't the kinda work I normally do. Now if one of ya had a lost friend or had a cheatin' lover . . ." He fell silent a moment more, studying our faces. "I'm tellin' ya, the police and the public are in an uproar about all this. I might not be able ta—"

"Please, Lou," said Kelly. "Could you at least look into this for us? Please?"

After staring at Kelly for some time, he began to slowly smile. "All right. All right, sweetie. Let's see what I can do."

I had just begun to breathe a sigh of relief when Lou caught me completely off guard with his next request.

"I'll have expenses. I'll need five hundred dollars up front."

My jaw dropped so far it ached. "You want what?"

"Do I stutter or do your ears flap, kid? I said I'll need five hundred ta start."

"You didn't say anything about an advance over the phone," complained Kelly.

"Ya didn't tell me what I'd be doin' for ya either," countered the investigator.

"But we—"

"What?" Lou interrupted. "Ya don't have that much on ya?"

"Of course I don't."

Lou then leaned forward and looked me square in the eye. "Well, I'm a pretty reasonable guy. How much *do* ya have on ya?"

Before Kelly had the chance to say anything, I reached into the pocket of my jeans. I still had a little over two hundred dollars left over from the ATM machine. "I've got a couple hundred." I held out the twenties and he snatched them from my hand faster than a robin grabbing a worm from the damp spring soil.

"That's a start." But before I could get a word out about what had just happened, he'd already leaned back in his leather chair and slipped the money into his shirt pocket. "Relax, kid. Ya've just hired the best. Now, whatta ya say we start puttin' things together?"

I glanced over at Kelly. I was really beginning to dislike this man, and I could tell from the expression on her face that Kelly felt the same way. Lou Marino may have sounded friendly over the phone, and his rates were probably lower than anyone else's in town, but I still wasn't sure we could completely trust the man.

From a side drawer in his desk he withdrew a worn yellow legal pad, its corners dog-eared and a few coffee mug stains on the first page. Lou didn't seem to notice. "All right," he said and then patted his desk until he discovered the pen he obviously knew was there. "Whatta ya say we start from the beginnin'?"

"The beginning of what?"

Lou lowered his pen. "Kid, yer not gonna make a habit of this are ya? Repeatin' everything I say? It's gettin' on my nerves."

I was beginning to lose my temper when Kelly suddenly took hold of my hand, giving it a slight squeeze.

I took a deep breath. When I felt calm enough, I began speaking again, once more detailing everything that had happened to me since Wednesday afternoon. Only occasionally, though, would Lou take notes. And, when he did, they were never more than a word or two. As I spoke, I spied a business license of some kind on the wall—a slip of paper jammed into a cheap metal frame. The realization that I was spilling my guts to a man I hardly knew was constantly gnawing at the back of my mind. After all, the guy seemed more like a used-car salesman than a private investigator. Of course, who was I expecting? Tom Selleck?

When I'd finished telling him everything, he glanced at the tablet a moment, holding it back as he read wide-eyed what little he'd written.

"Kid, whadda ya know about the Mafia?"

"What?" I caught the look of disgust on his face and spoke up immediately to cover up my mistake. "I don't know anything about the Mafia, except what I've seen on television or read in the newspaper. What would a bunch of Ital—?"

"I didn't say anything about the *Italian* Mafia," he corrected me, tossing his pen back onto his desk. It rolled beneath a few papers—back where he'd originally found it. "I'm talking about the *Russian* Mafia."

I glanced at Kelly's confused expression, then turned to Lou and shrugged. "I don't know anything about the Russian Mafia."

"Well, in that case, Teach, ya've got a little homework ta do."

Lou stood and made his way over to a laptop on a small student desk and raised the monitor, hitting the power button at the same time. The machine beeped and began booting up.

"Sensei Green lets me use the computer in his office next door when I need ta. Nice setup he's got, too. He's got one of those high-speed connections. Nice. I'm gonna look up a few things next door and yous two are gonna look up what ya can on the Russian Mafia—*Red* Mafia if ya want ta be politically correct about it. Gimme an hour. Use the Internet ta find out what ya can. When I get back, then mebbe we can have a more *educated* discussion."

With one thick finger he tapped in his password, connecting the laptop to the Internet. He then threw Kelly and me a wink. "I'll be back." He left his office and shut the door behind him.

I looked at Kelly. "I can't believe he trusts us enough to leave us alone in his office."

"Why not?" replied Kelly matter-of-factly. "He's got us both in one place, has his two hundred dollars, and now has a current physical description of both you and me. When we leave you can be sure he'll also have my car's license number as well. He knows we won't go anywhere."

I nodded, conceding the point. "Do you trust him?"

"I don't know, Jason. I think we've got to run with him for now. We'll have to stay on our toes, though."

"Yeah. I guess you're right."

I eyed the monitor. The home page was set on a search engine I was familiar with from school, but I knew my limits. I learned long ago, during our first project together, that Kelly had a genuine gift when it came to researching on the Internet, and I had no reservations at all about letting her get into the driver's seat. "Go ahead. You're the pro when it comes to this kind of stuff."

Kelly immediately reached for the dirty external mouse Lou must have preferred using himself. With his large fingers, it was easy to understand why. "All right, let's see what we can learn about the Russian Mafia."

We both leaned forward as she entered a few keywords. It took us only five minutes to begin to fully appreciate the breadth and scope of the trouble I was in.

If, in fact, a member of the Russian Mafia was after me . . . if even half of what we were reading was true . . . I didn't stand a chance.

CHAPTER 11

My eyes barely had time to focus on each new window as Kelly began pulling up a wide variety of articles from various magazines, newspapers, and websites.

"That should be enough for a start," she remarked. She then selected a reputable news magazine article first and brought it to the front of everything else on the computer's desktop.

The article didn't hold back any punches. Unlike La Cosa Nostra—the American Mafia—whose look and vernacular have become so much a part of our culture and entertainment, the Russian Mafia doesn't play by any rules. There are no specialized business ventures. With the Russian Mafia, everything from medical fraud to the selling of nuclear weaponry is fair game.

According to Russian police, cited in the article, there were two hundred organized crime syndicates operating in Moscow alone, and over three hundred operating in over fifty nations worldwide. There are at least thirty Russian crime syndicates just in North America—in almost every state. The article cited U.S. intelligence sources that estimate one million "soldiers" operate in the United States, the same number of men found in the ground forces of the Russian army.

Thanks to corrupt businessmen and officials, forty percent of Russia's Gross Domestic Product was presently controlled by the Mafia. They controlled all the banks in St. Petersburg and

Moscow, and laundered literally billions of dollars from drug sales through banks they've set up in the Caribbean and Panama.

I touched the monitor. "Look at this."

"'Over eighty percent of the businesses in Russia pay money for protection,'" she read. "What makes them tick?" Kelly asked.

She focused next on a website article that had originally appeared in book form. It had a more historical flavor to it, which was what she'd been looking for. We both began skimming through it.

Throughout Russia's history, peasants have rebelled against the all-powerful czars. From these rebellions an outlaw culture developed that neither Lenin nor Stalin could stop. A vast network of prisons were built and filled with what Stalin had deemed criminals, political enemies, dissidents, and Jews. In the wake of his death, however, some eight million of these inmates were released.

When corruption began eating into the Soviet empire, these thieves and criminals filled the voids with a black market. The Kremlin turned a blind eye to it, and the underworld thrived. Eventually the underground economy produced by the black market accounted for fifty percent of the average soviet worker's personal income.

By the late 1980s the Soviet Union was on the brink of economic collapse.

Then, in 1991, the Iron Curtain fell, and the nation's criminal element seized power before democracy ever had the chance of getting a foothold. By the mid-90s over six thousand crime groups were established. It was a free market free-for-all.

I turned and stared blankly at Lou's filing cabinets for several minutes while Kelly kept reading.

Eventually, I voiced what was running through my head. "They're the biggest, wealthiest, most well-equipped Mafia organization out there, Kelly. How do we fight against something like that?"

Kelly continued clicking the mouse, undoubtedly scrolling down the article while skimming the rest of its contents. Seconds later she spoke up, and I didn't like the tone of her voice.

"Uh, Jason?"

"Yeah," I answered rubbing my eyes with my thumb and forefinger.

"It gets worse."

"You're kidding." I looked at the screen and, when my eyes had finished focusing, began reading where Kelly's finger had been touching the screen.

According to the article, the KGB looted their own nation for party bosses who wanted to hold on to their wealth and power, knowing full well their government was on the brink of collapse. They'd set up over two thousand shell companies and false bank accounts. But that still wasn't enough to hide the amount of money they were stealing. They turned to Soviet criminal organizations for help, providing them, in exchange, with the latest in communications and computer technology.

"Okay. So how is this wor—?"

"Keep reading," encouraged Kelly.

Only after reading two more sentences had I caught on to Kelly's point.

When the Curtain fell, the article went on to point out, KGB members, government officials, and up-and-coming Russian entrepreneurs swelled the ranks of these modernized criminal organizations. These individuals had PhDs and included engineers, economists, and mathematicians. In no time they became the leaders of these corrupt organizations.

"Excellent," I muttered with sarcasm. "So what they're telling us is that we're not dealing with idiots here, or the kind of bumbling mobsters you see in low budget B-movies."

Kelly was nodding her head slowly. "That's putting it in a nutshell."

My eyes were still on the computer screen, though I wasn't seeing anything.

I'm not only in over my head, I thought to myself darkly, *but I've got a hundred feet of ocean on top of me.*

In the meantime Kelly began closing several of the open windows we'd already explored. I had turned to gaze off into nothingness when Kelly spoke up again.

"Hello. Now this is interesting."

I felt too numb to respond. When my eyes hadn't returned to the screen, Kelly began describing for me what she was looking at.

"This is the home page of an organization known as the Congress of Russian Americans. It says here that, according to the CRA, 'there are hardly any ethnic Russians in the Russian Mafia. Use of the term is therefore offensive to the over three million Russian Americans who have, over the last two centuries, contributed much to the U.S. in science, art, engineering, literature, and music.'"

"And that's supposed to make me feel better?" I asked.

"No, but now I understand what Lou had meant when he said that the Red Mafia was a more politically correct term than Russian Mafia."

Kelly went on paraphrasing more of the article. "In the 1980s, during the Cold War negotiations, when anti-Semitism in Russia was at its peak, Russia granted many Russian-Jewish citizens permission to leave the country. And while many of these good Russian Jews did, Russia took advantage of the opportunity by ridding their country of some of its worst criminals at the same time—falsifying passports to make them appear Jewish when necessary. Fidel Castro did the same thing. A compassionate United States suddenly received—with open arms—hundreds of thousands of criminals who had a new home."

Both of us jumped when Lou burst through the office door. Part of me was surprised he hadn't come back with the authorities in tow. *But then, he can't make any money off me that way,* I thought.

"So, am I speakin' ta the enlightened?" Lou dropped heavily into his chair and tossed a single sheet of paper onto his desk. It had only a few words scribbled on it.

Youthful shouts from across the hall filled the office, and I got up to shut the door. "If you mean, have we learned a great deal? The answer's yes."

He merely nodded as I returned to my seat. Kelly had turned her chair around, as well as my own, so that we faced Lou just as we had in the beginning.

"Well, Teach, let's hear what ya've learned."

I summarized what we'd read and watched as Lou sat silently, listening intently, nodding his head occasionally. When I'd finished, he seemed pleased.

"Very good. Ya shared some stuff that I hadn't heard before. But, like I say, ya learn something new everyday if ya wanna."

Lou cleared his throat and fished a pack of cigarettes from his shirt pocket. He hesitated, seeming to catch himself. "You guys mind?"

"Yes," I said, "we do."

He gave me a mischievous grin. "Just hope I never find out what your vice is, kid." He brought his huge hands back together, interlaced the fingers, and rested them on his desk.

"You were about to tell us something?" prompted Kelly, in an effort to change the subject.

Lou grinned. "Now, you I like."

Lou leaned forward and shared with us a few more things about the Red Mafia we hadn't read online. "La Cosa Nostra's built with a top down setup—modeled, I guess you'd say, after yer corporate America. In Russia, ya are—were—dealing with communism. The Red Mafia's modeled after that. Ya gotta take that into account when yer dealing with them."

"That makes sense," I added.

Lou grinned. "Yeah, it makes sense. But it also means that they're . . ." Lou's thick hands began to move around with his words. "They're what you'd call . . . fluid. Their networks I'm talkin' about. That make sense?"

We both nodded.

"Well anyway, they moved in when La Cosa Nostra was being thrown to the mat. Sure, La Cosa Nostra still has power in yer Northeast, but as far as branching out all over the world? Forget about it.

"And yous gotta remember, ex-KGB run the show today. I've heard talk they're still working for Russian intelligence, if ya can believe it. They're determined to destroy the good ol' U S of A. And the Mob assassins? Yous two are going to love this. I hear they're veterans of Russia's Special Forces."

I looked at Kelly. "That's comforting."

"I thought ya'd get a rise out of that one." He winked. "They're busy in cyberspace too. I hear they've hacked into Microsoft, NATO, and even the Pentagon. They've stolen millions just from Western banks."

Kelly nodded. "I remember reading about that."

"And ya want ta hear the weird part of it all?" As usual, Lou didn't bother waiting for an answer. "Most criminals try 'n' hide what they've done—so ta speak. They burn up the evidence or get ridda any trail. Not these guys. They're so proud of their crimes that they gotta record them all over their bodies as a kinda callin' card."

"Tattoos," replied Kelly with a nod. "I remember hearing something about that too."

Lou began gesturing toward his chest and arms. "The tattoo's shape and placement—it's all symbolic."

Kelly then added something I'd forgotten to mention in my summary earlier. "We also read how drug cartels in Mexico and cocaine smugglers from Colombia have teamed up with Russian mobsters."

"Ya bet they have. Why do you think heroin's become such a problem here? It's 'cause now yous got a route from Southwest and Southeast Asia to the U.S. and Europe. And, so as not to offend anyone at the other end of the route, cocaine and heroin from Colombia are now sold in Russia. And since yer Russian army is reachin' into their pocket and comin' up with nothin' at the moment, Colombians are gettin' their hands on weapons, information-gatherin' equipment, military hardware. It's all done in what yous call secret."

"Secret combinations," I muttered. Secret combinations, or vows, oaths, and techniques used to murder, rob, persecute, and destroy both freedom and property. I'd always associated them with Cain or the Gadianton robbers. And, as far as a modern-day equivalent was concerned, terrorists and evil dictators were what usually came to mind first. But this—this suddenly put the true evil and potential of secret combinations into a much greater perspective.

Lou obviously had no idea what I'd been referring to. "They call it *Omerta*. It's what you'd call their code of silence. When members of La Cosa Nostra broke it and started spillin' the beans, that's when they fell apart. It's still practiced in the Russian Mafia."

"*Red* Mafia," corrected Kelly.

Lou was beaming. "Now, see? This is what I call an educated discussion. Right ya are, sweetie." He leaned forward and clasped his hands together once more, his eyes locking onto mine. The expression on his face was grim. "That reminds me. Did you mention the word *musor* earlier?"

"That's what the guy on the phone called me! That's *exactly* it!"

"I was afraida that," Lou said, nodding his head.

"Why? What's it mean?"

"I made a few phone calls. One was ta a friend I've got at the Russian Consulate. He tells me it's a Russian word for 'rat.'"

"Rat?"

This time, if Lou was at all perturbed at my knee-jerk question, he didn't show it.

"As in, break the vow of silence—Omerta—and you're labeled a rat. A rat does anythin' it has ta do ta survive."

He sat back, stretched his arms, and placed his hands behind his head. He had a strange expression on his face.

"What, Lou?" I could tell there was more he wanted to say. "What else did he tell you?"

The investigator rolled his tongue around his mouth a few times before finally answering. "In the Red Mafia, when you're labeled a rat, it's . . ."

"It's what?" I asked, becoming not only more frustrated, but also more frightened.

"It's the mark of death, kid."

CHAPTER 12

Though I already knew I probably wasn't Lou's most favorite person in the world, the look on the private investigator's face appeared sincere. He hadn't liked sharing the significance of that Russian word with me any more than I enjoyed hearing it.

The room was quiet for some time before the shock gradually began melting away. It wasn't long before confusion and more than a little frustration took its place.

"Okay," I began, trying to wrap my head around this. "So it's already pretty obvious that someone wants to kill me. Now it turns out some foreign crime group has marked me for a dead man—supposedly because I'm a rat of some kind? Why?"

Lou sat up and again interlocked his fingers, resting them on top of his desk. "That's what I've gotta figure out. My guess is we've got a mistake in identity, assumin' ya have no connection with the murders."

"Which I—"

"Kid," interrupted Lou, "we get nowhere when we go in circles. Relax. I'm presumin' yer innocent."

"Only presuming?" Kelly asked. From the tone of her voice I could tell she was becoming just as irritated as I was.

Lou spread his hands out wide. "Do I think yer involved? No. Will I leave the possibility—as incredible as it might seem ta yous—open? I have ta." He held up a thick finger before I could interrupt. "Kid, ya *want* me ta look at this from both sides. If I don't look at this from the cop's side, I won't be lookin' for the strongest pieces of evidence that could save ya. Does that make sense?"

Unfortunately, it did. I could see his point, but I didn't like it and kept my mouth shut. I had to put my trust in him—albeit tentatively. I just didn't have the background or training he had to handle this sort of thing. I was hiring an investigator for a reason; I had to allow him to do what he was trained or experienced to do. I sincerely hoped the man knew what he was doing.

I nodded my head once, which Lou took as his cue to begin again. "Like I was sayin', mistaken identity. Somehow yer name or physical description has triggered somethin' in the Red Mafia."

He pulled his stained legal pad out and turned it to a clean page. "I want ta make a complete list of every place ya've ever lived. Countries, states, cities, counties—all the places where ya've lived in yer life. We can start with that."

His small request was satisfied in less than a minute. I was born and raised in Denver. Aside from a few vacations to the Grand Canyon and Washington D.C., I really hadn't traveled anywhere. I could see the disappointment in Lou's face.

"What about your mission?" prompted Kelly.

"Mission? You military?" asked Lou, his face brightening.

"No. She means the two-year mission I served for my church."

"Ah . . . Mormon, huh?" His face fell and he reached to scratch the back of his head. "Okay, I know about yous guys. What, yer eighteen when ya leave and can be sent anywhere in the world, right?"

"Something like that. But I was nineteen, and I didn't travel very far."

Lou offered up a tentative grin. "Please make this easy on me and tell me ya work—served—in Russia."

"I wish I could. No, I served my mission in the States. Missouri."

"Missouri?" From the look on the older man's face and the sound of his voice I could tell the private eye wasn't too impressed with the location of my old mission field.

"Right. Missouri," I said simply.

Lou eventually shrugged and, though it appeared he was simply doing it out of obligation, made a note of it on his legal pad.

When he'd finished writing the name of the state down, he looked up and stared over my right shoulder. "Of course . . . the fact they've got yer name . . . could purely be coincidental . . . a random error of some kind."

Kelly glanced at me, our earlier discussion of how un-random randomness, or chaos, really was, clearly coming to her mind as well.

"Well, I've got an idea. But it's a dangerous one." Lou sat back, his fingers still interlocked and cradling his balding melon of a head.

"Like what?" I asked.

"Well, it's more than likely that it's yer name that's attracted their attention. If I was to conveniently let yer name slip out on the street—in cyberspace too—there's a chance they could come ta us."

"Making Jason the bait of his own trap?" asked Kelly. The look on her face told me how little she thought of the idea.

"For now, I'm only askin' ya ta think about it," responded Lou, defending his suggestion. "The truth is, sweetie, in a situation like this, hidin' isn't gonna do anythin' for us."

"But it could keep Jason alive!" Kelly burst. "At least until we've exhausted all our other options!"

With the way I was being talked about, I was beginning to feel like I was already in my casket. "I can see your point, Lou," I added, jumping into the debate. "And I won't rule it out. But let's do a bit of digging first before we consider making a move like that."

Lou grinned and seemed to lean back even farther in his chair. "Interesting choice of words, kid."

I was confused, having no idea what I'd said exactly. "What words?"

"'Make a move,'" answered Lou. He leaned forward in his chair.

I was still confused. "I'm not following you."

"Do ya know what Russian mobsters do for fun, kid?" he asked with a grin.

"Of course I don't."

Lou's eyes narrowed. "They play chess, kid. They play chess."

Seconds later my head gradually began to nod. I was beginning to understand what the man was getting at. I could try to hide forever, but whoever I was up against would be patient, waiting for me to unexpectedly move into an inescapable checkmate situation. After all, hadn't the guy already declared "check" on the phone? How long would he wait to make his next move? Didn't some chess matches run for days before a winner was declared? The analogy was a good one.

I stood up and offered him my hand. "Well, we'll leave and let you get started, then. Thank you for seeing us, and thank you for your help."

Lou stood—clearly out of courtesy—and shook my hand again as though the very act of doing so was some quaint gesture he rarely saw these days. "Ya got a number where I can reach ya?"

"We'll contact you, if that's all right," responded Kelly.

"Sure, sure. That's fine with me." He reached for his wallet and withdrew a card. "Gimme a call tomorrow night, and I'll tell ya what I've come up with. My home number's there, the office number, and my cell phone number—if I ever find the blasted thing. It's my second one. Anyways, call any of 'em. I've got 'em all linked."

"Thank you," I said and opened the door for Kelly.

"Yeah. Get some rest." He threw me a knowing wink and grin. "I'm sure yous will find somethin' ta do ta keep ya busy."

Kelly had almost made it through the doorway when she stopped and looked sharply in Lou's direction. She clearly hadn't understood what this man with a wall full of indecent pictures had been alluding to.

Lou threw her a quick wink as well, and she continued to walk onto the landing, refusing even to respond to Lou's implication.

"If only I was younger," Lou muttered under his breath. Then he turned to me and said, "Don't let your girlie get away. She's a good one."

I stayed in the office, closed the door slightly, and approached Lou with annoyance.

"Look," I said, "I'd appreciate it if you'd keep your salacious thoughts to yourself. Furthermore, Kelly and I are just friends. And even if we were in a more serious relationship, it would be none of your business. Kelly's not 'a girlie,' and for that matter not your 'sweetie,' either. She happens to be one of the finest people I know. Do not—I repeat—*do not* insult her that way again. She's here to help me get out of this mess. That's all. Do you understand?"

Lou held up his hands in surrender. "Easy, kid. Relax. I didn't mean to insult anybody. I was jest pullin' yer chain."

"My chain I can handle. When it comes to Kelly, though, you're crossing the line."

The private investigator let his hands fall to his sides in capitulation. "Sure, kid. I get ya."

I turned and firmly closed the door behind me.

CHAPTER 13

Closing the antique store's wood-and-glass door, I jogged a few seconds to catch up with Kelly, who had already rounded the corner of the building on her way to the car. Traffic was light in this sleepy part of town, and there were only a few other people on the sidewalk.

I soon caught up with her and matched her stride. "Hold up, will you?"

"You didn't have to do that, Jason. I can take care of myself you know," she said as we walked.

"You heard all that?"

"The man's nothing but a vile knuckle dragger. He's only capable of thinking about the gutter. I'm amazed he's even able to stay in business. The guy's a creep . . ."

I knew she really wasn't talking to me. When we were dating, she used to do the same thing whenever she'd needed to vent. I learned then just to keep my mouth shut. She wasn't looking for a solution to her problem, she'd told me once. She just needed a minute to unload.

Kelly continued muttering and gesticulating all the way back to her car. When she'd unlocked the driver's side door, she got in and slammed the door behind her. I hesitated to get into the car and instead decided I'd be better off waiting outside. Since the street was deserted at the moment, I leaned against the side of the car, giving her all the time she needed to cool off.

Remembering what Kelly had said about Lou knowing our license plate number by the time we'd left, I started stealthily scanning the area, keeping an eye out for anyone who might now be following us, any drivers who expressed a sudden interest in Kelly's blue Lexus.

A minute went by before I heard the car door open and then close. It closed much more softly than before.

I remained where I was as Kelly slowly rounded the front of the car and leaned on the hood beside me. When I glanced at her, she had a sheepish expression on her face.

"You remembered," she said finally.

"Remembered what?"

"You gave me time to cool off."

I responded with a slight smile. "Oh, I remember a few similar reactions you had with two or three men in college. I knew if I left you alone for a minute or two you'd return to your imperturbable, professional self."

Kelly nodded, saying nothing.

I decided to change the subject just a bit. "So, this Lou guy, do you think we can trust him?"

Kelly straightened up and calmly walked back to the driver's side. She opened the door. "What do you say we step into my office?"

I nodded, and when both doors were shut, Kelly sat there shaking her head. "I guess that's the frustrating part. The guy sounded like milk and honey on the phone. I had no idea he was some greasy roach that only comes out at night."

She looked me in the eyes. "But the moment he recognized you, I felt trapped, Jason. If we didn't go with him, it would only take one phone call and we'd be finished. I'm . . . I'm afraid we're stuck with him for a while." She let out a short laugh. "I guess you do get what you pay for."

I nodded. "I suppose so. But I agree. We'll stick with him for a bit. By the way, Kelly, that was great thinking back there."

Kelly tilted her head to one side. "What do you mean?"

"Letting us be the ones to contact him. It's better if he doesn't know where we are. Besides, the more distance we keep between him and us, the better off we'll be."

Kelly groaned. "That's for sure. I'm totally sorry. I had no idea he was such a—"

"It's not your fault. Who knows, the guy might actually come through for us. Sure, I felt uncomfortable there, but . . . but somehow I get the impression the guy knows what he's doing. He just sees a side of the world that's been pretty much invisible to us, that's all."

Kelly nodded. "Yeah, I suppose so. I hope you're right."

I looked out the passenger window, again searching for anyone who might look suspicious.

"Tell you what," Kelly said, interrupting my search before I'd really had a chance to start. "What do you say we grab a bite to eat? We'll get some take-out and go back to the hotel."

I nodded. "Sounds great, Kelly. But I hate having you spend money like this. I promise you, when this is all over I'm going to pay back every cent."

She slipped the key into the ignition. "Don't be ridiculous. We have to eat." She took the car out of park and put it into reverse.

"I'm good for it," I added quickly, watching her as she checked her mirrors.

She smiled, suddenly looking as radiant as ever. "Of course you are." But before she hit the gas she looked at me once more. It was a different look, one filled with affection. "Thanks, Jason," she said, reaching over to briefly touch my arm. "Thanks for what you did back there."

This time it was my hand that went to her forearm. "Anytime. You know that."

My eyes held hers a moment longer before she eventually turned, looked over her right shoulder, and proceeded to back up.

* * *

When I first opened my eyes the next morning, I hadn't a clue where I was. Perhaps it was because I was warm, sleeping under a cozy but cheap flowered bedspread. Maybe it was because I actually had a pillow beneath my head. Whatever had triggered the initial jolt to my system, I was finally awake and knew exactly where I was.

I pulled my left hand out from under the bedspread and fumbled for the control lever for the driver's seat of Kelly's Lexus. Slowly my seat returned to the upright position and my hands naturally gripped the steering wheel. I tossed the pillow onto the seat next to me and ran a hand through my short hair and beard, wondering just how hideous my morning face was. That's when I remembered the rearview mirror.

I looked awful. Sure, my hair was too short to really require a comb or brush, and my beard was beginning to fill in quite nicely, but I looked tired. I still looked like a man on the run.

I sat there for some time, appreciating the warmth and comfort of the car. It was paradise compared to the hard, uneven ground of the foothills.

Kelly had offered me the floor of the hotel room. But after Lou's flippant comment, I just couldn't take her up on it. After we'd watched a movie on television in an effort to cheer ourselves up, I borrowed a pillow and the bedspread and told her I'd be sleeping in her car. I respected Kelly. It was as simple as that.

The movie had helped a bit, but by the time it was over, I was exhausted. Not just because it had been a long and stress-filled day, but because twice during the movie I had nearly jumped out of my skin.

The first time was when we'd heard a door slam from across the hall. It turned out to be a small child, excited for some reason, tearing down the hall; I could just imagine a SWAT team breaking in the door and taking Kelly and me by unnecessary force.

The second time I jumped was when someone had tried to use their key card in our door by mistake—finally opening the door next to us instead; both of us were breathless after that one.

The moment the sun went down I sneaked into Kelly's Lexus for some much-needed sleep. I suppose I should've felt more nervous in the car, considering I *was* being hunted. But for some reason I didn't. I reclined the seat back as far as I could so that I couldn't be seen and didn't stir once all night.

I sat behind the steering wheel for another thirty minutes until I decided it was time for me to sneak back into the hotel room. Although we had parked her car on the extreme end of the hotel parking lot, it wouldn't be long before the hotel guests started filing out of their rooms.

Folding the bedspread and mashing it and the pillow under one arm, I slipped through the back door and up the steps to Kelly's room.

I gave the door a few gentle knocks. "Kelly?" I called softly. "Kelly, are you up?"

I heard her fiddling with the door lock, and a few seconds later she opened the door.

Even though her eyes were a bit puffy and her hair flat on one side, Kelly still looked great. She noticed me looking at her and immediately dodged behind the door.

"Hey. No staring. I know I'm a sight."

I slipped through the door.

Like me, she was still wearing the clothes she'd been wearing the day before. "If you'll excuse me a moment," she said primly, and then walked into the bathroom, shutting the door behind her.

I walked over to the window and pulled aside the room-darkening curtain. Bright morning sunshine instantly filled the room.

Kelly came out of the bathroom a few minutes later. "Okay. It's all yours." She'd obviously run a brush through her hair, but she hadn't gone out of her way to completely make herself up. I thought she was beautiful the way she was.

She walked over to the foot of the bed and sat down, squinting against the sunlight that reached her. She glanced at the clock on the nightstand. "Well, it's seven twenty. Got any plans for today?"

When she'd mentioned the time, I automatically glanced at the watch I'd just put on. The digital clock was only a few minutes behind. But what suddenly grabbed my attention wasn't the time, but the abbreviated word appearing just above the minute hand of my watch. "It's Sunday."

Kelly's eyes scanned the ceiling a second or two. "Yeah. I guess you're right. It's Sunday."

I shook my head. "These past few days have really run together for me." I continued staring at the watch as an unexpected desire slowly began filling my heart.

"What is it, Jason?"

I looked at her, knowing full well the kind of reaction the next few words were going to get. "I want to go to church, Kelly."

"You're kidding."

"No, I'm serious. Could we?"

"I didn't exactly pack any church clothes, Jason."

"That's okay. We'll . . . slip into one of the back rows. If anyone asks we can say we're just visiting—passing through on vacation."

Her expression told me she'd need a bit more convincing.

"Kelly, I can't sit around doing nothing all day. I've done enough of that. Besides, Lou's in on this now. I . . ." I was having trouble coming up with the words. I wanted to tell her that I just wanted to take the sacrament, but I really wasn't certain she'd understand. Fortunately she spoke before I had the chance to fumble through a response.

"You're a man being hunted by the police and the Red Mafia and you want to go to church?"

A chuckle exploded out of me. "When you say it like that I guess it sounds pretty ri—"

But Kelly interrupted me and stood, smiling and surprising me once more. "Why not? It may well be the safest place on earth for you. You want to go to church? I'm game."

* * *

I found the nearest church house using the phonebook in our room. A phone call informed us that sacrament meeting started a little after nine. Kelly and I slipped into the back row of the overflow of the chapel just in time for the sacrament hymn.

Kelly had attended a few sacrament meetings with me before, of course, but it had been quite awhile and I wasn't sure how comfortable she'd be. She surprised me though. The moment we sat down she picked up a hymnbook, found the correct hymn number—after a quick glance over the shoulder of the chorister—and in no time we were singing together. We hadn't even finished the first line of the hymn when I realized just how much I had missed Kelly's singing voice. She sang beautifully, and for a moment I remembered back to many a picnic when we'd headed for the mountains in the red Omni, the windows rolled down, both of us singing as loud as we could to the radio.

Shortly thereafter I partook of the sacrament and was a bit surprised when Kelly did as well. Perhaps she did it to avoid drawing any attention to ourselves.

As it turned out, no one gave us a second look, except for a small toddler two rows up. The little guy was standing on his chair and, when his mother wasn't looking, was taking bits of cereal and secretly dropping them over the back of the pew. He had large, bright blue eyes and only a wisp of blond hair that was slicked back and plastered to the top of his head. His little white shirt was untucked and his tiny clip-on tie was askew. He looked as carefree as a kitten with a ball of yarn. But, of course, he did have at least one care. How was he going to slip the next bit of cereal over the pew without his mom catching him?

How would it be, I mused, *to have that as your only pressing thought?*

The meeting was more or less typical. The format and structure followed the same pattern I'd grown up with all my life. The hymns were familiar. The themes in the two youth talks that followed were similar to ones I'd heard many times before.

I guess a small part of me hoped that someone would just happen to say something that would give me an idea of what it was I was supposed to do next. I'd even flipped through the hymnbook, hoping the words of a hymn would jump out at me and offer me the precise direction I needed. But when my thumb came to rest on "A Poor Wayfaring Man of Grief," I closed the hymnal. The words in the title hit a little too close to home.

The first adult speaker was a missionary who'd just returned home from Brazil. He'd had a fantastic mission, and I could see in his eyes a look of determination I felt always accompanied those who'd served honorably and with dedication. But he looked very young. And, as with the toddler, I couldn't help longing for simpler days.

After the rest hymn, a member of the stake presidency was the final speaker. He gave a wonderful talk on the Word of Wisdom. But, again, it really didn't seem to apply to my situation the way I'd hoped it would.

It wasn't until we sang the first verse of the closing hymn that it finally hit me—the reason for wanting to attend church in the first place. There was order here. I knew what the meeting was going to be like even before I'd walked through the door. It would have been the same no matter where I had attended church. Whether in Chicago, Venezuela, or Ireland, the Church was run the same way. It was that order, that structure, I'd been craving.

It felt good.

When the closing prayer had been given, we immediately slipped out of the church and headed for Kelly's car. It's not that I thought anyone had recognized me, but I just didn't want to take any chances. Besides, I knew Kelly wasn't feeling too comfortable in her jeans and white sweater.

What would we do next? Probably head back to the hotel room and sit, catch some of the local news on TV, or maybe even catch up a bit on each other's lives.

"Feel better?"

Kelly had startled me, and I stopped walking. She was looking up into my eyes. "Yeah. I do. Thanks, Kelly. Thanks for bringing me . . . and coming along."

She rose up on her toes and gently kissed my cheek. "I'm glad we came. Hey, I noticed a park not too far from here. What do you say we get a bite to eat and enjoy some fresh air before locking ourselves up again," she whispered.

"Sounds perfect. Maybe we can even roll down the windows and belt out a few songs like we used to."

Kelly threw me a half smile. "I wish we could, Jason."

As Kelly walked the few remaining steps to her car and got into the driver's seat, I just stood there.

That was the moment I realized I was still very much in love with her.

CHAPTER 14

Tossing the bone from the last drumstick into the red-and-white bucket, I helped Kelly gather up what remained of our meal—compliments of the Colonel—and dropped it into a nearby garbage can. The taste of the chicken, potato salad, and buttermilk biscuits helped to lift our spirits. It was the closest I'd come to a home-cooked meal since this whole mess began. I savored every bite.

A golf course bordered the wooded park we'd chosen as our dining spot. The green was sprinkled with only a handful of players who seemed intent on trying to get in as many rounds of golf as they could before winter finally set in.

The park, for the most part, was pretty empty. The few families we could see in the distance had congregated at its center, where the covered pavilions and children's play equipment were. And, since a huge portion of the park bordered the golf course, both Kelly and I decided one quick lap around the park before shutting ourselves away for the day wasn't taking that big a risk.

Both of us remained in companionable silence as we walked, taking in the fresh air and enjoying the chance to stretch our legs. Of course, I wasn't feeling completely relaxed. I still tried to keep my eyes open for anything that appeared out of place, out of the ordinary. My head felt like that of a dashboard doll, bobbing constantly in all directions. And I still didn't quite feel like myself with sunglasses and a ball cap turned backward. Still, this was unquestionably far better than walking around the same trees and boulders—alone—in the foothills. Come to think of it, almost anything was better than that.

After five or so minutes, it was Kelly who first broached a subject I knew would eventually come up.

"So, Jason. Anyone special in your life right now?"

I grinned, feeling awkward. "I'm afraid I haven't found much time to date. I'm pretty drained by the end of the day. I tried a singles war—church for singles—for a month or two, but . . . I don't know. I just didn't feel right there. My friends and I sometimes do things over the weekend, but I guess you'd say my social life could use some improving." I swallowed hard. I felt like a complete idiot. *All she wants to know is whether or not I'm seeing anyone,* I thought. *Why can't I give her a simple no?* I wondered.

Was I seeing anyone? No. Did I want to? Yes. But I didn't want to come across as desperate. I had to get the focus off of me.

"How about you?"

"Well, I'm dating three men right now—a doctor, a lawyer, and an actor. I feel terrible about stringing them along the way I am. I guess I'm just trying to figure out who I'd be the happiest with."

Kelly began laughing at the expression on my face and punched my shoulder. "I'm teasing you, Jason. I've barely had time to eat, let alone date."

I chuckled, embarrassed at how relieved I felt at hearing this.

Companionable silence followed once more.

We stopped walking in the middle of a short wooden bridge that arched over a narrow creek bed. Leaning on the protective wooden side rail, we watched the water slowly flowing beneath us. An occasional twig or leaf would disappear beneath the bridge as the water gurgled its way downstream. It was a relaxing sight—the water ever moving, ever flowing.

After some time though, my mind lost interest in the stream and focused once more on Kelly. I'd forgotten just how beautiful she was. She appeared more focused than she had when we'd first bumped into each other as sophomores in college, but she was still the same strong-willed Kelly I remembered. Nothing ever seemed to faze her. I appreciated her company. I appreciated it a great deal. *How is it I let her go?* I wondered.

"Kelly," I said with some hesitation a few minutes later. "We . . . that is, a few years back . . ."

I suddenly lost the nerve to ask the question that had come to mind and fell silent.

"What was that, Jason?"

I just couldn't say it. I screwed up my face in discomfort. "Never mind."

Kelly, who was also leaning on the wooden rail of the bridge, turned her head and wouldn't stop looking at me. She reached up and removed my sunglasses. "Jason. You started to say something. What is it?"

I could feel my face beginning to turn red.

Kelly prodded gently once more. "Come on. What is it?"

I kicked at a small rock on the edge of the bridge, sending it plopping into the rushing water. It disappeared without a trace. "It's nothing." I plucked the sunglasses out of her hand and put them back on. "I don't think we'd better stay here. Let's keep walking."

Once we'd cleared the bridge, however, Kelly stood still. She folded her arms and gave every indication she wasn't going to take another step. "You can't start something like that and then not finish it."

"Why not?" I asked. I found sudden enjoyment in seeing her stubbornness surface once more.

After standing there for some time, I realized Kelly wasn't going to move until I shared with her what was on my mind. I really felt awkward. I kicked at a clump of grass near my foot and walked over to one of the thick oak trees that lined the path we were on and leaned against it.

I took a deep breath and began again. "We . . . had something once, didn't we, Kelly?"

Kelly grinned and it was her turn to blush slightly. She unfolded her arms and walked closer toward me and once again removed my sunglasses. "Yes. I . . . I think we did."

I reached out and took hold of her hand. It was cold but familiar. "So, what happened?"

She gave my hand a gentle squeeze and released it. "Life happened, Jason. Things just . . . got in the way. At the time, I think all either one of us could really think about was trying to graduate. To get through. I mean, you remember how it was. When we weren't studying we were struggling to keep our eyes open over dinner. You had finals to study for and projects to complete—so did I. We both had jobs, too. Think about it. We were both burning the candle at both ends back then. With that kind of pressure, how *can* a relationship survive?"

"I've seen others make it through," I countered.

Kelly smiled. "True, but everyone's different, Jason. What works for one couple doesn't necessarily work for another."

Deep down I knew that it wasn't simply the stress of college life that had broken us up, and I knew she knew that as well.

"Is that all it was?" I asked, kicking at the clump of grass near my foot again.

"What do you mean, Jason?" The hint of a smile on Kelly's face was slowly fading away and I knew her emotional shield was beginning to drop.

"Look, Kelly. I know I was a bit headstrong a few years back and . . . if I made you feel at all . . . inadequate, I'm sorry."

"Inadequate?" A forced grin suddenly surfaced and I knew her shield was back up. "What do you mean by *inadequate*?"

I realized I was digging myself into a hole and suddenly wished I'd kept my mouth shut.

I closed my eyes in an attempt to gather my thoughts.

"My religion," I finally blurted out. "My religion was—and still is—very important to me, Kelly. And I know having a church calling on top of everything else didn't help matters either—on Sundays or during the week."

"My religion is very important to me too, Jason."

"I know. I . . . know that. I . . . I guess what I'm trying to say is that if you feel I pushed you away because of . . . your faith—"

"But you did, didn't you?" Her words were blunt, but a genuine smile reappeared, taking out most of the sting.

"I just didn't want to force anything on you, Kelly. That's all. It just wouldn't have been fair to you. To us."

The grin disappeared again, though I still detected a spark of playfulness in her eyes.

"And you really think you would have been able to *force* anything onto me?"

I laughed and threw up my hands in surrender. "Okay. Okay, Kelly. I give up." I chuckled. "You know you're not making this very easy on me. I'm trying to apologize here."

I approached her and gently grasped each of her hands with my own. "It's just . . . seeing you again, spending time with you, I . . . I . . ."

"You what?" Kelly prompted.

I looked into her eyes. "You're going to think it's stupid."

Kelly gave my hands a squeeze, and I could see her emotional shield slowly begin to drop. "Tell me, Jason. I'm not going to think it's stupid."

"You're sure? Because I know how you sometimes get when—"

She gave my hands another squeeze. "Jason, please. I promise you, no flippant comments and no wisecracks. I promise."

I looked deep into her eyes. "I . . . I wonder . . . I wonder how in the world I could have ever let you go."

Kelly let go of my hands, which surprised me, and folded her arms. "I suppose it's probably because I wasn't ready for you yet."

She'd caught me completely off guard, and I couldn't help giving her something of an accusing stare. "You said no wisecracks, remember?"

"That wasn't a wisecrack, Jason. I meant it—I mean it seriously. I don't think I was ready for you . . . for us . . . yet."

I was confused and my face must have shown it.

"Look, Jason," she continued. "Before this conversation goes any further, there's something you should know."

I grinned, trying to cover up the anxiety I felt at her pronouncement. "It's the actor, isn't it? I knew it!" I teased.

I must have really raised my voice because Kelly was suddenly shushing me. So absorbed had I become in our conversation, I had temporarily forgotten that the last thing in the world we wanted to do right now was attract attention.

"Now who's not being serious?" replied Kelly. She was smiling though, which I took as a good sign.

"Then it's the doctor," I said, nodding my head.

Kelly laughed, shaking her head. "No, Jason. I'm not married or engaged to either one of them." Another sly grin appeared. "Of course if the *lawyer* ever approached me the way I want him to . . ."

We burst into laughter, which I think we both needed.

A few seconds later, however, Kelly's expression became more serious and she folded her arms once again.

"Jason, you might find this hard to believe, but . . . I was baptized three months ago."

I felt a tingling in my chest. Was she saying what I thought she was saying?

"Into what church?" I asked.

Kelly punched me on the shoulder—just like she used to.

"The same church as you, you idiot," she replied, beaming.

"You're right. I don't believe it," I quipped, still trying to process the enormity of the news.

"Well, don't look *too* shocked."

Truth be told, I felt like jumping up and down with joy. Instead, I settled for smiling and giving her a quick hug.

"I'm only kidding, Kelly. That's great! It really is." Along with happiness, I was also full of questions. "So, why? I mean why the sudden change of mind? Our discussions used to get pretty heated, if you'll recall."

"Oh, I recall them alright. And based on what I knew then, I still think I did a fine job of defending my faith."

Both of us were smiling, but it wasn't long before I could see Kelly's emotional shield begin to lower once more—her emotions close to the surface.

"It wasn't all that sudden, if you really want to know the truth. And it's really not all that complicated. A year after we stopped seeing each other I noticed that something was missing in my life. In the beginning I thought it was you."

I grinned at what I knew had been an unintentional jab. "Oh, well, thanks a lot."

"No. What I meant to say was that, even though I did miss you, it was more than that. It was . . . being *around* you that I missed too."

I remained silent as *she* now struggled to find just the right words.

"There was always something different about you that I never was able to put my finger on when we were together. Anyway, one Sunday morning I drove by an LDS church and just for fun I thought I'd attend—just sacrament meeting. I guess I thought it would be a way to have a little piece of you near me—for old time's sake."

I returned her smile but remained quiet, allowing her time to share what was in her heart.

"Anyway, by the end of the meeting, and thanks to one of

the talks, I knew exactly what it was I'd been feeling when we were together."

"And?" I prodded when she'd fallen silent.

For a brief instant I could see her resisting the urge to fire right back at me with some flippant remark. But her mouth closed and she took a deep breath before finally answering me. "It was the Spirit, Jason. It was the Spirit I'd been feeling when we were together."

I was about to reply when she interrupted me.

"You asked me if I thought we had something, relationship-wise. Yes, Jason. I think we did. We always had a great time whenever we went out and I really felt like I could open up to you. I just . . . I just don't think I was ready for you yet."

I shook my head. "And I wasn't ready for you either, Kelly. I had a lot of growing to do. Still do."

This elicited a grin from Kelly. "Oh, I don't know." She stood straight and placed herself directly in front of me. "You're about the same height you were a few years ago."

But when she looked up into my eyes, what had probably been meant as another flippant remark melted into something completely different. I suppose it was the closeness of our faces, or the fact that we were looking directly into each other's eyes.

When she closed her eyes and tilted her head back, I found my lips naturally drawn to hers.

After a long and meaningful kiss we looked once again into each other's eyes.

"And you haven't changed as far as that goes either," Kelly said with a grin.

"I still tingle your toes?"

"You do." She laughed. "You remembered."

I smiled. "How could I forget? You were telling me all about how meaningful a kiss was—that it said a lot about the other person, and that if your toes didn't tingle, then that was a sign to move on. Talk about pressure."

"But you passed the test with flying colors back then." She blushed slightly. "You passed the test now."

"Well, when it came to kissing, I don't seem to remember us having a problem with that at all."

Kelly nodded. "I suppose you're right."

Both of us fell into companionable silence. Finally Kelly spoke up.

"So you're really not at all surprised I was baptized then?"

"Oh I'm surprised. I think it's wonderful, Kelly. I really do. I . . ." I couldn't help flashing a wry grin of my own. "I just pity the poor missionaries—"

I dodged a playful punch.

"I didn't grill them too badly," defended Kelly. "Of course, it took a few sets of them to answer all of my questions."

I nodded. "I'm not surprised. I know how you love to take things apart and really study them."

Kelly nodded. "That's just what the elders said. Or was that the team of sister missionaries? Anyway, it was a quote they shared from President Hinckley that really caught my attention. He invited others to investigate the Church and to more or less bring with them what they already had so the LDS Church could *add* to it.

"I guess what really appealed to me was the fact that he wasn't discounting what I'd already learned—what I'd already been taught. He viewed it as being of worth, and all he wanted to do was add to it."

I nodded my head, appreciating once again the wisdom behind the words of a prophet. "And you're happy?"

Kelly's slight smile faded again. "I feel more focused on spiritual things and what's really important in life. And my ward has been very supportive and welcoming. I still have a lot to learn."

I was shaking my head before she finished her first sentence. "We all do, Kelly. But that's not what I was asking about. I asked you if you were happy."

Kelly studied my eyes for several quiet seconds. "To be honest with you, it's been rough, Jason. My parents were pretty upset with me when I told them about my decision to be baptized.

"My sister, Alicia, has been really supportive. I think with a little time she might actually investigate the Church herself. At least she's been willing to hear me out.

"But the rest of my family . . . they're pretty upset with me right now. Hurt, I guess you'd say."

"I'm sorry, Kelly. That's got to be rough."

"It is."

An uncomfortable silence followed, neither one of us looking the other in the eyes.

Suddenly I brightened when I finally thought of something positive to say. "But they've got to be awfully proud of you working on your master's degree. That's definitely quite the accomplishment." I finished with a smile, my hands up. "Not that I'm surprised, mind you . . ."

Kelly stepped back and folded her arms once more. She turned her face away from me, and I knew she was upset.

"Look, Kelly. I was just trying to . . . I'm sorry."

When she turned around I could see tears in her eyes—which was rare for Kelly. "I know, Jason. I'm sorry. You mentioned how you feel your life has fallen into chaos. It just seems like ever since I was baptized . . . my life's been thrown into chaos too. And even though you say there's order, I don't see any pattern at all when it comes to . . ."

I really didn't know what to say. "Whatever the problem is . . . I'm sure your family will . . ." I was at a loss here.

Tears spilled down her cheek and she wiped them away quickly with her hand. She was also shaking her head. "I'm not really worried about them. Really I'm not. I'm sure they'll come around eventually."

"Then I guess I just don't quite understand what you're saying."

Kelly wiped at her eyes. "Well, it's like I was telling you earlier. I've barely found time even to eat over the last two years. I guess it's finally catching up with me. That's all."

Kelly knew I wasn't buying it, but I didn't want to press her. Now she held out her own hand, which I accepted, and we resumed our walk. After a couple minutes, she started to explain the situation that was causing her so much distress.

"When I left the teaching program, I went into business administration, as you know. But I already knew I would want to pursue a master's degree after graduation. I did a little research and eventually set my sights on public relations. It had a good ring to it."

"What do you mean?"

"Well, it's solving problems, mediating between opposing groups, advising. The bottom line is it can still be service-oriented, which was what attracted me to teaching in the first place."

I smiled. "Wanting to make a difference."

"I guess so."

I nodded my head. "So you'd work for the government or a company?"

"Either one, really. That's the beauty of it. You work with businesses, hospitals, universities—anyone wanting to contract out for services once handled by a full-time staff. It's less expensive for them, and your assignments vary. You could be dealing with an organization and its policies toward employees one month, or dealing with some public issue—like nutrition, health, energy—the next. The variety sounded appealing."

I nodded once more. "I can understand that. And you'd work in some kind of firm?"

"Right. I interned with a public relations firm in Chicago last summer. They represented mostly corporate clients. With my undergrad in business administration, it worked out really well for me, so I would probably go with a company like that. A lot of firms are actually based in larger cities, but then they like to scatter their employees throughout the nation to expand their customer base."

"Sounds interesting," I replied.

"Interesting?" She took a deep breath and let out a massive sigh, shaking her head at the same time. "I believe it is when you actually hit the trenches, but getting there . . . that's a whole different story."

"What do you mean?"

She stopped walking and really looked me in the eyes. Kelly again seemed unsure of what she wanted to say, and I could see it in her face.

Finally, with a sigh, she turned and started to walk once more—picking up where she'd left off. "The master's program I was in could take five to seven years to complete, unless you've got the means to attend full time."

"Which you did, right?"

"Yeah. My parents not only picked up the tab for tuition, they gave me my Lexus. They've been super supportive of my educational goals." She sighed. "Anyway, going full-time gets you through the program in about two years. The problem is that the courses are taught by PhDs who are determined to make sure you've earned your degree. It's the whole tear-you-down-and-then-build-you-up concept."

"A real-world feel, huh?"

Kelly was shaking her head. "No. I'd probably list it in the 'No Heart Whatsoever' column."

I had started to laugh but caught myself. Kelly wasn't even smiling.

"There was a lot of weeding out going on, Jason. For example, in a marketing class I had a professor that seemed quite pleased with himself when by the end of the semester the number of students he taught had dropped from seventy to twenty. They'd all bailed—dropped out. And that was just *his* class."

"Sounds rough," I added.

"Rough makes it sound pleasant. Try *grinding*. Most of my professors demanded ten hours out of class for every one hour spent in their class."

"Why do they come down on you so heavy?"

"From what I understand, they're going to make sure you've got what it takes to survive. Or, at least what they think it takes. The truth is, a lot of them haven't even been outside the classroom. Now, Chicago? I enjoyed that. Real people, with real situations to deal with."

We were coming up on her car, now a little over fifty yards away.

"But you showed them, didn't you? You've proven you've . . . Kelly?" From the look on her face I could tell she was stubbornly fighting back even more tears. "What's wrong? You did make it, didn't you?"

"I don't want to talk about it."

When we'd finally reached the car, I opened the driver's door for her and then took my place across from her. When she went to put the keys into the ignition, I snatched them from her hand.

"Tell me, Kelly. What is it?"

At first she appeared angry, startled at what I'd just done. "Jason, give me the keys."

"After you tell me the rest."

"But I told you. I don't—"

"Want to talk about it," I finished for her. "I know. But, Kelly, I'd like to help if I could. You've taken the time to help me out, maybe there's something I could—"

"There's nothing you can do, Jason," she whispered.

Both of us sat silently, her words suspended in the air around us.

After sitting in silence for some time, Kelly finally gave in. "Aside from the course work, there's an oral presentation you give during your final year. They give you a topic or case and it's up to you to define the problem, find a solution, and make a recommendation. You have two weeks to write a response. It then goes before twenty individuals for review. It takes about three days for them to review it. If it's good enough, you move on to round two where three professors listen to you—one each from the English, math, and business departments."

Kelly bit at her lower lip, a sure sign that she was struggling to keep her emotions in check. "You've got forty-five minutes to an hour to present. Afterwards, you find out if you passed. That's it."

I struggled, trying to put the pieces together.

Soon I stumbled upon the only conclusion I could make. "And you didn't pass? I can't bel—"

"They set the date, the time, and the place," interrupted Kelly, staring off into the distance.

At that moment, I felt my stomach begin to drop. "And if you miss it?"

I watched her eyes carefully, struggling to read what was in them. She just sat there staring at her car's steering wheel.

She bit at her lip and finally answered me. "Then you wait six months and hope you can try again," she finished.

My stomach was really churning, so hard that I was actually dizzy and nauseated. "Kelly, when were you supposed to present?"

She looked up at me. "Yesterday. Yesterday morning."

"And there's no way they'll reschedule?" My stomach felt like it was free-falling.

"A woman, who worked while going to school, was taking classes on the side for five years. Just before her presentation last year she took a small trip—I'm not sure of the reason why. Well, her flight home was bumped. It was something she had absolutely no control over. But they wouldn't let her reschedule. And, when she finally did get the chance to present, six months later, she didn't pass."

I sat there, speechless.

Kelly quickly swiped the tears from her eyes and held out her hand. "What do you say we find a pay phone and give Lou a call? Maybe he's got something."

I handed over the keys, and she immediately started up the car.

We drove in silence after that, looking for a pay phone.

I'd never felt worse in my life.

CHAPTER 15

Lou *had* stumbled onto something, and he wanted to share it with us in person.

We agreed to meet at ten o'clock that night. I chose that particular time for two reasons. The first, I figured, was obvious. In the dark we had a lot more freedom to move around. Granted, it might have been a false sense of security, but I felt safer anyway. Second, it varied our routine. If we accidentally slipped into a habit of some kind when we did leave the hotel, it wouldn't take long, in my mind at least, for someone to notice. I guess I just wanted to mix things up a bit.

The street running directly in front of the antique store was empty for the most part. Stores in this older section of town had closed much earlier and, aside from the occasional security light left on in some businesses, the street was almost dark. On the second floor, above the antique store, I could see a light on in Lou's office. Though the blinds remained closed, we could see the shadows cast by the large filing cabinets in front of the window.

I had Kelly drive by the place several times. Of course, I really didn't know what I was looking for, but I did my best to account for every shadow, every parked car, every human. I was looking for a trap. After all, if the police were offering a reward for information leading to my capture and arrest, I had little doubt our conniving private investigator would jump at it; the man had nearly taken a few of my fingers with him when he'd snatched the money from my hand the day before. The guy certainly didn't come across as the salt of the earth, and neither Kelly nor I felt completely at ease with him.

"What do you think?" asked Kelly as she rounded the corner, preparing to make another pass down the narrow street.

We'd both gotten some rest at the hotel—this time I slept in the passenger seat of the car, which I discovered was far more comfortable—and we were more alert because of that. I was still wrestling with the guilt I felt over causing Kelly to miss her presentation. I had tried to bring it up a few times, but Kelly didn't want to discuss it any further. She insisted that I just let it go, that there was nothing we could do about it.

The last thing she said concerning the matter was that after a great deal of thought and prayer, she felt deep in her heart that meeting me was something she needed to do. At first she logically chalked her desire up to the fact that if it had not been for me she probably never would have found the gospel, never been baptized—which was the beginning of that journey back to her Heavenly Father and worth more than anything she would ever find on earth. But late into the night she realized it was something more than that. Deep within her heart she knew she had to help me and that her Heavenly Father wanted her to. She'd made the decision to come but admitted she was still very scared and unsure of what lay ahead of her in the future. After all, she was tossing two years of her life away on nothing more than a "feeling" in her heart. But she'd learned now just what that feeling really was. It was the Spirit. And, scared as she was, she knew she had to trust it.

Her faith was incredible. Still, in my eyes, her sacrifice on my behalf had been extreme, and I could only hope I could do something about it when I'd finally gotten out of the mire that engulfed me.

"I don't see anything odd. And I haven't seen anyone on the street," I finally said, pushing myself beyond the guilt.

"Did you check the parked cars?" Kelly asked.

"Yeah, I did. I didn't see any movement at all. Let's do it."

With only a nod, Kelly pulled her car over to the side of the curb, shut off the engine, and killed the headlights. Both of us scanned the street, the shadows, everywhere we could imagine a person capable of hiding, but saw no movement anywhere. I glanced at my watch. It was five after ten.

We both exited the car and in no time had made our way to the blue door of the antique store. Sure enough, Lou had left it open, just as he said he would, and we slipped into the darkened building. I quietly shut the door behind me. My hand, however, lingered hesitantly on the doorknob as Kelly began climbing the stairs to the second floor.

Something didn't feel right. But in my current state of mind I couldn't determine whether it was just my paranoia or an actual physical indicator.

Through the door's glass panes, I studied the street once more. Everything seemed so terribly ordinary. I chalked up my unexpected feeling to paranoia. I then headed up the stairs, two at a time, to catch up with Kelly.

The door to Lou's office was wide open, and the light spilling from the open doorway did a fairly decent job of lighting the landing at the top of the steps. The darkened windows of the martial arts school seemed strangely out of place. No lights, no shouting, nothing. We stepped into the light of Lou's office and found him seated at his desk. That is, his feet were propped up on the desk and he was tilted back in his chair asleep. There was someone without a care in the world.

I closed the door behind us, which startled him. He grinned as he withdrew his feet, stretched his hairy arms, and rubbed his eyes. "I was beginnin' ta think ya weren't gonna show."

We again took our places in the two chairs directly in front of his desk and watched as he fumbled with a flimsy paper coffee filter he'd pulled from a side drawer, tamping it down in a small coffee maker. "How we doin' today? Hmm, make that tonight."

I swore the man was still wearing the same shirt and tie he had on the day before.

"Still being hunted by the Mafia and sought by the law," I quipped, rather dryly. "How about you?"

My response elicited a grin from the grizzled investigator, who paused just before dumping a scoop of ground coffee into the percolator. "Ah, but ya've got yer health, kid. That's somethin'." He finished setting up the coffee maker and switched it on. Only then did he give us his complete attention. "It's good to see ya, Jason. Kelly."

The fact that he hadn't called Kelly "sweetie" so far on this visit didn't go unnoticed. She seemed to visibly relax a bit. "Thanks," she said. It came out soft, rather than terse, and I decided she was subtly thanking him for his apparent effort at showing her a bit more respect.

Lou received the subtle message. A truce had been called, and he too seemed to relax just a bit more as a result.

"Before I share with ya what I've come across, I want ya ta sign somethin' for me, kid." From somewhere near his hand, Lou produced a small slip of paper—a business card from the looks of it. He held it as a magician would between the index and middle finger of his right hand. He grinned at my hesitation to accept it. "Don't worry. The card's blank on the back. In fact you can keep it when we're through here. Whatta ya say?"

I cautiously plucked the card from his fingers. It belonged to a dry-cleaning business. "What do you want me to do with it?"

He pulled a worn ballpoint pen from his shirt pocket. "Sign the back of it."

I'd been in the process of reaching for the pen, when my hand froze in midair.

"I told ya, kid. You can keep it. Tear it up if ya'd like when we're through here."

I nodded and accepted the pen. I glanced at Kelly, who looked just as confused as I was.

I slipped the card in front of me on the desk and without any hesitation scrawled my signature.

"Good," replied Lou. "Hold it up so I can see it, will ya?"

I did.

"Hmm. Kinda sloppy for a teacher, don't ya think?"

I got that a lot from people and, out of habit, offered up my knee-jerk comeback. "You try signing hundreds of report cards and see what happens to your signature."

Lou grinned slightly, nodded, and sat back in his chair, apparently satisfied with whatever it was he'd seen. "All right. You can put it away or destroy it if ya'd like." He leaned back in his chair, once again resting the back of his melon head into the space made by his interlocked fingers.

When I'd folded the card and slipped it into my wallet, he spoke to me again. "Well, Jason, I found yer vice."

In the background the coffee maker gurgled. The pungent smell of coffee in such close quarters surprised me as much as Lou's assertion.

"Excuse me?" I asked.

Lou grinned. "You heard me. I found yer vice."

He seemed so sure of himself, I was almost anxious to prove him wrong. "And just what is that vice supposed to be?"

Though I was genuinely curious as to what he'd come up with, I wasn't at all prepared for his rapid answer.

"Vodka."

Before I could ask my obvious question, he pulled a color picture from a drawer. I could tell he'd printed it himself on a cheap ink jet printer. He dropped it on the desk in front of me. "Take a look at this."

The picture featured what looked like two stone buildings placed side by side, one building rising slightly higher than the other. Behind the buildings, towering over both of them, was a large white grain elevator. Two tall, silver, cylindrical storage tanks sat adjacent to the buildings. The buildings—in fact, the entire property—looked starkly utilitarian.

I glanced up at the investigator as I handed the picture over to Kelly. "I'm supposed to recognize this place?"

His response was to toss a second picture across the desk. It depicted a large sign framed in stone, the kind you'd see before entering an upper-class neighborhood or subdivision. It read, "MCALLISTER DISTILLING COMPANY: Producing quality spirits since 1856." Seconds later, I handed this over to Kelly as well.

"I still don't get what this—"

"They're located in western Missouri. A small distillery, but productive."

"Alcohol?" I asked for clarification.

"Right. Scotch, whiskey, and brandy. Pretty good stuff. I'm thinking this here's yer tie ta the Mafia."

I looked first at Kelly and then back at Lou.

"Then would you mind elaborating, because I'm not seeing one."

"Sure, kid. Well, I've been rackin' my brain for hours tryin' ta figure out how in the world a connection could exist. It's not like yer a globetrotter or involved in business that would have connections ta the Mafia. But Missouri. Now *that* kept gnawin' at me. There was somethin' about Missouri and the Red Mafia that kept ringin' bells for me. A little web searchin' and a phone call to the agent in charge—"

"What do you mean, agent in charge?" I interrupted. "You talking FBI, CIA?"

"Naw. This guy's a special agent for the Bureau of Alcohol, Tobacco, and Firearms—the ATF. We worked together years ago in Philly when I was a cop. I'll tell ya, he was one—"

Kelly interrupted the private investigator. "All right, Lou. What do you say we backtrack a bit? What does this distillery have to do with the Red Mafia?"

"Well, swee—Kelly," he corrected himself, throwing me a smile along with a knowing wink. "In '98, hundreds of 55-gallon drums were discovered in the port of Elizabeth, New Jersey—along the waterfront. They were marked 'industrial solvent'—had flammable stickers and everythin'."

"And they were filled with vodka?" Kelly ventured.

"Nope. Grain alcohol. Corrupt American distillers added blue dye ta it, makin' it look like windshield washer fluid. Gangsters would then ship it ta Russia and Ukraine. Each container was marked with an industrial label. So ya see, they could ship the stuff without payin' the heavy duties on liquor that's imported into those countries. If a nosey customs agent opened one of 'em, all he'd find inside was a blue, smelly liquid."

"Washer fluid," Kelly said.

"Right. Once it passed through customs, smugglers would get ridda the dye using instructions from the distillers. Add a little flavorin', put the liquid in bottles, and sell it as vodka. And, since it'd already cleared customs, no one could tell if the liquor taxes had been paid. Pretty ingenious. In the old days, contraband alcohol was smuggled in bottles with trucks and boats. Now, with a little chemistry—"

I started to interrupt him to get him back to my case, but he cut me off. "The average Russian citizen drinks mebbe six ta twelve gallons of vodka a year. That's their drink of choice. More than any other nation accordin' to my friend in New York. Six containers of the stuff, he says, are worth half a million dollars on the black market in Europe. Now, take 100,000 containers and yous can kinda appreciate how much money's at stake. Millions a dollars were lost when the whistle was blown on that one."

"But what's this got to do with Missouri?" I asked.

"Well, the Russian mob had at least six American companies involved in the racket—providin' the grain alcohol."

"And McAllister was one of them," I ventured.

"Correct. They were the first to be charged. They pleaded guilty ta tax fraud and managed ta get off easy by payin' only two million in fines."

"*Only* two million?" Kelly asked, incredulous.

Lou grinned. "Chump change when ya consider that jest what they'd been supplyin' coulda brought in a billion big ones on the street."

The room was silent as Kelly and I absorbed this information.

After nearly a full minute went by I finally asked the one question Lou hadn't answered yet. "Okay, so this distillery was shipping grain alcohol to Russian mobsters. What's this got to do with me?"

"Quite a bit, actually."

"How?" I asked, frustrated at the investigator's apparent desire to keep me in the dark as long as possible. I was tired of his games.

Without so much as a flinch, Lou withdrew another sheet of paper from the top drawer of his desk. It was a faxed copy of some sort of invoice. "See for yourself. Internal records tell it all."

I took the paper and tried to make sense of it.

"The bottom, Jason. Look at the bottom," Lou said.

Kelly leaned over to get a glimpse of the paper herself. When the investigator knew my eyes had found what he'd wanted me to see, he spoke once more, smiling slightly. "It was you, Jason Harrington. You prepared the shippin' manifests for the blue grain alcohol from McAllister."

The private investigator leaned across the desk, enunciating his next words very clearly.

"Every gallon of it."

CHAPTER 16

The name "Jason Harrington" was written on the bottom of the form in front of me, but it wasn't my signature. In fact, it bore no resemblance whatsoever to my scribble.

The relief I felt at that moment probably increased my seated stature by two inches. Of course, I had nothing to do with anything I was being accused of, but to finally see my name written by some other hand was, to say the least, vindicating.

I passed it over to Kelly, who was now grinning from ear to ear.

"So, this is what we've been looking for, right?" I asked.

Lou was pouring himself a cup of coffee, his face now stern and resolute. "I wish it were that easy, kids. I really do. But remember, they've got DNA evidence against ya. That's gonna be tough to beat. Some might view this as physical evidence, others . . . circumstantial. I'm afraid we're gonna need more than this signature ta get ya untangled from this little dilemma. Coffee?"

We both shook our heads.

"No? And, of course, this won't do anythin' ta save ya from the Mafia." He leaned back in his chair, resting the edge of his black coffee mug on his ample middle. "I wanna do a little more diggin' into this signature. I got no idea who signed it and whether he really shares your name. I just thought ya might enjoy knowin' that ya aren't goin' crazy."

I took the fax from Kelly and stared at the signature once more. I ran my index finger over it as if to make sure it was real. Finally, I raised my head. My eyes met Lou's. "Thank you. Thank you so much."

Lou sat up, apparently a bit befuddled by my sudden display of gratitude, and set his mug on his desk so he could be free to gesture, as he often did, with his hands. "Hey, uh, this ain't much. Really. But it's a start."

I nodded. I understood that.

"But why Jason?" Kelly asked. "Why his name?"

"Believe me, that's what I'd like ta know. It's clearly a mistake in identity, but there's more ta it that doesn't make sense."

"What do you mean?" I asked, returning the fax to Lou.

"Well, yer name's obviously the stickin' point here. Like I said, this guy may or may not even exist. Sure, ya served your mission at the same time the vodka scam was blown, but ya've got a professional hit man on your trail. It's not like he's gonna find his target by simply openin' the phonebook and goin' after anyone with the same name. There's gotta be more ta it than that. These Mafia guys may be ruthless thugs, but I doubt they'd wanna attract the attention of an outright killin'. Especially in this little area. We're not New York, ya know? Unless . . ."

"Unless what?" encouraged Kelly.

"Well, I've been mullin' over everything and the pills—the drugs, I'm thinking that's where he expected to get ya."

"I don't follow," I replied.

"Well, it's the way they went after ya at the motel and that article in the newspaper ya told me about. 'Gang-style shooting' is how they described it, right?"

I nodded.

"Well, then forcin' you out in the open and then makin' it look as if you'd been taken out by a gang would be one way of gettin' rid of ya. Police would find the drugs, figured you'd gotten into a habit that had spiraled out of cont—"

"But an autopsy would show I'd never taken the stuff," I countered.

"Yer sure about that, kid?"

My short laugh came out as a snort. "Of course I'm sure."

Lou sat back and laced his fingers over his middle. "What if over the past several weeks you've been taking it in small doses without even knowin' it?"

"You're serious, aren't you?" But before I had the chance to protest any further, Lou barreled on.

"And even if you're not takin' the drug, who's ta say ya weren't intendin' on maybe sellin' the stuff? You are around children at the perfect age—"

"That's nuts!" I shouted.

Lou's eyebrows shot up at my sudden outburst but soon relaxed—his familiar grin emerging once again. He reached for his coffee mug. "Look, all I'm doing is throwin' out ideas here. What yous teachers call hypothesomethin'."

"Hypothesizing," I corrected.

"Right. That too." He took another sip from his mug.

My mind was spinning, struggling to even start to wrap itself around Lou's outlandish theory when suddenly he threw out another.

"Then again, we could be lookin' at a rogue agent tryin' ta score points with those at the top. He manages ta take out the *musor* that cost them millions and his station in life changes significantly. I hear life in those rows of gray cinderblock apartments in Moscow is pretty miserable. They make the projects in yer inner cities look like Club Med."

"Assuming he is Russian," Kelly pointed out.

"Correct. Assumin' he's Russian. Which in this case I'm bettin' he is."

My eyes were closed and I was shaking my head back and forth. "So the guy's going to kill me for better living accommodations."

"They're just guesses, kid. That's all. You've got ta get them out of yer head and air them out and give them a final sniff before pitchin' them completely, ya know?"

Both Kelly and I were nodding. Lou made sense. The bottom line was that it was clear we'd hit merely the tip of the proverbial iceberg. I was just grateful that others finally knew an iceberg even existed.

"So, what do you suggest we do next?" I asked, as a newly found respect began to develop for the short, unusual man before me.

"Well, obviously I wanna dig a little deeper into this." He picked up the fax and returned it to the drawer he'd pulled it from. Lou apparently had some kind of filing system, perhaps something like drop and search, though I doubted anyone else in the world could have figured it out. "Call me in a couple days and I'll let ya know what I've come up with. I wanna talk some more with my friend at ATF, and I know a few people that might have some more info for us."

The man stood, signaling unmistakably that our meeting was over. Kelly and I stood as well. I offered my hand to Lou, who again took a second to regard the gesture before actually shaking it.

"Thank you," I said, pumping his hand. I could feel emotion welling up within me and couldn't trust myself to say any more. His handshake, in return, was warm and firm.

"Sure, kid. Don't ya worry. We'll get this worked out. But, remember, we're not outta the woods yet. Things could still get ugly. Yer sure ya wanna go on with me?"

I nodded, as did Kelly.

Nothing more needed to be said.

* * *

I shut the passenger door just as Kelly turned the engine over. I again felt uneasy, as if we were being watched.

It's late, is all, I told myself. *Relax, Jason. Relax.*

"So, what do you think?" I asked.

"Well, for a roach, he seems to be doing a pretty good job." Kelly smiled broadly. "It's a start."

She put the car in drive and in no time we were headed back to our hotel room.

"You know, it's funny."

"What is?" Kelly asked.

Red, white, and green lights reflected erratically off the hood and windows of the car as we drove, bringing life to an otherwise dark evening.

"Oh, I don't know. Just what he said back there about the vodka and the corruption and the stuff we read on his computer yesterday concerning the release of criminals into this country." I sat back and rubbed my eyes. "It makes it sound like the collapse of the Iron Curtain was a bad thing."

Kelly nodded. "That's one way to look at it. You could make the argument that the 'curtain,' so to speak, was also acting as a 'shield.'"

"What do you mean?"

Kelly bit at her lower lip a few seconds before responding. "According to that last article we looked at on the computer, Russian criminals are taking advantage of the West's open access. They've definitely taken advantage of their country's lack of financial regulations. Under the Iron Curtain, citizens had to endure a great deal of hardship, but in spite of all the corruption, apparently there was less outward crime. I guess the Mafia is simply the ugly side of making the switch to a free-market economy."

"Opposition in all things?" I suggested, remembering the scripture in 2 Nephi.

"Perhaps. I suppose that's one way to look at it. But I don't think what we're seeing taking place in Russia is a hopeless situation. Doesn't the Church tell us there's always hope?"

"What about all of the corruption?" I countered, playing devil's advocate.

Kelly was silent for nearly a minute. "Well, think of Russia as being a newly planted lawn. Sure, in the beginning weeds infest the ground and spread throughout the lawn. Soon, though, if conditions are right, the grass begins to grow. As it thickens, it eventually chokes out the weeds. Right now we're in the weed-infested stage."

I nodded. It made sense.

Both of us remained silent until we'd reached the next traffic light.

"Jason?" Kelly began quietly, the only other sound coming from the turn signal on the dash.

"Yeah?"

"Have you thought about giving your parents a call? I'll bet this news would do wonders for them."

"Of course I've thought about it. I've thought about calling the school, too—at least my principal."

Kelly pressed on. "Because I'd be willing to make a few calls if you wanted me to."

The traffic light turned green and we were moving forward again.

I nodded, understanding perfectly where she was coming from. I, too, wanted to let them know what we'd stumbled on, let them know this really was one gigantic mistake. But the very act of calling them seemed dangerous somehow. *Right now, by having no contact with me, they are completely in the dark about everyone and everything,* I thought. *And, for their safety, isn't that best for them right now?*

I finally shook my head. "I'll think about it. It's late. There's nothing anyone can do about it tonight."

"Do you still believe there's order in chaos?"

I couldn't help grinning. "'Disorder being channeled into certain patterns.' That's how the scientists describe it. Study the patterns and you discover that a common underlying theme emerges."

"What kind of scientists are finding Chaos Theory useful?" asked Kelly as she looked over her shoulder and changed lanes.

"That's what makes Chaos Theory so powerful. Biologists, physicists, even mathematicians are all finding chaos everywhere. The way a flag flutters in the wind, politics, economies, the weather, even traffic jams when broken down follow certain laws. Nature is a mixture of complexity *and* simplicity."

"Fascinating—even reaffirming," Kelly admitted, hitting the gas once more.

"I've always thought so. And that's the beauty of it. Everything obeys simple laws—we just haven't figured those simple laws out yet. It's right in line with what the gospel teaches."

Kelly grinned. "And our dear, sweet Lou, in this case, has found the pattern."

I grinned. "What Lou found is a start. In fact, a very good start to finding a pattern and unraveling this mess."

Kelly didn't argue with me. Instead, she patted my leg with her hand. "I want to help you celebrate. Tonight, you take the bed and I'll take the car. What do you say?"

Of course, I wouldn't take her up on her offer. I couldn't. But I appreciated the gesture and reached for her hand—holding it and giving it a gentle squeeze.

We held hands all the way back to the hotel.

CHAPTER 17

It's funny how the mind works. You keep telling yourself you'd relax if only you had the answers to a few simple questions. Then, when you finally start getting a few answers, your mind conjures up new and improved questions to take their place.

I felt fairly certain I was being hunted because of mistaken identity. I was being confused with someone who'd worked at the McAllister Distillery in Missouri. That person, if Jason Harrington really was his name, appeared to have worked at McAllister at the same time I was serving my mission. And, to keep me from getting any law enforcement help, the Mafia had somehow planted DNA evidence at the scene of the police murders to implicate me in those. Whoever this man was that was after me, it was clear he was going to do anything it took to get me.

But why not just take me out with a bullet? I thought. *Why run me around like a mouse in a maze if all he wants to do is kill me? Does he want to kill me? He's already tried killing me with a bullet—hundreds of them—that first night at that cheap motel. What does he want? Does he want me dead or alive?*

I was confused, and I knew I was running out of time. The police had surely thrown out a large, secure net in their search for me, and that net had to be shrinking with the passing of each day. The police weren't stupid. They'd eventually find me. I couldn't hide forever. The net they'd thrown out was meant to box me in. This I understood. The problem was, I had a free-roaming assassin trapped in the net with me. And as the law enforcement's net grew tighter, I would have less and less room to run—from a man trained, perhaps, by Russian Special Forces!

After talking the matter over with Kelly the following morning, we decided to leave the hotel room once more. We were planning on stocking up on some food and making one quick trip to the local library. The information Lou had stumbled on about the grain alcohol kept bothering me, and I wanted to know a bit more about this distilling plant I had supposedly worked at. Just where was it on a map, and was I even near the area during my mission?

Nothing new was being reported on the local news channels, at least the three we watched that morning in our room, and both Kelly and I felt that if ever there was a time to slip out among the public once more, it was immediately.

I of course donned the sunglasses and baseball cap, which, to Kelly's credit, did alter my appearance. But I still felt as if I was walking around naked. I remembered a friend once telling me that wearing glasses for the first time felt as if you were experiencing life behind some kind of shield. I could see now that he was right. I only wished it was a very big shield—and bulletproof.

Under a lead-gray sky we pulled into the library's near-empty parking lot. There were only two other cars near the old brown brick building. I had little doubt they belonged to the two women I could see through one of the library's many windows. My guess was they were preparing to open the doors. We'd arrived at ten o'clock—precisely the hour the library opened—hoping to avoid any crowds.

When the short, gray-haired, heavyset woman in her late fifties finally unlocked the doors, we were the first and only ones waiting to enter. And, given what we'd seen in the parking lot, it looked like we'd be the only ones for at least a while.

"Good morning," the librarian said. Without waiting for a reply, she turned and headed off in the direction of a matching set of locked doors on the other side of the library.

The library's layout was simple. Children's books ran along the south end of the building, adult books on the north. We walked toward the center where the large help desk was located. To the right of the desk was our target—a bank of eight computers. We read over the rules of the machines that were printed on a small sign hanging directly above them.

"All right, let me see about getting us a terminal," Kelly said as she headed purposefully toward the library's help desk. I immediately made myself at home in front of the terminal nearest me.

I watched as Kelly's smile was quickly returned by the librarian's assistant. Kelly had a way with people. There was no doubt about it. The assistant was a great deal younger than the librarian, but she seemed very competent. She tapped a few keys on her desk terminal. The terminal I was sitting at instantly sprang to life, and the password-protected screen saver vanished and was replaced with a web browser.

By the time the popular search engine had loaded completely, Kelly had pulled a chair from another table and sat closer to me. "All right, Jason. We've got it for thirty minutes. What do you want to look up first?"

I moved over a bit more so that Kelly had full access to the keyboard.

"For starters," I replied, "let's see just where on a map this distilling plant is."

"Right."

In less than a minute Kelly had brought up a map of Missouri, a star marking the precise location of the distillery.

Unfortunately, it was located near an area I had worked in. I say unfortunately because I was hoping the plant would turn up on one end of the state, with me on the other. And, to make matters worse, it was situated in the area where I'd spent the longest stretch of my mission. I couldn't remember anyone mentioning the plant at that time. But considering that I had been a missionary at the time, why would I have known about it?

In ten minutes we'd learned more than we would ever need to know about the distillery itself, its founder, history, and product line. There were plenty of articles praising McAllister's moderately priced products as the reason behind the company's growing success. And there was no shortage of products either. Aside from scotch, whiskey, and brandy, they produced gin, rum, tequila, and vodka. A new line of alcoholic eggnog was coming out soon for the holidays, and already the taste-testing reviews were positive.

Kelly then began pulling up what she could about the Mafia scandal. Again, it was easy finding information. Most of what we discovered corroborated what we already knew. Prosecutors had indicted several of the smugglers, including the informant. The informant pleaded guilty to one count of conspiracy to commit wire fraud and, through a plea bargain, agreed to remain in place working as the eyes and ears of the ATF. Should smuggling operations pick up again, authorities had a man on the inside who could tip them off. The article concluded with an ominous statement regarding the ingenuity of the Red Mafia and its remarkable ability to always remain one step ahead of authorities—not only in the U.S., but around the globe.

Lou's reference to chess and strategy naturally came to mind.

I tapped my finger on the monitor, pointing to a reference listed at the end of the article. "I'd sure like to read the whole article that stuff about the informant was pulled from."

"Our time's about up," said Kelly.

I looked around and, for the first time, noticed others had filled the empty terminals that surrounded us. It was as if the entire library had awakened, and I doubted we'd get back onto a terminal for some time. No sooner had I opened my mouth to answer Kelly than the monitor's screen saver activated once more.

"I wonder if this library holds any back issues of that magazine?" I asked.

"I'll check." Kelly headed toward the help desk as I moved out of the way of a thin, grim-faced woman in gray sweats who'd come to claim every single one of the thirty minutes she'd been assigned at our terminal.

I saw Kelly and the library assistant heading toward a storage room. Kelly's quick thumbs-up let me know I'd probably have the article soon.

I wandered over to the end of a book aisle and leaned against one of the tall shelving units to wait.

"Jason?"

I flinched. At the help desk, out of the corner of my eye, I could see the older librarian holding a telephone receiver in one hand, her other hand over the mouthpiece. *Relax, Jason. There's more than one Jason in the world. Lou's proven that. Relax.*

I began looking around the library, doing my best to ignore her.

"Jason?" she called once again. I forced myself not to look in her direction.

A few seconds later I was startled when I suddenly noticed the older woman standing beside me.

"Excuse me, sir. Is your name Jason?"

"I . . . uh . . ."

"There's someone on the phone that's asking to speak to a man with a short beard, wearing a blue T-shirt and a baseball cap named Jason. You match his description."

I felt naked. No one knew we were at the library. We'd only decided to come a few hours earlier. I doubted even Lou would have figured out where we were. But if it wasn't Lou, who in the world was it?

My mouth felt dry, and I could barely feel the floor beneath my feet. I nodded, finally, and followed the older woman back to the help desk . . . and to the telephone receiver sitting innocently on the counter. I picked it up and, like an automaton, brought it to my ear. "Hello?"

"*Musor!*" The thick Russian accent was unnervingly familiar. "So nice to see you again!"

CHAPTER 18

I just stood there, holding the telephone receiver—frozen in place like an iced-over January snowman.

"*Musor*, I see you are at loss for words. That is okay. I want you to listen."

I was hearing him, but my unfocused brain was straining in a hundred different directions. *How did he find us? Am I going to die? Does he know anything about Kelly? Has he seen—*

That thought spun me around. Instantly, my attention was riveted on the conversation. When I'd answered the telephone, his first words were "Nice to see you." My eyes darted around the interior of the library and then from window to window— at least, the ones I could spot from where I was standing.

"A little to your right, *Musor*."

I turned and there, just outside a narrow window on the eastern end of the building, just behind the large fish tank, I spied him. Tall and well built, black leather jacket, and a head shaved completely bald. He wore dark sunglasses, didn't appear to have much of a neck, and was holding his cell phone to the side of his head while grinning like a jack-o-lantern. Seeing him standing there, an actual person, just about knocked me senseless. I became cold and clammy. The hair on the back of my neck prickled. But something in my head clicked, overriding all my other physical sensations, and I found my tongue. "Look, there's been some misunderstanding here. I'm a school teacher for crying out loud. You're making a mistake. I'm not the person you think I am."

"Missouri was not your home for while?"

"It was. But I was a missionary. A missionary for my church."

"Your name is Jason Harrington. Yes?"

"Yes, but—"

"Well, *Musor,* that's good enough for me."

"Listen, I—"

"No! You have said enough. You are going to step outside and come with me. We continue discussion somewhere else."

I turned and looked to see if Kelly was on her way back. Did he know about her? Had he seen us together? How long had he been following us, and did he know the kind of car Kelly drove?

"Are you hearing me, *Musor?*"

"Wh—what's that?" There was no sign of Kelly, but I knew what I had to do next. I had to get the assassin away from the library and as far away from Kelly as I could.

"You are going to hang up telephone and meet me outside. If you do not, then you force me to come inside. Many could die, *Musor.* No tricks. Clear?"

"Is everything all right, young man?" asked the older librarian, who hadn't moved since she'd handed me the phone in the first place. She had a genuine look of concern on her kind face, and I imagined she made a fantastic grandmother.

I looked into the old lady's eyes and knew I looked like a deer caught in the headlights of an oncoming car. No, make that a Mack truck.

"Let me think," I said into the phone, then I placed my hand over the mouthpiece and whispered, "When my friend gets back could you please tell her I couldn't find the book on *camping* I wanted, so I'm going to have to *rough it?* Tell her . . . I'll see her *early in the morning.*" I hoped she had heard the emphasis I had applied to those words.

The woman looked at me as if I'd gone mad. Nothing in my response tied in at all with what I'm sure she'd overheard, but I didn't have time to repeat the message. And if I didn't get moving instantly, Kelly could be harmed. Somehow I didn't think the man I could still see in the distance would bat an eye if he suddenly felt she should disappear as well.

"All right," I said into the phone. I tried to remain calm so as not to panic the old woman. "Here I come." I handed the phone back to the librarian who hung it up for me.

"Son, are you sure you're—"

"I'm just fine. Deliver that message—all of it. Will you?"

"Message? Oh, yes. Camping. Sure I will."

I forced myself to smile kindly. "Thank you. Thank you so much."

I turned on my heel and glanced out the narrow window once more. I could see the assassin pacing outside in watchful waiting.

I started to head for the exit nearest him but abruptly turned and walked briskly toward the exit on the other end of the building.

I'd caught the assassin's attention immediately. He ran for the door and stalked into the library, his pace and body language letting me know that he had every intention of stopping me before I ever reached the door.

I was only five feet from the exit when he picked up his pace and started jogging. At that moment, I bolted for the door.

I'd made it across the parking lot in no time and could easily have made a beeline for the nearest cross street, but I hesitated. I had to. For Kelly's sake, I had to make sure he was following me. When I stopped to look over my shoulder, it took a few seconds to realize that the assassin had already cleared the library doors, spotted me, and was running full tilt in my direction.

I raced on a bit farther before coming to a busy intersection. I hesitated only a few seconds as I gauged the lanes of traffic. I ran into the middle of the street, dodging an SUV and hesitating only long enough to let a yellow pickup truck pass by. By some miracle I made it to the other side of the street without getting hit. I thought such a stunt would have slowed the man chasing me, but he plunged into the traffic as if it wasn't even there.

I ran hard, my eyes darting from side to side as I struggled to find a place where I could hide. Running through a subdivision, I cut through several front yards and backyards. Track had never been my forte in high school, particularly not the high hurdles. But with my adrenaline level almost overflowing, I powered over a couple of brick walls, chain link fences, and even a hedge.

As I passed a car parked in front of one of the houses, its rear windshield suddenly exploded. A quick glance over my shoulder confirmed what I thought had happened. The man had drawn a gun and was firing at me! The fact that I hadn't heard the shot fired hadn't even registered as I dived into an alleyway that eventually opened up onto a bustling, business-lined street.

My eyes spotted the name of a store, towering above the other businesses half a block away. It was in a big, two-story shopping mall. Although I'd never been to that mall, I was instantly reassured that I needed to be there.

I ran across the busy street and chanced another look over my shoulder. He was still behind me. Since we'd essentially resurfaced in public, however, his gun was gone. I continued to run, trying to focus on my breathing. Although I was in pretty good shape, my breathing was labored and ragged. I had to really concentrate to get it back under control—inhaling through my nose and exhaling through my mouth.

As I neared the mall's immense parking lot, my leg muscles and lungs were on fire. I glanced over my shoulder and noticed that I'd managed to put some distance between us. In fact, the assassin was walking. Clearly, he wasn't in the best shape either.

I slowed to a jog and then began walking. I was breathing so heavily that I could feel the blood rushing to my head and legs, pounding through the arteries in my neck, thrumming against my forehead and behind my eyes.

I kept peering over my shoulder, knowing I didn't dare let him get a chance to reduce the distance between us. If he suddenly got his second wind and began running, I wanted to be ready to run again myself.

Two minutes later I'd reached the doors that led to the mall's food court. I didn't like the idea of involving complete strangers in this threat against me, but the fact that he'd holstered his weapon the moment we'd left the subdivision told me he wasn't too keen on creating a big scene in public.

The smell of pizza, chow mein, and cinnamon rolls washed over me as I scooted past the various vendors lining both sides of the food court. Set up down the center were tables and chairs, and I received some strange looks from the lunch crowd. I suppose it was to be expected. I was drenched in sweat, still breathing pretty hard, and jerking my head around like the carriage of an old manual typewriter being returned to the left-hand margin.

I took a right at the end of the food court, pausing briefly to see just where the assassin was.

He'd barely entered the food court, stood still a moment, and finally spotted me. Only then did I start to walk again. I'd lured him into a mall, achieving my first objective of putting some distance between him and Kelly. By that time I was praying that she'd gotten the message I'd left with the older librarian and was headed someplace well out of harm's way.

As I power-walked through the mall, it didn't take me long to realize that any store I passed to my right or left was a dead end. The moment I darted into one of the craft boutiques or shoe stores, I was finished. And so I headed toward a large department store I could see at the end of the mall. I no longer took the time to look over my shoulder. What I had to do was concentrate only on losing him.

My breathing had almost returned to normal, though sweat still poured down my face and arms. I wiped what I could off my cheeks. My short whiskers had trapped the sweat and were beginning to itch something fierce.

The first thing that caught my eye in the department store was the escalator. My goal was the mall's second level. If I could get him to follow me and then somehow double back, I could find another exit, leave the building, and then try to lose him again outside.

Taking the slow-moving steps of the escalator two at a time, I reached the men's wear section on the second floor. I brushed by the clothing racks, dodging several shoppers, and headed back to the open mall area. When I glanced over the thick wrought iron railing of the second floor, I could see a variety of shoppers milling around far below on the first level. How I longed to have the freedom I felt certain they were taking for granted.

That's when our eyes met once more. There was the assassin. He hadn't followed me up the escalator. He seemed to know I was headed for the second floor and decided he could keep better track of me by watching from below. Obviously, I had to come down sometime.

I considered just keeping my eyes forward and running, sprinting for the other end of the mall, but I stopped myself. I was reacting again, and I couldn't do that. Instead, I jogged back into the department store, stopping only when I knew he could no longer see me from below.

I hesitated and counted down the seconds. After thirty, when I was confident he had to be making his way to the escalator, or at least making sure I wasn't attempting an escape through the department store exit, I bolted out of the department store once more and headed for the open mall.

I hoped he was on the escalator, since I couldn't see him below on the first level. Dodging baby strollers, mall walkers, and engrossed shoppers, I covered a lot of territory. I passed by the food court and just ahead could make out a large set of stairs leading to the first floor, with a few elevators behind it. The walls of the elevators were made of glass. Automatically, I discarded them as a source of concealment. By that time the natural man in me was begging to look back, to figure out just where in the world my hunter was. By sheer force of will, I refrained. I knew if I did that, I would only be sacrificing time and distance, both of which I was sure I had in very limited quantities.

I spotted a door marked *Stairs* next to the elevators and headed for that. Flinging open the door, I barreled down the first and second flights of stairs to the first floor and was surprised to discover a third and fourth flight. *Are there three levels to this mall, instead of two?* The thought buzzed through my mind.

Sure enough there was a third level, though it was obvious that most of the shops specialized only in novelties. One store, which looked like it had changed hands at least three or four times in the past year, sold only items found on television infomercials. A noisy, flashing arcade and game room, packed with teenagers, took up quite a bit of space to the right. Beyond the black lights and flashing neon signs, however, everything came to a dead end, walled off by large sections of plywood and plastered all over with *Coming Soon* and *Please Excuse Our Progress* signs. A flimsy wooden door had been installed to give workers access to the area. Like a homing pigeon, I flew toward it.

It was unlocked.

I passed a group of busy carpenters without a word or glance and headed toward the end of the construction. I was doubling back, which was what I wanted, though I kept expecting the assassin to emerge in front of me at any time. I wasn't running, and I think that was why most of the workers I passed hardly gave me any notice.

The renovation project was a large one—interminable, it seemed. New stores were being built, as well as a play paradise for kids—with plenty of things for children to crawl through and over, and bold, vibrant colors to stimulate them even more.

Finally, I reached the end of the construction. What lay beyond the next door—a much more permanent looking door—was clearly the managerial portion of the mall. Doors designated those rooms assigned to employees, managers, first aid, and . . . security.

I hurried past that door and followed the exit signs until I finally found a stairwell and a door that led to the outside. I opened it, peering tentatively around the corner. I saw no sign of the assassin.

I think I lost him, I thought to myself warily. The only people I could see were shoppers walking to and from their cars.

One thing had changed since I'd been in the mall. It was raining. Not hard, but a steady sprinkling of rain that in time would drench me.

I ran across the parking lot, contemplating my next move. If I dashed into another retail store, I'd be boxed in again should the assassin suddenly decide to give each business a thorough search. Besides, at some point stores would have to close their doors. When evening fell, I'd be stuck in the cold once more without shelter.

Back at the library, when I'd left my message for Kelly, I'd thought of heading back to the foothills somehow. But at that moment, standing in the rain, it just didn't seem like the best move. Golden was miles away, and by the time I reached my tent and sleeping bag I'd be soaked.

A passing RTD bus gave me a new idea as I suddenly remembered the city's light rail system. If I headed west, I knew I'd hit tracks. A station couldn't be too far up or down the line.

Though I'd given Lou almost everything I had, I still had a few odd bills and some change in my pocket. Perhaps it would be enough.

As I broke into a slow jog, the idea of getting back to my tent gradually began making the most sense. I seriously doubted he'd find me there—he hadn't before. Sure, it would be a long trip, but at least I knew what was waiting for me when I finally got there: shelter, food, and a nice warm sleeping bag. Besides that, it was not only far away from Kelly but probably the only real place we would be able to find each other again, assuming, of course, that she understood my cryptic message.

With a new determination, I began weaving my way through the streets, following a circuitous path, varying my directions as much as possible, wary of every approaching car.

When I finally found myself safely seated on the light rail, my attention and concern about running into the assassin began to subside. My new concern was for Kelly. Somehow the assassin had learned we were at the library. If he knew I was there, then it was a pretty safe bet he'd spotted Kelly at some time. When she got my message, would she even understand it? I prayed for her safety, pleading with the Lord to help her. All I could do was hope she'd realize I'd been spotted and would immediately clear out of the hotel we'd been staying at. The thought of her lying in bed that night, with bullets streaming through the window, kept haunting me. Kelly was smart. She'd know to get away—to put as much distance as she possibly could between her and the assassin, wouldn't she? Then Kelly and I would get back together again in the morning. This was what I hoped, anyway, and hope was all I had to cling to right then.

Switching to a regular bus in Denver, with only thirty-two cents left in my pocket, I finally got off in front of the Colorado School of Mines in Golden. The rain came down steadily, and when I finally reached the base of the foothills, my body was shaking from the rain and the cold, my teeth chattering so much that I kept biting the inside of my mouth. The trail was empty, which came as no great surprise. Taking a bike ride or hike in this weather would be just plain stupid.

A bike would have sped things up a bit, but even if I did have my mountain bike, the path was too muddy and there was too little light left. So I continued walking, stopping only occasionally to do a few jumping jacks, clap my hands together, and rub my bare arms in a desperate effort to fight off the cold.

By the time I'd reached my old campsite, dusk was approaching.

I was never so happy to see boulders in all my life. They weren't really shelter, but they were big and nestled near a thick stand of pine. The fact that they appeared so solid and immovable provided me with at least a sense of protection.

I recovered my tent from where I'd stashed it and, with great struggle, managed to set it up in the rain—hardly according to Dutch military regulations, but standing nevertheless.

The pines provided some cover from the rain, but I was still wet, and as the minutes rolled by, I imagined I could feel the evening temperature already beginning to drop into the low forties or high thirties.

Weaving my way through the trees, I found the brush I'd wedged the sleeping bag under, only the bag was gone.

My eyes darted all about, searching frantically for the one piece of comfort I'd been visually clinging to with the passing of every wet, cold mile.

After ten minutes of searching, I found what was left of the bag behind a thick stand of brush. It had literally been ripped to shreds by an animal of some kind. I considered collecting some of the larger pieces, but they were soaking wet and I was tired of wet.

I then went to my third hiding place and with some relief found my red survival kit intact. I plodded back to my tent.

Inside, I opened the survival pack and immediately pulled out the 100-hour candle. I didn't care about being seen anymore. I just needed to feel some warmth, even if it came from a single tiny flame.

Once the candle was lit, I ripped open an MRE. Whatever it was, it was cold and chewy, and I was simply grateful I had something to eat.

After finishing off two water pouches, I began to take inventory once more.

I had an extremely thin emergency blanket, which I unfolded and wrapped around my body. I doubted it would actually warm me, but at least it would help trap any heat my body managed to produce.

I found the hand-warming cloths next and opened them. The package warned not to place the cloth directly on my skin, so I pulled off my shoes and wrapped one around each sock-covered foot, slipping on my wet, muddy shoes to help hold them in place. I unwrapped another one and used it for my hands. I had three more I could have used, but if Kelly and I, for some reason, couldn't get back together in the morning, I wanted them on hand—just in case.

As minutes slipped by, I could slowly begin to feel the warmth from the cloths seeping into my skin. It was now dark outside, and I stared blankly into the single flame of the emergency candle while the sound of the rain hitting my canvas tent gradually began lulling me to sleep.

In my fatigue and worry I found my mind naturally beginning to freefall—freefall toward frustration and despair.

What am doing? I wondered. *I just barely escaped the claws of a man who wants nothing more than to see me dead and . . . and I nearly got Kelly killed in the process!*

My tired eyes studied the dancing flame of the candle—its movement, its pattern.

Chaos, I thought to myself darkly. *What was I telling Kelly about it last night? Everything obeys simple laws. There are patterns to even the most chaotic of systems.*

A shiver went through me and I pulled the crinkly emergency blanket tighter around my body, willing warmth into my skin. *So what's the pattern here?* I thought, discouraged, my thoughts now bordering a prayer. *The only pattern I see is that someone's out to kill me, and I'm pulling Kelly right into this mess with me and ruining her life in the process!*

Is that the pattern? Is every move I make going to . . . ?

The image of a chessboard suddenly came to mind, which in turn triggered my memory—a comment Lou had made during our first meeting together.

"Do ya know what Russian mobsters do for fun, kid?" he'd asked with a grin.

I told him that I didn't.

"They play chess, kid," Lou had replied, his eyes narrowing. "They play chess."

As the flame of the candle continued to sputter and dance, I recalled learning somewhere about how most amateur players find it extremely difficult to "see" four or five moves ahead. But an expert at chess—grandmasters—have learned between fifty and a hundred thousand moves and patterns.

I squeezed my eyes shut at the seemingly staggering numbers and found myself becoming even more discouraged.

I'm an amateur, I thought to myself with despair. *And I'm playing this game with a grandmaster.*

On the heels of this thought, however, I remembered something I'd also learned from the same mission companion who'd been so infatuated with Chaos Theory. He, too, had shared something with me about chess.

I now struggled, probing my tired mind to locate that thought, as it seemed very important. I took a deep breath and tried to let the fear, anger, and frustration roll away from my mind.

I had started to offer up a small prayer, when suddenly I remembered the conversation.

"Life is like a giant chess game," my companion had said.

"What do you mean?" I'd asked.

"Well, God has only so many pieces—no more and no less. Some of those pieces are valiant and eager to help in the cause. Others are not. Well, God has to play every piece He has, even if the good is included with terrorists and murderers. And He has to do it in such a way as to bring about the success of His plan while at the same time allowing for our free agency."

At the time I remembered shaking my head at the enormity of what my companion was saying. "I don't think I can even comprehend the magnitude of such a task," I finally responded.

My companion laughed and then shared with me a statement I didn't think I'd ever forget. "You're not supposed to, Elder. You're only a mortal. There isn't any *way* to comprehend it now."

When my eyes opened they naturally returned to the tiny flame of the candle.

The same had to be true of chaos, I finally decided. While I knew order had to exist, I simply wasn't capable of seeing the entire pattern, or the big picture, myself. I couldn't. I was only mortal. But my Heavenly Father could—Grandmaster of all grandmasters.

I closed my eyes and offered up a prayer—for my safety, for Kelly's safety, and for help in pulling myself out of what felt like a literal nosedive.

What I had at the moment wasn't exactly what I'd been hoping for, and I knew it would probably be a long night, but for a moment I had a little warmth, food, and shelter. And I should be grateful for that. More importantly, I was still alive.

Is Kelly? I wondered when I'd finished my prayer.

I tried hard to anchor myself to my newfound outlook on my situation, to try and keep positive about Kelly, but I found myself so completely exhausted—mentally and physically—all I could catch were brief flashes and images of her face: a mental snapshot of her laughing over a candlelight dinner I'd splurged on in a fancy restaurant back in college for our second month anniversary, images of her cuddling with a puppy or baby kitten at an animal shelter we'd visited a few times, her energetic contributions to a few group study sessions she attended before switching her major, the tears in her eyes the night we'd discussed our drifting apart and what I was certain would be our last real meaningful conversation together, and a vision of her lying in a coffin, the guilt of knowing she'd died because I'd involved her in a nightmare meant only for me, feeling frightfully real and tangible.

I struggled to force myself back to happier images, to cling to my earlier feelings of hope, but I found the effort too draining, too exhausting.

Thankfully fatigue finally caught up with me, and I fell asleep.

It would be a long and fitful sleep.

CHAPTER 19

Wrapped in my flimsy emergency blanket and concealed behind a few almost leafless trees, I just stood shivering at the corner where Kelly first found me. Finally, in the weak, early morning light, her blue Lexus rounded the hairpin turn and pulled over to the side of the wet road. I made a dash for it. My clothes were still wet and the heat being generated by the hand warmers had waned. When I opened the passenger door and threw myself inside, all I could do was sit in my crinkly blanket and shake. My finger lashed out at the car heater. In seconds, heat—satisfying, life-preserving heat—began rushing over me. I glanced over at Kelly, who just sat calmly watching me. "Rough night?" she ventured.

From the look on her face I knew Kelly was scared and more than a little relieved to see me again in one piece. Her wry remark, I figured, was simply her way of holding herself together.

I looked at her and finally I began to chuckle. Her hand reached for mine and I accepted it, enjoying both the warmth and softness of her touch. "I've had better," I managed through chattering teeth.

"Come on," she said with concern in her eyes. "Let's get you warmed up. A good, hot breakfast should do the trick."

I didn't answer. I couldn't answer. I just sat there shivering.

A few minutes later the bright, cheery colors of a fast food place beckoned us. Rather than use the drive-thru window,

Kelly parked some distance from the restaurant and left me in the car, the motor running, the heater still on high.

When she returned several minutes later, she killed the engine and we ate our meal in the car. I knew I needed to eat. Chilled and fatigued as I was, if I didn't keep my strength up I could easily fall ill. And being sick was pretty much the last thing in the world I needed right then. I appreciatively sipped the cold orange juice in spite of the resulting shivers.

"What happened, Jason?"

Kelly took a bite of her breakfast sandwich. Only then did I take a moment to study her face and hair. "Where did you sleep last night?" I asked, ignoring her question altogether.

"The car. I wasn't sure from your message whether I should be using a credit card anywhere, so I decided to lay low."

I closed my eyes and slowly shook my head. "I'm sorry, Kelly. I'm so sorry."

"Hey, come on. You've been doing it the last few nights. At least I had a heater part of the time and a blanket from my trunk. I'm fine, Jason. I'm just fine. Now, what happened back there?"

"I . . . I don't really know. Somehow he found me."

"The guy on the phone?"

"Yeah. He was there at the library. I saw him. Tall, dark sunglasses, black leather jacket, and completely bald."

"And he chased you?"

"Chased and shot at me. I lost him in a mall."

Kelly stopped chewing the food in her mouth. "Are you okay?"

A few minutes earlier, when Kelly brought our breakfast to the car, I'd tossed the wet, flimsy emergency blanket in the backseat. It still felt as if it was clinging to my arms and I reached up and scratched them—something I'd been doing all night.

"I'm . . . I'm fine," I said, as convincingly as I could.

Of course, I wasn't fine. I'd been chased and shot at and had just spent a miserable night in a wet and soggy tent. From the look in Kelly's eyes, I knew she could sense my frustration, fatigue, and discomfort.

Several minutes later, without saying a word, Kelly started picking up the mess we'd created with breakfast and left the car to deposit it in a trash can about twenty yards away. I watched as she stretched out her back a moment before slipping back into the car.

"I'm sorry, Kelly."

She reached over with both hands and gently rested them on mine. "It's not your fault, Jason."

I shook my head and closed my eyes. "I shouldn't have called you in the first place. I had no right to—"

"Jason." Kelley's voice was firm and she began squeezing my hands with her own. "I'm here because I chose to come. Now, we can spend the day basking in your pity party, or we can try and get you out of this mess."

"Pity party?" I asked, arching an eyebrow.

Kelly grinned. "That's what my mom used to say whenever I started feeling sorry for myself."

I returned her grin, nodding my head.

It was silent for some time as I just sat there, thinking. Kelly must have thought I was tired and eventually shifted in the driver's seat to start the car. The engine turned over immediately.

"Wait. Wait, Kelly."

She killed the engine. "What is it?"

"We need a different car."

Kelly's eyes widened. "Excuse me?"

"There's a chance that whoever's after me now knows what kind of car you drive. Should we happen to pass him somewhere in our travels . . . I just think it would be better if we got ourselves a new car."

Kelly appeared stunned. "And just how do you propose we do that? Look for an empty one that looks like it could use a good owner?"

I grinned at her sarcasm. "No. Of course not."

"Well?"

"I taught a student last year whose father owns a used car lot south of town."

"And you think he'll just give us a car?"

"No. I doubt it. But I'm hoping he'll let us drive a loaner or something for a few days. It's worth a try."

"Can you trust him? I mean, you're an alleged cop killer. Why wouldn't he just turn you in?"

"I really don't know."

"What about your family? Don't they have an extra car they could let you borrow?"

Kelly's family lived back East. Consequently, she had always seemed to get a kick out of how close many families in our area were. If you had a problem, help was only a phone call away. Clearly now she was beginning to see the value in it.

"No good. Something tells me I'd be putting them in danger if I tried that."

Kelly was silent a moment, digesting what I'd said. "So, this student of yours," she began with some hesitation, "you and he really hit it off, huh?"

"What? Oh, no. No. As a matter of fact, it seems all we ever did was lock horns. I think he left my class with a C or a D+."

"And you're going to ask his father for a car?"

I nodded silently.

"You got along with the father, right?" ventured Kelly.

"No. I wouldn't say that. We locked horns a few times ourselves."

Kelly sighed, sounding frustrated. "So what makes you think he's going to want to lend you a car?"

"Nothing," I admitted. "Other than the fact that I can't get the man's face out of my mind this morning. Just like I couldn't get your name out of my mind a few nights ago."

We fell into companionable silence until Kelly finally began shaking her head, a small smile playing at the corners of her mouth. "Why not?" she mumbled. "Let's give it a whirl." With a quick flick of the key, she turned the engine over.

I reached for her hand once more. "Hold on, please."

She killed the engine again and turned to me, grinning. "You know, for a man who's on the run, you sure like to sit and talk."

We both laughed at her flippant remark, which was something I knew we both needed.

"Last night I had a lot of time to think. I barely escaped yesterday. Another foot and he would have hit me instead of that car window. Had he caught up with me in the mall, I know I wouldn't be alive talking to you now."

"What are you saying, Jason?"

"Would you mind if I used that pay phone over there?" I pointed to the one affixed to the side of the fast food place. "I want to call my parents and at least tell them how big a mistake this is. I may not get another . . ."

Kelly was patting my hand as if warning me not to finish such a gloomy thought. "Go ahead. I understand. I'll wait here for you."

"Uh . . . you know, that bus and light rail . . ."

"Spit it out, Jason!"

"I . . . I'm completely cleaned out. You wouldn't happen to have fifty cents I could borrow? I'll pay you back, I swear."

Kelly was grinning as she dug for coins in her purse. She said nothing about the small loan, which I appreciated very much. I felt horrible enough as it was.

Pulling myself stiffly from the car, I made my way over to the pay phone. In less than a minute I could hear my mother's very familiar voice.

"Mom?"

"Jason?"

"Listen to me, Mom. I don't have time to talk. I . . . I just need you to know that all of this is one giant misunder—"

"Jason, sweetheart," her voice was strained as though she'd been crying for some time. "Please come in. I know we can work this out. Please, won't you come in? We can help you."

I found it odd how she hadn't said, *Please come home. Please come in* sounded like something a cop . . .

"Mom? Where's Dad?"

"He's left for work already. Now, please, whatever's happened I know if we sit down . . ."

I wasn't listening to a word she was saying. Instead I was straining to pick up the strange sounds I could hear coming from the background.

"Mom," I interrupted her, "who's with you?"

"We want to help. The police are on our side, Jason. I'm convinced of that now. Please—"

"Mom," I interrupted her once more. "Are the police with you now? Are they tracing this . . . ?" My question died away as I could suddenly hear in the far-off distance the sound of police sirens.

My mother, apparently uncomfortable with my silence, started once again to plead with me. "Honey, please come in, will you? Don't fight them when they get there. I'm sorry it has to be done this way, Jason, but it's the only way we can help you."

I nodded silently. "I know, Mom. I . . . I don't blame you for any of this. I love you. I just wanted you to know that." I hung up the phone as the volume of distant police sirens continued to increase.

I jogged back to Kelly's car and plummeted into the backseat.

"Jason, what's wrong?"

"Police, Kelly. They traced the call. They're on their way."

Kelly nodded and I could see her biting at her lower lip as she struggled to start the car.

"Just pull out slowly and get onto the freeway, Kelly. They're looking for me, not you, remember."

Kelly seemed to take the hint that panic, over everything else, is what draws attention. I took several deep breaths myself in an attempt to relax.

I dropped to the floor of the backseat, yanking the emergency blanket over me in an attempt to remain invisible.

I was on the run. I had to get that through my thick skull. If I was going to survive—if Kelly was to survive—it was something I just couldn't afford to forget.

CHAPTER 20

My jeans and blue T-shirt were nearly dry, and I was actually beginning to feel civilized again. I wasn't quite up to what I was about to do next, but I knew I really didn't have much choice in the matter. If I wanted to remain free, and if I wanted Lou to have a little more time to untangle my pretzel-shaped life, it had to be done. We needed a new car. And if not for my own safety, then for Kelly's.

We were parked across the street from a small used-car lot. Multicolor pennants, strung from light pole to light pole, fluttered in the scant morning breeze, advertising yet another MONEY-SAVING EVENT. A large white banner hung from the lot's business office, boasting a 98 percent credit-approval rating. And, if those weren't enough to bring in customers, free frozen beef was being handed out—according to a few strategically placed posters—with every vehicle purchase.

After watching the lot for half an hour, I was pretty well acquainted with every written word I could see. Kelly and I had been waiting for the owner of the car lot to arrive. I didn't know what kind of car the man drove or if he was even coming in to work that day. Nonetheless, I had a strong impression that I should try finding him at the lot first, rather than at his house. I learned long before that day not to question such impressions.

"Do you know his name?" asked Kelly, who at the moment

was running a brush through her short hair, doing her best to "freshen up a bit."

"Yeah. It's . . . Mr. Shepard."

Her brush froze in mid-movement. "You *don't* know his name."

"With the number of kids I see in a day, I'm lucky to know the student's name, Kelly."

She nodded in understanding—rather unconvincingly, I felt—and continued brushing her hair.

My eyes returned to the used-car lot, though there wasn't much going on at eight o'clock in the morning. A salesman who'd arrived fifteen minutes earlier turned on the lights and unlocked the office doors. We could see him now, through one of the many windows, sitting on the corner of a small wooden desk, talking with someone over the phone.

"Here comes someone."

I turned and spotted the shiny red pickup truck Kelly must have been referring to. It slowed down as it approached the lot, almost as if the driver of the vehicle was inspecting the place. Eventually the pickup pulled into the lot and parked adjacent to the lot office.

"That's him," I said, sitting straight up and checking out the passenger window both ways for any oncoming cars. "Wish me luck."

I opened the door and jogged across the street. I wanted to catch the man before he entered the business office. The fewer people I had to deal with, the better. I had no idea what I was going to say to the man, but since my business was with him, I wanted to have to worry only about our conversation. The closer I got to Mr. Shepard's pickup, however, the less sure of myself I was beginning to feel.

Just as I reached the pickup, he was opening his cab door to climb out, reaching for his brown cowboy hat on the passenger seat at the same time. It was easy to see this was Cody Shepard's father. They shared the same lean build and angular facial features. As a teacher it's always fascinating to meet the parents of students. At times it's downright spooky; if you didn't know any better, you'd swear science had, in some cases, already sanctioned cloning. Of course, Cody's father was dressed a bit more formally in his western-cut sports jacket and jeans, white shirt, and turquoise choker. But he had the same down-turned eyes that made him appear tired. He also shared his son's perpetual grin that I presumed came in handy as a used-car salesman.

"Mr. Shepard?" I called out, as I rounded the bed of his red pickup.

He slipped his cowboy hat over his dark, thinning hair before turning on his boot heel to address me. I could tell, at first, that he didn't recognize me, but it didn't take long for him to see past my short beard and haircut. "Mr. Harrington?" he said, in his slow country drawl.

"Yes, sir."

And then I could see recognition cross his face and his normally friendly expression suddenly went stern. "Say, aren't the police looking for . . . ?"

He didn't finish his sentence. Instead, he began marching toward the front door of the lot office.

I jumped in front of him, beating him to the door, and held out my hands.

"Wait. Please! Listen."

He stopped, glowered at me, and I knew at any second he was prepared to shove me aside.

"Give me five minutes. If after five minutes you still want to call the police, I'll understand."

He stared hard into my eyes, and I knew I wasn't getting through.

"Mr. Shepard. You and I haven't always seen eye to eye on things, but you know I never sugarcoat anything. I tell it like it is, and I'm honest with you."

As I made the final statement, I remembered the first time Mr. Shepard visited my classroom. Without any preamble, without even so much as a greeting, he'd entered my classroom—cowboy hat and all—after school, walked right up to my desk where I was working, and demanded that I justify why I was giving his boy a D. When I told him I wasn't *giving* Cody a D, he seemed taken aback.

"If I was going to *give* him a grade," I responded, "I'd probably give him something else, like a C or B, maybe an A."

Mr. Shepard then pulled Cody's first semester report card out of his shirt pocket and tossed it on my desk. "You gave him a D."

I calmly picked up the report card and unfolded it, studying it for a while. "No, Mr. Shepard. I didn't give it to him. He earned it. There's a difference."

What followed was a long discussion on Cody's work habits.

We both worked hard the rest of that year trying to help his son improve. Cody did make some progress, though it was a struggle. He probably got a C- or a D+ in my class, but I knew—as did Mr. Shepard—that his son had earned it.

Both of us had really put in a lot of extra time on the boy, and I had little doubt it was the giving of my time previously that kept the man from shoving me aside that morning.

"You've got five minutes."

"Mr. Shepard, I know this is going to sound ridiculous, but I'm very close to tracking down the evidence that proves I had nothing to do with those cop killings."

His head tilted to one side. "You've been framed," said Mr. Shepard dryly.

"I know. It sounds like something you'd hear on TV. But, yes, I am being framed. And the man who's doing it is out to kill me. I've barely managed to dodge him twice already. And he's good."

"Who's good?"

"The man that's after me."

Mr. Shepard let out a sigh. "What I mean is, who is this man that's chasing you?"

"I . . . I really don't want to say any more about him—for your own safety."

Mr. Shepard rolled his eyes.

"Look, I don't know how I can convince you that what I'm telling you is the truth, but think about it. If I did have something to do with those murders, why in the world would I still be hanging around here? Why haven't I fled the state or even the country?"

"Well, I . . . I don't know."

"That's just it, Mr. Shepard. I haven't run anywhere because I'm not guilty. I'm just trying to prove that, and I'm really close to doing just that. All I need is a few more days."

"You didn't kill those men?" He was looking straight at me, enunciating his words carefully.

I knew what he was doing. "No, Mr. Shepard. Of course not." I looked him straight into the eyes, enunciating my answer as clearly and honestly as I could. "I had nothing to do with those murders."

It was quiet for several seconds.

"I hear there's evidence."

"If there is, then it's planted evidence, Mr. Shepard. And . . . look, the truth is, that's all I dare tell you about it."

"Why? It's the police that are after—"

"No, Mr. Shepard. It's much deeper than that. I'm being set up to take the fall for something I never did, and all I'm trying to do is prove I'm innocent."

"Then go in and prove your innocence! That's what the justice system's all about. If you're innocent, then you have nothing to worry about."

"We're talking about four cop killings here, sir. You've seen the news. The public, the state, both are hungry to have someone to prosecute."

"I don't think you're giving the cops enough credit here. Just because—"

"I don't fault the police at all. But they're acting off planted evidence. They didn't plant it. Someone else did. The police can't help but see it the way they see it. It's not their fault. Like I said, it goes deeper than that."

"And you can't tell me anything about it?"

"No, Mr. Shepard. I could, but then you might be running for your life as well. You've got a family to think of. I'm thinking of them, believe me."

He studied my face for the longest time. I held his stare without flinching. Finally he said, "What can I do to help?"

I grinned. "I know the moment I tell you, you're going to think the worst."

"You let me worry about what I'll think."

"Fair enough. But first I want you to take a look at that Lexus my friend and I are driving."

Mr. Shepard followed my index finger across the street. There he found the blue Lexus and noticed Kelly waving. He nearly waved back before catching himself. "Who's driving?"

"You don't see her, Mr. Shepard."

"What?"

"I said, you don't see her." It was my turn to hold his eyes. He seemed to get the message.

"Right. What about the car, then?"

"I think the man who's hunting me has spotted our car. He knows what we drive. We need something to get around in that he won't recognize."

"You want a car? Are you nuts? Have you ever heard of aiding and abetting—"

"Mr. Shepard, I don't want a getaway car. Believe me, the Lexus would do just fine if that's what I really wanted it for. Give me the worst car you've got, as long as it's reliable. I can't pay you because I gave all my cash to a PI, and my other accounts are frozen. But you can hold on to our car. Strip its plates and throw it on the lot. He'll never find it. I just need something different that he won't spot."

"But the police—"

"The police don't know anything about that car. They've never seen me with it, or with her. Believe me, I don't want to see anyone get into trouble over this, but I know when I need help. And, as hard as it is for me to do, I'm asking for it."

"But how do I know you won't flee the country?"

"You don't, Mr. Shepard. You don't. You're just going to have to decide whether or not you trust me."

He removed his brown cowboy hat, ran a hand through his thinning dark hair, and glanced off into the distance. I knew this wasn't easy for him.

"If you don't feel good about it, Mr. Shepard, I'll turn around and walk away. I'll never bug you again."

His eyes returned to mine. Inwardly I couldn't help but see the irony. Here I was trying to sell a used-car dealer an unknown bag of goods.

"I'll hopefully only need it for few days, a week at the most. I give you my word I'll repay you when I'm able." I was guessing on the time frame, of course, but I knew I was close to swaying him.

"I sure hope you know what you're doing, son."

I remained silent, because I didn't.

"But, tell me, how do you know I won't call the police the moment you and the girl drive off—tell them exactly what they're to look for."

"Well, Mr. Shepard," I began, a slight grin coming to my face at the sound of his concession. "I guess that's where I'll just have to trust you."

CHAPTER 21

The gray Saturn Mr. Shepard let us borrow wasn't the greatest car, but, to his credit, it wasn't the worst either. It was probably only five or six years old, and even though the upholstery was torn in a few places, it had low miles on it and seemed to run well. I could tell by the way Kelly was driving, though, that it would take her a little while to get used to its unique ride and handling. At least I had peace of mind knowing her car was in good hands. And, I was clinging very hopefully to the feeling I had that she'd be getting it back—in one piece—very soon.

We decided Kelly should continue to do the driving. If I had to suddenly disappear, I could duck without endangering anyone around me—including myself.

"Kelly, I really feel bad about—"

"Don't say anything, okay? You know how I feel about all this. There's nothing to apologize for."

I nodded. "Thanks."

Kelly reached over with her hand and gave my hand a quick, reassuring squeeze. "So, where to next?"

I stared out the passenger window, watching the houses and yards rush by, not really focusing on anything. "Well, I think we should give Lou a call before we do anything else. Maybe he's stumbled across something new. We'll tell him what happened at the library. Maybe he has a suggestion on what we should do next."

Kelly nodded and started to slow down, preparing to stop behind a long row of cars at a stoplight just ahead. Everyone outside the car looked so calm. Again, I was almost positive it was a normalcy that most of them had to be taking for granted.

"Good idea," agreed Kelly. "But how about letting me make the call this time? Considering how your last call went . . ."

I appreciated her good-natured jab. "You won't get any argument from me."

The gas station we eventually pulled into, just off Highway 58 on the Denver side of South Table Mountain, looked like it hadn't been open for some time. What windows remained unbroken were painted over, the four gas pumps long since removed. Of course, we wanted someplace out of the way, but I wondered whether the pay phone just outside the rundown station would still be in service. Although, if the phone wasn't working, the phone company was generally on top of those kinds of things and would've probably removed it.

Kelly put the Saturn in park and left the motor running. I pulled Lou's business card from my wallet and handed it to her. "Good luck."

As luck would have it, the phone was working just fine. I watched as Kelly gave me a thumbs-up after picking up the receiver and then punched in the number.

She really is incredible, I reminded myself for the umpteenth time. I honestly had no idea how I would ever be able to repay her for her help—if I ever could.

It wasn't long before Kelly was gripping the phone and looking at me, smiling wide. She nodded a few times and quickly hung up. When she reached the car she was literally beaming. "Guess what?"

"I couldn't if I wanted to," I replied.

"Lou says he's found it! He's found the evidence we need! He wants us to come right over and take a look at it."

I was hearing Kelly's words. I just didn't quite understand them.

"What are you talking about?"

Kelly slipped her slender form back into the driver's seat, buckled her seatbelt, and put the Saturn into drive before answering me. "He's got what we've been looking for, Jason. He's got it!"

I just sat there—numb. *Could he?* I thought. *Could he really have wrapped up this giant mess already?*

I didn't have to say it, but it felt good just the same. "Then let's get over there, Kelly. Mr. Shepard just might get his Saturn back sooner than he imagined!"

* * *

As excited as both Kelly and I were to find out just what it was our private investigator had discovered, we forced ourselves to tamp down that excitement and err on the side of caution. After all, somehow this man from the Red Mafia had found me at the library. How? We didn't know. But he had. And, as far as I was concerned, if he could find us there, then he was capable of finding us anywhere. We drove past the antique store twice, both of us searching for anything that seemed the least bit irregular.

Only a handful of people were out. Many of the stores were still closed and wouldn't open for another hour or two. Of those people we could see, I didn't notice anyone who appeared out of place or who seemed awkward in what they were doing.

On the second floor of the antique store, Lou's blinds were closed—as usual. If he was there, we wouldn't know it for sure until we'd entered the building and checked. At night we at least had the benefit of being able to look for light struggling past the outer edges of his blinds. But in the bright morning sunshine, and with his blinds pulled shut, there was just no way to tell. We rounded the corner and prepared for yet another slow pass down the narrow facing street.

"Tell you what," I said, pulling down the sun visor this time to deflect some of the blinding sunlight pouring through the windshield, "let's park a hundred yards past the store this time. We'll leave our car and double back on foot."

"Come in from a new direction?"

"Right. No one knows what kind of car we're driving, and I'd kind of like to keep it that way for a while."

Kelly smiled. "Good idea. Say, you're getting pretty good at this cloak-and-dagger stuff."

"No. I think it's more like the mouse is just accepting the fact he's in a maze."

Kelly pulled over to the side of the curb and killed the engine. Both of us sat in silence and just looked around, keeping an eye out for anything that looked as if it didn't belong—out-of-state license plates, shadows, people hanging around places they looked like they normally wouldn't.

"All right. Let's do it." I opened my door and stepped out of the car. Together Kelly and I crossed the street and began walking back toward the antique store. I had a headache, and I knew it was from eyestrain. I don't think I've ever relied more on my eyes in my life. But it couldn't be helped; I had to remain alert and try to see everything—for Kelly's sake.

We reached the blue door and found it unlocked. According to the sign in the window, the antique store wouldn't open for another hour. And as far as I could tell, the martial arts school seemed to operate only in the afternoon. The unlocked door did tell us one thing. Lou was there and waiting for us.

Once again I found my hand lingering on the doorknob as I closed the door and rechecked the street for any strange movement. Something wasn't quite right, and I couldn't put my finger on it.

As we began climbing the narrow wooden staircase, my feet felt heavier for some reason. I almost stopped to mention it to Kelly, but I wanted so much for Lou to have the answer I'd been looking for—the silver bullet that would put an end to this nightmare I was in—that I shrugged off the feeling, my feet gradually picking up speed the closer I got to the second floor landing. Progress reports, in-service training meetings, piles of papers that needed grading, and seating charts all sounded so wonderful now, so comfortable. More than anything I just wanted my old life back.

At the top of the stairs I could see Lou's door was open slightly. The aroma of coffee brewing and a hint of cigarette smoke was yet another clue that the man we were looking for was in. I opened the office door wider and stepped inside. Kelly followed. Just as I'd imagined, Lou was seated in his desk chair—though his feet weren't up on his desk this time. Instead, he was hunched over his desk, dressed as he usually was, his stubbled chin resting on the clasped fingers of his thick, hairy hands, his elbows resting on his desk. There was no greeting. His eyes simply followed us as we made our way into the office and headed for the familiar chairs in front of his desk.

"How ya kids doing?" he finally asked when I'd closed the door behind me and had taken a seat myself.

I'd toyed with the idea of immediately filling him in on what had happened the day before, getting his opinion on where we should go next, but I was much too excited to find out what he'd discovered. "We're okay. What did you find out?"

He unfolded his hands and leaned back in his leather chair, his expression grim. "I found out exactly who's been chasing ya. That's what yous two have been payin' me for."

"That's great, Lou," I said. "Who is it?"

I didn't notice the doorknob begin to turn until it was too late. And, when the door to Lou's office opened and a solidly built bald man in a black leather jacket, silk shirt, and dark sunglasses entered the room, my heart seemed to explode in my chest.

Only then did Lou finally answer my question. "It's him."

I stood immediately, placing myself between Kelly and the assassin. I was too stunned to speak, too frightened to do or say anything else.

"Ah, *Musor!* At last we finally are together." His eyes went from me to Kelly, and then back again. "And look here. He thinks he can protect young girl from me."

The assassin took a few steps forward until his face was mere inches from my own. "I can shoot right through you, *Musor,* and she still dies."

I felt the business end of a huge pistol jab against my ribs. I tried to keep from wincing but failed. "Do you want that to be your last memory, watching her die? Because if you move, I kill you both. I grow weary of chasing you."

I turned my head in Lou's direction but found only a placid set of eyes looking back at me. "I warned ya this was serious stuff, didn't I, kid? I told ya things might get ugly."

"Thanks to you, *Musor,* I will start living what you call the 'good life.' Who knows," he added, eyeing Kelly with a peculiar grin, "Maybe I get a Lexus of my own. Hmm?"

It appeared Lou's theory of personal advancement within the organization as a motive had been right. *But why wouldn't it have been right?* I thought to myself. *Lou's probably known the assassin's true motive from the very beginning.*

I was confused. The man we'd hired, the man we'd put our trust in, had just sold us down the river like so many board feet of lumber.

Kelly had been right. The man was a roach.

The sound of an envelope hitting Lou's desk with a thud was like a splash of ice water in my face. I watched as Lou sat there and opened it, flipping a thick thumb through a wad of bills that had to total thousands of dollars. I couldn't imagine where the man had gotten so much money.

"Your help is much appreciated," said the assassin. "I tell others of your efforts."

Others, I realized. *He's got an entire criminal organization behind him, Jason. Where'd he get the money?* That's *where he got the money!*

Lou grinned. "Glad I could help. And if yer ever in need of my services in the future . . ."

Everything around me seemed to be swirling in slow motion. When I caught the terrified expression on Kelly's face, when I saw her eyes going from the gun to my ribs, only then did the full impact of what was going on begin to crystallize in my head.

We were about to die.

Despite our careful planning and effort, we'd been captured. And seeing the pistol and the money seemed only to confirm how pitiful our attempts had been. How could I have been so arrogantly stupid? Who was I to think I could compete with an organized criminal organization? Why hadn't I turned myself over to the authorities in the first place? Sure, I might not have had anyone to turn to for help, but at least I would have been alone. Now Kelly was with me. And she, no doubt, would have to now be dealt with as well. And what would happen when they eventually found our car parked only a hundred yards from the building? It wouldn't take them long to trace it back to Mr. Shepard. Would they deal with him as well?

My mind was jumping from one worst-case scenario to the next as my fertile imagination painted picture after picture of failure and defeat. So when Lou stood and offered me his hand—along with, "No hard feelin's, kid. Business is business"—without thinking, I reached out and accepted it. I was unprepared for such a move on his part, unprepared for the quick wink that accompanied it, and even more unprepared for the slip of paper that moved from his hand to mine. If it hadn't been for that small, tangible slip of paper, I don't know how long I would've let my emotions and imagination run wild.

"Let's get going, *Musor*. You first. Go downstairs. Get in white car across street." He gripped Kelly's arm hard enough that she cried out. "Don't try anything. If you do, she dies."

I was ushered out the door quickly and never got the chance to make eye contact with Lou again.

As we were led down the stairs, I did manage to get a peek at the single word written on both sides of the slip of paper before thrusting it into my jeans pocket the moment we reached the blue door at the foot of the steps.

Crossing the street, the assassin opened the back door of a white sedan and motioned impatiently for me to get in. Then he roughly shoved Kelly into the backseat next to me. When the door slammed shut, I had only a second to utter the word I'd glimpsed on the slip of paper. I then reached over my shoulder, as did Kelly, and found the shoulder strap of the seatbelt. I'd just about clicked it into place when the assassin opened the driver's side door. I said nothing, not wanting to draw any attention to our movements.

When he shut the door, he held up the pistol and looked directly into my eyes through the rearview mirror. I felt irrational surprise when I saw they were human eyes—blue—though cold, hard, and menacing. "Try nothing. Understand?" He held up his gun. When I nodded, letting him know his threat had been received loud and clear, only then did he lower the gun, placing it, I assumed, in his lap.

Starting the car, he gave his mirrors a quick glance and pulled away from the curb and into the street.

I had no idea where we were headed. That he wanted to kill us was obvious, and my only guess was that he was taking us someplace where our bodies wouldn't be found too easily.

I had just taken hold of Kelly's hand and was looking through the windshield when I first spotted the car coming toward us. That the driver was driving down the wrong side of the narrow street really hadn't registered. Contemplating one's imminent death seems to take priority over all other thoughts. But I did notice the unusual fact that the driver in the oncoming car wore a helmet. I suppose, at the time, I thought it odd. I also suppose I knew, at some unconscious level, what was coming next. I can remember seeing the car in front of us speeding toward us. I can recall thinking only seconds before impact how odd it was that he was coming at us in our lane.

A bone-jarring collision followed.

Instantly, I was swallowed up into darkness.

CHAPTER 22

Kelly's voice was distant at first, almost imperceptible, but it increased in volume rapidly. What felt like someone tapping either side of my face with drumsticks suddenly became the slaps they really were, and in no time Kelly's face came into focus.

"Please, Jason. Wake up! Wake up!"

I shook my head to clear it, but the pressure on the right side wouldn't go away. I just wanted to close my eyes again and remain inert.

"Come on, Jason. Come on!"

I felt my arm being pulled, my body hesitantly trying to move with each tug.

A chance glimpse toward the front seat showed our assassin slumped over the steering wheel, blood dripping steadily from his head.

An accident, I thought. *I've been in an accident. Kelly?* "Kelly!"

My final thought must have found its way to my mouth because suddenly Kelly was chattering like a child at her first circus. "I'm so glad you're okay. Come on! We've got to move! The guy who hit us told me to get out of here fast. Come on! We've got to move!"

I willed my feet to do just that, though with each step I took I felt like I was walking through a thick, suffocating fog. I held tightly to Kelly's hand and watched the pavement rushing beneath my feet. I didn't dare look up for fear I'd lose my balance completely.

Seconds later I recognized the Saturn we'd picked up earlier that morning. At first I wondered why we were running for that and not for some kind of help. I swallowed my questions. It was easier.

Kelly threw open the driver's side door, and I lunged awkwardly for the passenger seat. I'd barely gotten my legs out of Kelly's way when I felt the car start. Pulling myself upright, I lay my head back and tried to give my brain time to catch up with my body.

After only a few minutes I was beginning to see things a bit more clearly. I could also feel the bucket seat beneath me and decided that was yet another good sign.

I reached up to ambush an annoying trickle of sweat running down the right side of my face. When I pulled my hand away, my heart skipped a beat. It was blood, not sweat.

Kelly must have noticed my reaction to the discovery. "I think your head must have hit the window when he slammed into us," she said. "Just sit back and relax."

She reached in back of her, between the seats, and grabbed one of the duffel bags she'd brought with her—was it only four days ago? Unzipping it with her free hand, she dug out a yellow T-shirt and flung it against my chest. "Here, get pressure on that. Once we get a little farther out, I'll stop and take a look at it." She tossed the duffel bag back into the backseat.

I held the shirt against the side of my head and closed my eyes, which was about the only thing I could trust myself to do at that point.

Several miles later I pulled the shirt from my head and gently touched the wounded area with my fingertips. A goose egg was no exaggeration for what I had on the right side of my head, near the temple. Sticky blood had collected around the wound, matting the surrounding hair and, I'm sure, making the injury look worse than it really was.

I heard an ambulance and looked around to find it. It was some distance off, however. I wondered if it might be headed for where we'd just been.

After another three or four miles, Kelly pulled into a supermarket parking lot, putting the Saturn in park at the extreme end. There was no one around us, and Kelly parked the car so as not to be facing the street.

"Here, let me take a look at that," Kelly said, and I turned my head so she could inspect the wound.

"What happened, Kelly?"

She first checked all around my head and then focused on the wound itself. I could feel her fingers pulling my hair aside. "Nothing's broken—that's what I was worried most about—and the cut isn't deep."

"I think you're right. I must have smacked it against the side of the car when that guy hit us."

Kelly handed me the yellow T-shirt, which I reapplied to my head. "Well, keep that on it and we'll get it cleaned out when we find a better place to stop." She settled back into the driver's seat and put the car back into drive. "I want to get away from here."

Minutes later we were headed north on Highway 85, each of us lost in our own thoughts, but hopefully putting as much distance as we could between us and Lou, the accident, and the assassin.

Only when we'd driven several miles did Kelly finally find her voice again. "It was all a setup."

Her comment had come out of nowhere. "What are you talking about?"

"Lou. He set us up! He took what he could from us and then sold us out the moment he realized he could get more."

My head was throbbing and my vision far from adequate. Sitting back, leaning forward, or even leaning to the side seemed to do little to alleviate the pain or clear up the blur around me. But my brain was finally functioning again. "I don't think so, Kelly."

I knew she was close to tears. She was angry and frustrated. Both were emotions I was very much familiar with, but I'd learned over the last few days the importance of putting my emotions on hold, stepping back from a situation, and trying to study it from different angles. Kelly was also very good at this type of analysis, but shock has a tendency to befuddle you. I was sure that's what she was experiencing now. "I think something went wrong," I continued in Lou's defense.

Kelly glanced over her left shoulder. Holding down the turn signal a few seconds, she moved the Saturn into the next lane. "What makes you think something went wrong?" she asked when she was settled in the new lane. It was said with sarcasm, but with a weak smile as well.

"I don't know. Maybe this assassin got wise to Lou—put pressure on him to turn us over."

"But how? No one knew we were going to the man for help."

"I don't know, Kelly. But he knew. The man's a professional. Somehow he figured it out."

"And the money he tossed Lou? You saw how thick that envelope was. Are you telling me Lou just had to take the money?"

"I think he did."

"I guess I'm lost, then. From where I'm sitting, it looks as if the day after we hired Lou he made a phone call. Finally, when the asking price was met, he and the assassin exchanged property—namely, you and me—for cash. Now would you mind explaining to me just how you're able to draw a different conclusion out of all this?"

I held up the blood-stained yellow T-shirt I'd been pressing against the side of my head. "The accident, for one thing."

Seeing that she wasn't making the connection, I backpedaled a bit. "Kelly, the guy who hit us was traveling in the wrong lane."

"But—"

"When he crossed lanes, he was aiming for us, Kelly. He meant to ram us. Did you see what was on his head when he hit us?"

She shook her head. I could tell she wasn't following where I was headed with all of this. "He was wearing a helmet, Kelly. He meant to hit us."

"He wasn't wearing a helmet when I saw him," countered Kelly. "He was crawling out of his car shouting at me to get out . . ."

Recognition slowly began to spread over Kelly's face, her eyes suddenly narrowing as she started thinking instead of panicking. "He was telling us to get away! So he . . . he was . . ."

"Sent to hit us—to give us the chance to escape," I said, finishing her thought for her.

"And Lou arranged it?"

"He must have."

"We could've been killed! If you hadn't told me to put on my seatbelt . . ." She looked at me. "How did you know about the seatbelt anyway?"

Only then did my collision-addled brain remember the slip of paper Lou had passed to me during our parting handshake. I threw the yellow T-shirt onto the dash and dug into my pocket. It was still there.

"What is it, Jason?"

I turned the paper over a few times in my hand before holding it up to show her.

"Seatbelts," she read. "That's what made you tell me to put on my seatbelt? Where'd it come from?"

"From Lou. When he shook my hand he slipped it to me—threw me a wink, too."

"Why didn't he just warn us over the phone? If he hadn't been able to slip us that note, we'd have been killed!"

"I guess he figured he didn't have any other choice. When that assassin sets his sights on you, he's pretty hard to shake."

"So Lou found himself boxed in by this guy. And . . . the only way he could escape from the box was to lure us in and then try and . . . I'm lost."

"I don't think we'll ever know what really happened until we're able to talk to him again."

"Jason?"

"Yeah?"

"The assassin. You saw him didn't you?"

"Slumped over the wheel?"

"Right. Well, if what you say about Lou is true, then it's over now, right? Lou reports the accident, explains to the police what's been going on, and then, whoever that guy in black is, he gets taken to the hospital and held under police observation. That's it, then. We've got the guy who's been after you. You can turn yourself in now."

While Kelly had been talking to me, I had grabbed the T-shirt again and was holding it against the side of my head, not because it was still bleeding, but because I had nothing better to do. Kelly was right. Assuming help arrived immediately following the accident, there was a good chance the man was now in custody, with helpful Lou filling in the blanks for the authorities. Perhaps that had been Lou's plan the whole time. But the more I thought about it, the more it just didn't seem like it could be wrapped up so easily. After all, the fact that the man was even after me was simply my word against his, wasn't it? If Lou testified about whatever he knew and showed the police the money, would that be enough? For kidnapping maybe, but not murder. No. Something was missing from all this. Something—

"What's it say inside?" asked Kelly.

I was startled, suddenly yanked from my thoughts. "What?"

Kelly nodded toward the note I was unconsciously turning over in my hands. Until that moment I thought it was just a small slip of paper. But with Kelly's question, I realized it was in fact a slightly larger piece of paper folded over. "Open it up. Is there anything written on the inside?"

I slowly unfolded it as Kelly once again signaled, preparing to change lanes.

"What's on it?" she asked, her curiosity clearly piqued.

"Three addresses."

"Addresses?"

"Yeah. Three addresses. That's it."

Kelly looked as confused as I felt. "What does Lou want us to do with them?"

I sat silently for a minute before an idea surfaced. "Of course," I muttered.

"Of course what?" asked Kelly.

"Lou couldn't warn us over the phone because our assassin friend might have been with him."

"So."

"So, maybe he knew we needed this information and he wanted to make sure we got it—personally."

"So, it's a clue or a lead?" asked Kelly.

"Maybe."

Kelly nodded. "You think one of these addresses belongs to the whistle-blower in all this?"

"It might. I haven't the slightest idea. But they must be important if Lou risked our lives to get them to us. The whistle-blower's address would make sense, I guess."

"But if Lou's found the whistle-blower, why not just call up the FBI himself and clear everything up—at least get the authorities to know you're being set up in all of this?" asked Kelly, looking as confused as I was. "They could put you in some kind of protective custody."

The thought of Lee Harvey Oswald taking a bullet in the gut while in "protective custody" flashed through my mind again, as it had when I'd first contemplated turning myself in. But I decided not to bring it up.

"Maybe he's protecting his source," I finally said. "I don't know. He's obviously taking the backdoor approach to all of this for some reason and wants us to stay clear."

Maybe Lou's simply trying to get us as far away from here as we can, I pondered.

Kelly shrugged her shoulders. "We can try to call Lou later. If our assassin is in the hospital, he should be free to speak with us."

"Not necessarily," I said, staring once more out the passenger window at nothing and everything at the same time.

"What do you mean?"

"Sure, our assassin friend may be laid up for a while, maybe even dead, but he's only one cog of many in that killing machine. We're assuming he's only a rogue agent in all of this. But what if he isn't alone? If the Red Mafia suddenly decided to call for reinforcements to help clean up the mess, I doubt we'd have much of a chance. Getting away from one of these guys is hard enough. I'd hate to see what a whole army of them could do. Maybe Lou wants us to stay clear until he's had the chance to unravel everything."

"But then why not just tell us that in the note?" countered Kelly. "Why give us three addresses?"

"I don't know," I replied, folding and refolding the note several times. "I do think we need to clear the area for a while anyway."

Kelly was nodding her head. "Well, the guy didn't mention the Saturn at all. Maybe we're safe that way. For a while. So, what do you suggest we do next? Because I don't think we should stop until we put a bit more distance behind us."

"I think we should try the addresses on this note. Lou's given it to us for a reason." I stared out the passenger window once more. "And somehow I get the feeling we haven't got much time to unravel this."

Kelly bit at her lower lip for a time before finally answering me. "All right. It makes sense. What's the closest address you've got on that list?"

"Well, for starters, you're going to need to turn around. We're headed in the wrong direction."

"So, where are we headed?" Kelly asked, clearly frustrated.

"You're not going to believe it."

"Try me."

"All three addresses are in the same place—quite a ways from here."

"Where, Jason?"

"New Mexico."

Kelly just looked at me. "You're right. I don't believe it."

CHAPTER 23

    I'd never been to Farmington, New Mexico. In fact, I'd never even heard of it before. Kelly knew a little bit about it from an article she'd read in a travel magazine several years before and informed me that it was in the northwest corner of the state—the Four Corners area. She also remembered the article mentioning the town as a takeoff point for lovers of the outdoors. The Navajo Reservation and National Historical Park are only a stone's throw away. Whether you're into kayaking, hiking, fly-fishing, or skiing, a short drive from Farmington, New Mexico, is apparently all you need to get you started.

    Getting to Farmington, though, is the challenge. There's absolutely nothing to see on Highway 285 southbound, unless of course you count the occasional car, semi-truck, scrub brush, and acre upon never-ending acre of rough, dry desert. Of course, the nice part about being in the middle of what feels like nowhere is that there's hardly anyone around to notice you. Hence, I was finally able to spot Kelly from time to time on the driving. Concerned that I probably had a mild concussion, she allowed me to drive only an hour at a time. She wanted to make sure I got the rest I needed, but I could tell she greatly appreciated the moments when she could turn the Saturn over to me, rest her eyes, and relax a bit.

    The Saturn ate up the miles, but the hours rolled by slowly on the seemingly endless highway. Though we took turns napping, neither one of us ever really woke completely rested and refreshed. Aside from having to stop twice for gas, or to switch places in the driver's seat, we pretty much made the eight-hour trip in one straight shot.

We'd long since given up speculating on the three mysterious addresses. Both of us agreed that one of them had to belong to the whistle-blower but decided it was probably best to wait until we could get a local map of the area before guessing any further. So we traveled in relative silence, broken only occasionally by small talk or the few stations we could tune in on the car radio. Both of us, I think, were still trying to sort out, in our own way, what we'd just been through.

We found a local map at a gas station just outside of Farmington, off Highway 550. During the remaining forty-five minutes of the trip, I worked at locating the three addresses on the map while Kelly drove. Two of the addresses, it turned out, were located only a mile apart—as the crow flies—at the northeastern end of the town. The third address was farther south—by two or three miles—on the other side of what the map had labeled the Animas River and Willett Ditch.

"I vote we start with the first address on the list," said Kelly. "It has to be our whistle-blower's most current address."

"That's assuming the list runs from present to past," I pointed out. "The third address could just as easily be the current one. Or for all we know, these are addresses for three different people."

"Yet another pattern to decipher in all of this chaos, hmm?" Kelly bit at her lip. "I guess you're right. Okay, then let's take the southernmost address first. If we don't find anything there, at least we'll be headed in the right direction if we suddenly need to break for home."

Despite our catnaps and the junk food we'd had along the way, I was tired. And I knew Kelly was too. I wanted to point out how crazy it would be to try to lose a guy on a lonely stretch of desert road that went on for hours, but I held my tongue. Fatigue was catching up with us, and I was sure that bringing up such a point at that moment would be as counterproductive as trying to extinguish a fire with flour. On the other hand, I knew that a good night's rest was probably the best thing for us.

"Tell you what," I began. "It's almost seven. I don't know about you, but I wouldn't mind getting a little rest first before we start exploring." I glanced down at the map and moved my finger along the road we were on. "When we hit . . . South Butler Avenue . . . what do you say we pull off and find us a hotel?"

I could see Kelly's face brighten at the suggestion, but then it darkened just as quickly. "We'll have a better chance of catching him home at night than we will during the day."

She was right, of course.

"All right. How about a compromise? We'll get some sleep now and head out before dawn."

She brightened once more and threw me a look of immense gratitude. She'd wanted a compromise—wanted some way to get some rest—and I'd just given it to her.

Upon entering Farmington's city limits, we learned a bit about the town from several strategically placed signs along the highway. The population was said to be near 37,000, and it was quite apparent that those 37,000 were very much spread out over a fairly vast area of land. Farmington must have been a lush area by New Mexico's standards. On a few billboards, as well as around the edge of the map I was holding, were several photos taken of the five parks along the San Juan River. Apparently they were the crown jewels of the town.

Kelly checked herself into the motel as she'd done before, though this time she surprised me by purchasing an adjoining room for me. When I'd started to question the wisdom in that, she held up a finger. "Jason, we're both exhausted, and we need the rest. You're not going to get what you need sleeping in the car. Call it splurging, call it reckless. I don't care."

I said nothing. Instead I carried her duffel bags and followed her into the small but adequate room and watched as Kelly collapsed on her back on the nearest bed. Her right forearm covered her eyes.

I put my key in the lock of the adjoining room, opened the door, and headed for the bathroom. I looked a mess! I'd tried to clean myself up at the first gas station we fueled up at, but there was still blood on my shirt and hair that had since dried out and become dark, hard, and crusty. I also knew I was sorely in need of a shower. I had little doubt Kelly knew it as well.

The shower was heaven-sent. I watched as blood and dirt from the last few days darkened the water at my feet, disappearing forever down the drain. I adjusted the showerhead, letting the water pummel me. Another adjustment brought the stimulation of water needles. I relished every sensation, thinking, *I feel; therefore I am.* I was alive.

I doubt that falling into bed after completing the Ironman Marathon feels any better than I felt when I finally climbed into bed.

A small tap on the adjoining room door surprised me. I quickly pulled on a pair of jeans and, standing to one side of the door, opened it a few inches. "Yes? You okay?"

Kelly peeked around her side of the door and smiled, though she looked completely exhausted. "I'm sorry I ignored you when we came in. I—"

"Don't worry about it, Kelly. You were just tired, that's all. I understand."

Once again our faces were close to one another, and I could see in her eyes the same longing I was feeling.

"I . . . I just wanted to tell you . . . good night," she whispered.

We were both exhausted, and I knew the desire we were both feeling for each other was stronger because of it. We'd had similar feelings before, but it had been some time ago. It seemed like only yesterday. I leaned down and kissed her lips—probably waiting a bit longer then I should have to break it off.

"I . . . um," I finally stammered. "I'll see you in the morning." And with some reluctance I closed the door, my heart pounding in my chest.

I slipped back into bed and had to force my mind to become aware of the room once more—quiet, dark, and peaceful. The sheets were clean and cool, and it felt so good to have a mattress—even a hotel mattress—beneath me. Seconds later I was fast asleep.

Once again, Kelly had been right. We both needed a good night's rest.

CHAPTER 24

"Jason, wake up! Wake up, Jason!"

I guess Kelly had been shaking me for some time because by the time I finally opened my eyes, she looked panic-stricken. Remembering the hit I'd taken on my head, I couldn't blame her.

"What time is it?" I mumbled.

"It's a little after five o'clock in the morning. I knocked on your door, but you wouldn't answer." Her voice was filled with relief. "Come on. We ought to get moving."

I watched as she disappeared through the open doorway that joined our rooms. She left the door open, and I could see her grab her shoes and then sit at the foot of her bed to slip them on. When she'd finished and I still hadn't moved, she picked up one of my own shoes near the door and tossed it at me. "Let's go, Jason!"

Kelly began rummaging through her duffel bag.

I rolled onto my back. The room was still quite dark and felt quiet, warm, and safe. Now I had to get up and leave it. When Kelly disappeared into her room, I reluctantly swung my feet over the edge of the bed, slipped back into my jeans, and held my head in my hands.

"Five o'clock in the morning never felt like this," I mumbled.

"Well, come on. We're running out of time." Kelly tossed me a small plastic bag before disappearing with a bag of her own into her bathroom, shutting the door behind her.

Inside the bag was a tan souvenir T-shirt we'd picked up in a gas station on our first stop for gas. I'd forgotten all about it. I had just slipped it on when Kelly opened the bathroom door and came back into my room. She had on a similar simple white T-shirt. I had to admit, though, that she looked much better in her shirt than I did in mine.

"Here. Let's take a look at that head of yours." She stood beside me and probed gently around what I was sure was, by then, a large bluish bruise.

"You did a good job of cleaning it out last night. In a week or so you won't even know it was there." She ran a hand over my head and laughed. "I would suggest running a comb through your hair, though. Rooster tails—even small ones—don't look as cute on a man as they do on a little boy."

Self-consciously I fingered my hair and growing beard.

Kelly smiled and started to walk away when I reached out for her hand. She stopped, hesitated, and then sat beside me on the bed. "What's wrong?" she asked.

"Are you okay? Last night you seemed really quiet."

Kelly looked down at her feet a moment before making eye contact. "Like I said last night, I was tired, Jason. I was very tired. But I'm okay. The sleep helped."

"Kelly, I—"

"Hey, no apologies. Okay? Let's just get a move on. I really think we're close to getting to the bottom of all this." She gave my hand a squeeze. "Let's go."

She went to stand but I still hadn't let go of her hand. Slowly she sat down again and this time placed her head on my shoulder.

"I . . . I've got to keep moving, Jason. If I don't . . ."

When I looked into her face I could see a few tears falling from her eyes, spilling over her cheeks.

"Thanks again for all of your help, Kelly," I whispered.

She leaned over and kissed me softly on the lips. After days of dirt, grime, and blood, it felt warm and incredible . . . just as it had last night.

When she started to pull away I returned the kiss with just as much softness and tenderness. When we parted the second time, she again gave my hand a squeeze. "Come on. Let's get your life back."

* * *

Highway 64 took us back over the Animas River. As far as the town itself was concerned, there was nothing architecturally that really jumped out at you. It was what it was: a shopping center—with a strong Navajo influence—for those living within a hundred mile radius.

Minutes later we found ourselves on Elm Street and, with no trouble, located the first address on our list. It belonged to the Western Village apartments. The complex looked relatively new and well-managed. Three four-story stucco buildings wrapped around a kind of plaza, the weight room and laundry room at the center of it all. Nearly every window was dark when we pulled into the visitor's end of the parking lot, but I knew it wouldn't be long before people began waking up, getting ready for the day, and ultimately leaving.

I shut off the engine and studied the corners of the buildings where large signs offered some guidance as to how each floor and building was numbered.

"There it is," I said. "You can just see it from here. Second floor, fourth door from the end."

"There's a light on. A good sign."

"Yeah." Whether it was or wasn't a good sign, I couldn't tell. "Okay, I'll go knock on the door. You're staying right here."

Kelly let out a short laugh as she opened the passenger door. "Yeah, right. We go together, Jason."

We held hands as we worked our way across the plaza to the nearest stairwell. The thick cement steps were surrounded by strategically placed brick that, for the most part, allowed what might have been a stuffy, dark stairwell to remain fairly exposed to air and light. The heat of the desert had obviously been taken into consideration during the complex's planning. It was a relatively cool morning, but I figured by noon we'd know we were in the middle of a desert.

Drapes were pulled on both the small window to the left of the door and the large picture window to the right. And although light was finding its way through the fabric curtains, we couldn't really see a thing from the outside looking in. I hesitated knocking.

"Kelly," I whispered. "I'd feel a lot better if you waited in the car."

"I'm sure you would. I, on the other hand, would not." Her index finger reached out and stabbed at the doorbell—the familiar two-tone signal barely audible from our side of the door.

In spite of her brazen action, I felt Kelly's grip on my hand tighten. Here we were, without a name or description, and no clue as to whether this individual could help us or not. Of course, I also was very much aware of the fact that even if this was someone who could help us, he could easily feign complete ignorance and send us off with nothing. Or worse. What if the fact we had found him ticked him off?

The rattle of a door chain and then the movement of a deadbolt snapped me back to reality. When the door finally opened a few inches, I was unprepared for the elderly face that looked at me with what appeared to be genuine curiosity.

"Can I help you?"

It was such a simple question, and yet I had no idea how to respond. It was Kelly who found her voice first. She leaned her head over. "We're sorry to bother you this early in the morning, but we're looking for someone very important."

The old man's eyes softened when he saw Kelly. "Just a minute." The door closed and we could hear him fiddling with the door chain. The door opened much wider the second time and revealed an elderly man in a very comfortable blue bathrobe. Diamond-patterned pajama bottoms poked out from beneath the robe and a well-worn pair of brown slippers covered his feet. He reminded me a lot of Jim, my own apartment manager back home.

This time it was Kelly's turn to hesitate, and so I cleared my throat and phrased my words carefully. "Sir, we're looking for a man that used to work at a distillery plant . . . in Missouri. McAllister Distilling?" I watched his eyes closely as I uttered each word, searching for any sign of recognition or surprise triggered by my words. If this was the man from McAllister, if he was in fact the very person we'd been looking for, there wasn't even the slightest hint of it in his eyes or face. He allowed me to ask my question and then, without any hesitation, responded.

"I'm sorry, young man, miss. I'm the only man who lives here and I can assure you I've never been to Missouri."

"How long have you lived here, if you don't mind us asking?"

"Oh, a little over two years now, I guess. After my wife passed away I thought it would be an easier way to live. Less maintenance, you know."

"And you wouldn't happen to remember who lived here before you?" Kelly asked.

"Heaven's no. It was a clean slate when I moved in."

All of us remained silent for some time. I knew Kelly had to be doing the same thing I was doing—I was desperately waiting for this old man to flinch, to cave in for only a second or so, to let us know we'd stumbled onto something that would help us. But he just stood there looking into our faces, his eyes narrowing during our prolonged silence. "I'm sorry I can't help you."

His words caught Kelly's attention first. "Yes. Thank you, sir. We're sorry to have bothered you."

The old man grinned at her glowing smile. "No bother. Have a good day."

When the door had closed, I turned around and placed my arms on the short brick half-wall that ran along the edge of the second floor. It echoed the design of the stairwells, and I could feel a slight breeze stirring at my pant leg. "Well. What do you think? A dead end?"

Kelly turned and leaned against me. "I think so. Come on, it's chilly. Let's get back to the car."

Once I had the car heater started, I pulled out the local map, along with the slip of paper Lou had given me, and switched on Kelly's reading light. The next address on the list was also an apartment building. And although it was only an inch and half to two inches away from us on the map, it would probably take us a good twenty minutes to weave our way over there.

"My vote's on the third address," said Kelly.

"What makes you so sure?" I asked.

"Well, look. It looks like an actual house address and only five minutes north of this second apartment."

I wasn't seeing the connection.

"He was probably moved here by the FBI and given this apartment first. He later moves to this second apartment complex, likes the area, and finally decides to settle down in a house of his own."

I nodded. "Yeah, I guess that makes sense. All right, we'll try the house first. If no one's there we'll run over to the second apartment complex. Sound good?"

"Only if we follow that up with a big breakfast. I'm starving."

"You got it."

It was just after six o'clock when I made a left on 20th Street and made my way up North Skyview Avenue. It looked like a nice middle-class neighborhood with modestly built homes lining both sides of the street. The neighborhood couldn't have been more than fifteen, maybe twenty years old. Kelly was counting the house numbers as we drove slowly up the quiet and deserted street. The sun was beginning to rise and, with the sky as clear as it was, I had no doubt we were in for a warm afternoon.

It turned out the address belonged to a small, one-level brick home. A two-car garage jutted forward on the right side of the house, making it appear bigger than it probably was. It looked similar to the other homes on the street, although the lawn in front was dry in several spots and badly in need of some TLC. It was now bright enough outside that it was difficult to tell whether a light was on inside or not. The closed, white garage door offered up no clues.

I parked across the street, and both of us sat there staring at the front door and the few windows that lined the front of house.

"See any movement at all?" asked Kelly.

"Nothing. Whoever lives here might already have left for the day."

"Hmm. Maybe. Maybe not. There's a rolled-up newspaper in front of the door."

Sure enough, there was. I couldn't believe I'd missed something as obvious as that. "Well, there's only one way to know for sure." I opened the car door and Kelly did the same on her side. Once more we found ourselves walking hand in hand toward what we hoped just might be the end to this nightmare I—we—seemed to be stuck in.

The moment we stepped onto the driveway, however, I found my pace suddenly slowing. We were almost to the front door when I stopped walking altogether and just stood there staring at the front door. My heart was on fire, pounding within my chest, almost suffocating me.

"You okay?" asked Kelly, giving my hand a reassuring squeeze.

"I think so," I muttered. I swallowed and began to take a few deep breaths.

"Do you see something?" asked Kelly. Her hand tensed and her arm had become rigid.

"No. No, I don't see anything. But I have the strongest impression this is the place we've been searching for."

Kelly stood there studying my eyes and biting at her lower lip.

"Then I suppose we should knock on the door," she finally suggested.

"Yeah. I . . . I guess we should." I swallowed hard and walked to the front door. When we'd reached it, I raised my hand to knock, but the door opened before my knuckles ever touched wood.

CHAPTER 25

Once again the person standing before me seemed out of place. I guess I had been expecting a thick-necked bruiser, a man who looked like he belonged in the back room of a distilling plant throwing freight around. Instead I was looking into the eyes of a little man, no taller than five feet. Mid-forties, perhaps. A bushy mustache and long, nut-brown hair—slicked back—reminded me of an old black-and-white picture of General Custer I'd seen back in elementary school. He was dressed in flashy cowboy attire that made him look even more ridiculous.

"Is there something I can do for you folks?" he asked in a nasal tone that seemed to suit him perfectly.

I quickly cast my eyes from side to side out of habit, checking for anything out of the ordinary. Then I pulled myself together, remembering just why it was we were there in the first place. The burning in my heart hadn't diminished. If anything, it had only intensified. I took a deep breath.

"We're sorry to bother you this early in the morning, but we're trying to find someone very important."

"I was just about ready to head for work anyway. Saw you standing here. Who are you looking for?"

Kelly jumped right in. "We're looking for a man who used to work in a distilling plant in Missouri. McAllister Distilling Company."

For just a fraction of a second I thought I saw the corner of the man's mouth twitch.

The small man brought his hand to his mouth, and with his thumb and forefinger began to tug at one end of his moustache. For maybe a quarter of a second he had a look of consternation on his face, but then it was gone. I knew—without a doubt—this was the man Lou had meant for us to find. The trick now would be to figure out just how we were going to convince him that we needed his help. His initial response wasn't leaning toward either fight or flight, and I took that to be a good sign.

"No. No, I'm sorry," he finally responded, his hand dropping back to his side. "I don't know anyone around here that used to live in Missouri."

He was smooth. He'd managed to tamp down his panic. Had I not felt the warm burning in my heart, he just might have convinced me. He honestly looked as if he had no idea what we were talking about.

"Sir, I really don't know how to say this, but I know you can help us."

"Well, son, I would if I could. I work down at the Trading Post in town. It's a souvenir shop. A lot of people come through. I can ask around if you'd like."

The entire time he spoke he never broke eye contact with me. Missing now were all the signs I was used to looking for in my students who held back the truth—darting eyes, nervous twitches, the rocking back and forth that unconsciously occurred when one felt uncomfortable. Aside from that first twitch and momentary look of concern, this man was a blank slate.

When Kelly and I hadn't responded to his offer, his grin widened. "Sound good? Why don't you leave me a number where you can be reached, and if I run across anybody I'll give you a ring?"

The ball was once more in our court. I decided a solid return was in order.

"My name is Jason Harrington. That name mean anything to you?"

Our eyes remained locked for several seconds, and for the second time I could see his defensive shield beginning to crack. Not giving him the chance for rebuttal, I powered forward. "You used my name, sir. You used it on shipping manifests that—"

The man's defensive shield dropped instantly. He shushed me, grabbed hold of my wrist, and pulled me toward the door. "Get inside!"

Though I had little doubt I could have easily broken his grasp, I allowed him to pull me forward. I felt Kelly reach out and grab my other hand and guessed she'd been caught completely off guard by this sudden move.

"It's okay, Kelly. It's okay." I gave her hand a reassuring squeeze as I pulled her through the doorway with me.

The small man, seeing we were now inside, released my arm and made a quick dash to close the door. He bolted it and leaned back against it. The scene would have been comical if what we were going through wasn't so grave.

"Jason Harrington?" he asked, his face askew, his eyes genuinely filled with confusion. "But you don't exist!"

The irony of his words hadn't been lost on me. "You hear that, Kelly? This whole time I've been trying to figure out how to prove to everyone that they're after the wrong guy. Now it turns out I don't even exist."

The little man—I momentarily thought of him as a tufted titmouse—ran both his hands over his head, grabbed handfuls of the longer hair that fell around his neck, and pulled, shaking his head. "This is crazy. Crazy!" When his hands came away from his head he seemed to be in better control of his emotions. "Please. Have a seat." He turned and glanced out the living room window once more.

The home decor was simple and functional. A long leather couch and recliner lined one wall, a small entertainment center another. A feeble attempt had been made to decorate the walls of the room, but the few embellishments revealed him to be a no-nonsense individual. He lived here. It was as simple as that.

Kelly and I took a seat on the couch while he sat on the edge of the matching recliner.

"You said your name is Jason Harrington?"

I couldn't keep my eyes away from his wringing hands.

"That's right, sir," I responded.

"So what is it you want? Why are you here?"

I attempted to answer him, but he continued to rattle off one question after another in news reporter fashion.

"Who sent you? Where did you get this address? Were you followed? Is this some kind of a trick you feds like pulling on witnesses?"

"Sir, please give me a chance to explain."

The little man shut his mouth, although by the way he repeatedly brought his lower lip up and over his mustache, it was taking all his effort to remain silent. His eyes were wide and, with all the fidgeting he was doing, I found myself becoming more nervous as well.

"There's a man out there looking for me. He thinks I'm Jason Harrington, the same Jason Harrington that showed up on your shipping manifests. He's been chasing—"

"Chasing?" interrupted the little man. "What do you mean *chasing*? What's he look like? Do you know his name? What was he driv—"

"He's tall, completely bald, and wears a black leather jacket," I interrupted. As I gave my description, I could almost hear him mentally eliminating possible suspects. I continued speaking, though his reactions to my words made me feel uneasy. Kelly glanced at me and I could tell the man's agitation was beginning to rub off on her as well. "He has an accent—a foreign accent. We think he has connections with the Red Mafia."

The man's face went white. For a moment I thought he was going to pass out. Instead he surprised me by standing and suddenly pacing back and forth. "I knew it! I knew it was too good to be true. I told them they'd find me."

"You're him, then?" began Kelly. "You're the whistle-blower?"

He stood still and stared blankly in Kelly's direction. A tiny smile played at the corners of the man's mouth and the edges of his small but earnest-looking eyes. Then he started to laugh.

Kelly looked at me. I could see she wasn't sure how to react to the man's outburst. I shrugged and watched as he continued pacing. When the laughter finally subsided, there were tears in his eyes. "I was told no one would ever find me. My lawyer assured me that I would disappear, that no one would . . ." His voice trailed off, and when he noticed us staring at him, he made his way back to the recliner and sat down.

"How did you find me?" he asked with a new and determined expression on his face. "What do you want?"

I found it ironic that I was feeling the sudden impulse to calm him down, to assure him no one had followed us. But of course the truth was I couldn't. Were we followed? Who knew? Every time it seemed like I was alone and secure, that's when the world suddenly blew up in my face. "Look, I promise you, we're not here to hurt you, and we have no intention of disturbing the life you have now."

No sooner had the words left my mouth when it suddenly dawned on me why Lou had perhaps led us to this man in the first place.

"How thoughtful of you," he added sarcastically. "The Red Mafia's tailing you and so you come here. Perfectly understandable. Why should I be upset?" He stood and cautiously tiptoed to the window once more, peering from around the wall as if doing so would protect him against a sudden stream of bullets.

I really hadn't heard a thing he had said, so absorbed was I in the sudden realization I'd inadvertently stumbled upon. Lou must have realized that going through proper channels would only serve to expose this man to intense scrutiny. No doubt in the process of an in-depth examination, the man's newfound life would come crumbling down around him. If, however, Kelly and I could persuade the whistle-blower to point out to law enforcement officials what they were clearly overlooking, then perhaps the assassin's path of destruction could be stopped without yet another life needlessly being destroyed in the process.

"Look," I began, digging deep within myself for patience. "All we want is for you to get in touch with the lawyer, or whoever it is you report to, and tell them all about the name you used."

"I've already done that."

"But I need you to remind them specifically about *my* name, because it's obvious no one's remembered it."

"I made it up. I . . . pulled it out of the sky. I had no idea it belonged to you."

I found myself losing patience once again. "And I had no idea you were going to use my name to illegally smuggle alcohol out—"

"Okay. Okay. I get it, all right? I get it." He stood once more and began wringing his hands. Kelly and I remained silent, watching him pace back and forth again. I knew deep down there was a much simpler solution to my problem. I could blackmail him. I could threaten to expose him, force the man to completely start over in rebuilding his life.

But I couldn't do that. And neither could Lou. Yes, the whistle-blower had done something wrong, but he was trying to make amends. Who was I to erase what little he'd built up? And, thanks to Lou's note and foresight, I was now being given the chance to prevent that destruction from happening.

"Look," I began. "All you have to do is tell whoever's over you all about your using my name. That person can then bring that evidence forward to police on his own."

"And if that happens," Kelly continued, looking at the little man who continued to pace back and forth, "then you can keep the life you've built here."

Based upon her comment, as well as the look on her face, I could tell Kelly had figured out, just as I had, Lou's intentions for contacting the whistle-blower directly.

A few minutes later the man finally stopped pacing and sat on the edge of the recliner again. "It was such a stupid thing to do. I still don't know how in the world I thought I could get away with it." He looked into our eyes as if pleading for understanding. "They said it would be easy money, a sure thing. So I picked a few more names to use on the manifests. I thought if I used a few others, besides my own, it wouldn't draw as much attention."

He fell silent.

"What turned you?" I asked.

"Things were moving way too fast. I blew the whistle while I knew I still had something to bargain with. I was kept on as eyes and ears, but when the feds finally decided to let the hammer fall, everyone thought I'd been rounded up and sent to prison too. That's when, according to our deal, I was supposed to have disappeared."

"Look, we meant what we said," added Kelly.

"That's right," I assured him. "We just want to clear this up. I think we can do that without destroying your life here. Whoever's after me has managed to convince the police I'm a cop killer. I don't know what kind of evidence he's planted, but he's kept me from turning to the authorities for help. If you could help remind them of the phony names you used, they just might begin to entertain the idea that I'm being set up."

"But you two know who I am. I'm going to *have* to start all over."

"We don't even know your name. Look, all I'm asking you to do is make one phone call. I need you to at least open their minds to the possibility that I'm being framed as well as hunted. I'm the victim here!"

"I don't know. I—"

"Look, I've lost my job, my reputation, my life because you used my name." I pointed at Kelly. "She's lost her master's degree over this."

"But I told you. I made up that name."

"That doesn't matter now. Someone's taking advantage of that and running with it. Please. I just need you to make one phone call. I'm running out of options here. I can't keep running. I would like the chance to start over, too."

Silence hung throughout the room like cobwebs as the man—long hair, cowboy suit, overgrown mustache, sullied past—buried his head in his hands. I glanced over at Kelly, who just shrugged. Deep down I didn't want to threaten the man, but this mess didn't stop with just my life. Kelly's life had been affected and the lives of my parents and my students. I had to do whatever it took to clear my name, didn't I? I shut my eyes and silently offered a prayer for help.

"Promise me you'll never darken my door again?"

The little man's voice seemed powerfully large and it had startled me. He was staring at me, his small eyes boring into me.

"I . . . I promise."

"Then get going. I'll see what I can do."

I closed my eyes and at the same time closed my prayer.

Kelly and I stood and watched as a small smile began forming on the man's mouth, all but hidden behind his ridiculously bushy mustache.

"Thank you."

I stood and offered him my hand. He shook it without hesitation. "I may have been greedy once, but I'm no killer. I'm real sorry you got wrapped up in all this. What do they say about the tangled webs we weave?" He then began looking all about him and grinned. "It don't look like much, does it?"

I knew he was referring to the sparsely decorated house and furnishings. He spoke before I had the chance to answer him. "I made a mistake. I got in over my head. I've tried to turn it around and start over. The feds gave me a second chance. A phone call is the least I can give you. You're probably right. All that the fed I report to has to do is point out the oversight. Could save both our skins."

"Thank you. Thank you so much."

After Kelly had thanked him herself, we headed for the door and left without saying another word. All I had was the man's word. Yet, deep down, despite his past actions, I felt I could trust him.

When the door shut behind us, Kelly cleared her throat as we continued walking. "You think he'll do it."

"I don't know. I—"

We'd just walked around the front of the garage when my eyes came to rest on a man leaning against the side of a car parked behind our Saturn.

He had a grin on his face.

Lou.

CHAPTER 26

I approached Lou with some trepidation. He was dressed as he always was—worn slacks, a white shirt with the sleeves rolled to the elbows, and a rumpled, loosened tie that looked as if it hadn't been removed for days. Only when we were a few feet apart did I speak. "I don't know whether to shake your hand or punch you in the mouth."

Lou's lopsided grin was quick to appear. "I get that a lot. Personally, I'm hopin' for the handshake." He winked. "I've just started getting used to 'em."

We shook hands.

"So, that the guy?" Lou asked, his stubbled chin quickly indicating the house from which we'd come.

"The whistle-blower? It is," replied Kelly. "How on earth did you find him?"

"Hold on, Kelly," I interjected. "No offense, Lou, but first I want to know exactly what happened back at your office."

Lou again leaned against the side of the navy blue car. From the sticker on the back bumper, I knew it was a rental. I figured he must have flown in, though he still looked tired. "I told yous. We're in a sandbox with some pretty ruthless people. It's tricky business. I did what I needed ta do. I drew him out."

"And if he'd killed me, or Kelly? What then, Lou?"

"But he didn't," responded Lou sternly. "I knew ya'd get

away. That wasn't the first time me and Baker have pulled that little stunt, and I'm sure it won't be the last."

"Baker?"

"The guy who hit ya. He owns a body shop just up the road from me. Drives in a demolition derby. I'm one of his biggest sponsors."

"You'd have to be," muttered Kelly.

"Nah. He loves that kinda stuff. He woulda done it for free if I'd asked him to. Look, kids, if ya want ta know the truth, the only one that was in any real danger back there was me. If our assassin friend suddenly decided ta rub me out ta cover his trail, I wanted yous to at least have the lead I'd discovered."

I hadn't considered the matter from that angle, and it placed things in a different light. I immediately felt guilty about attacking him earlier. "So how did you find this guy?" I asked, repeating Kelly's earlier question.

Lou crossed his arms, which took some doing with his ample middle. "First things first. Is that guy in the house going ta help?"

I nodded. "He says he'll make a call for us and see what he can do."

Lou nodded. "Did he happen ta give ya the name of the person he was gonna call?"

"It sounded as if he was going to be calling the agent assigned over his protection."

Lou nodded. "Perfect. Ya know I was going to come down here and handle this myself, but that assassin of yours moved in quicker than I thought he would. I was lucky ta find time to jot down those addresses before he showed up at my office. Watched me like a hawk after that."

"All right, Lou. Now it's my turn. How did you find him?"

"Hey, I told yous from the start that ya hired the best." His grin widened. "All right. Look, the guy was using yer name on the manifests—as well as a few others—to muddy the water, right? Okay, police records show that he admitted to using phony names. And, as far as the police were concerned at the time, that was that. After the guy spilled his guts, he was later placed into protective custody for his willingness to cooperate. Ya with me so far?"

Kelly and I nodded in unison.

"Well, I called in a few favors. I've got a friend in the Bureau. He supplied me with the last three addresses they had on file connected with this guy, but only if I promised to go backdoor on all of this." His chin once more indicated the house behind us. "He couldn't guarantee they'd pan out, but it looks like they have. Of course, he'll have no recollection of our conversation, but he's a good man. I took his sister to the prom."

Kelly arched an eyebrow. "And because you took his sister to the prom, he's willing to risk his career by leaking you that kind of information?"

"Now you're putting words into my mouth, swee—Kelly. No, the sister connection might have been the motivator, but the truth is, after I explained things to him, he just didn't wanna see an innocent man killed or sent ta prison. Both of us agreed the only way we'd get anyone's attention was if we had the whistle-blower make the call himself. And if we could preserve their whistle-blower's identity in the process, even better. Right? But he also said it mighta been the only chance we'd have at catchin' our assassin. He's about as old as I am and just as sick of the bureaucracy. Besides, he only gave me the addresses—no names."

"And as long as the three of us remain quiet," finished Kelly, "the guy has a second chance on life without costing the taxpayers a thing."

Lou threw her a quick wink. "Right. Smooth, huh?"

"So, what happened to the assassin?" I queried. "Last time I saw him he was slumped over the steering wheel of his car, bleeding pretty badly."

"He was taken by ambulance ta the hospital. I hinted at how dangerous he was ta the police and staff there. He's being watched. Of course, it's not just him I'm worried 'bout.

"Come on, jump in my car and we'll beeline it to the airport. We can probably make police headquarters by noon."

"Lou, I promised the man I borrowed this car from that he'd get it back without a scratch. I can't just leave it here."

"Kid, I appreciate yer wantin' ta keep yer word. It's commendable, but we've gotta move on this. The drive would set us back eight or nine hours."

"How about a compromise?" suggested Kelly. "Why don't we park the car in the airport's long term parking lot? In a few days, when things have blown over, we can fly down and pick it up. No one's going to bother it there."

Lou grinned. "Nice. Whatta ya say, kid?"

I glanced at the Saturn. "I guess that would be all right."

Lou clapped his hands together. "Great! All right, stay behind me in yer car. Let's get movin'!"

* * *

The flight home was much less monotonous than the trip down had been. The plane was divided by a narrow center aisle. Kelly had the aisle seat, Lou the middle, and I had the window seat. Very few passengers were on the flight. The moment the plane leveled off after takeoff, Lou, in a hushed voice, explained to us what he'd managed to piece together so far.

Lou was now convinced that his earlier theory had been right. The assassin wanted to score points within the Red Mafia. By locating and eliminating the man responsible for blowing the whistle on one of the biggest scams in history, he was sure to do just that. But Lou figured he'd have a tough time locating the real whistle-blower, figuring his identity most likely had been changed and he was presumably protected by the police.

"He musta stumbled across the same manifests I found. It probably didn't take him long to figure out the names our buddy was usin' were fakes. The gold mine for him woulda been when he discovered ya shared the same name and had lived a few years in Missouri at about the same time all of this was takin' place."

"But how in the world would he have made that connection?" asked Kelly.

Lou glanced in my direction. "I take it you drove on your mission."

"I did a few times."

"Any tickets or accidents?"

"Well, there was a small fender-bender at an intersection, but I wasn't found to be the one at fault."

Lou grinned. "Doesn't matter. A basic records search woulda connected your name with that location."

"And so the once phony Jason Harrington was suddenly resurrected," concluded Kelly.

"Right. He'd pass Jason off as the whistle-blower and then take credit for rubbin' him out. He'd have to make it look legit, though. By pursuing you the way he did, he'd have the manifests and phone records to back up what he'd done. It's the kinda hit a Red Mafioso woulda been proud of."

"What do you mean?" I asked.

"Well, ya'd be set up, psychologically tortured, and then killed. Sophisticated and satisfyin'."

"I appreciate the honesty," I said dryly.

"Kid, ya gotta face facts here. He tracked ya down and figured ya'd be an easy person to erase. Yer a school teacher for cryin' out loud. Who would have figured ya'd put up this much of a fight?"

"And so my link to Missouri, with my mission, was really all he had to work with?"

"Probably. I'm sure he's fabricated one heck of a story ta go with it. It's all one strategic game ta them, kid."

"Including the killing of the four police officers?" asked Kelly, sounding a bit incredulous.

Lou nodded. "To us it all sounds like overkill, but I'm tellin' yous, that's all part of the game with these people. He built ya up a bit there in the beginnin' only ta take ya out later. If he'd managed ta pull it off, he'd be one rung higher on the ladder of success."

I suddenly remembered something Lou had mentioned earlier about the Red Mafia and chess. "I was an expendable pawn," I muttered.

"That's one way a lookin' at it."

"But what about that DNA evidence the police have?" I asked. "Have you been able to figure out just what it is they've got?"

"As a matter of fact, I have. It turns out all they've got are a few strands of hair and a couple of partial fingerprints."

My heart sank. "That's all they've got?" I asked with some sarcasm.

Kelly bit at her lower lip and canted her head to one side. "Hair is easy enough to get and plant. I can see that. But fingerprints?"

"It's not as hard ta do as ya think. If our man got hold of a glass, or television remote, he'd have more than enough prints ta work with."

"And because our state fingerprints teachers when they apply for a teaching license, it wasn't difficult at all for the police to figure out just who those prints belonged to," added Kelly.

"Exactly," confirmed Lou. "Our assassin musta known this too."

"But how are we going to get by that?" I asked.

"By usin' DNA evidence of our own, kid."

Kelly grinned and nodded her head. "The blood from the accident."

"Very good! Yer quick, Kelly. But I'm telling ya, that blood was purely a lucky break. I had no idea ya were gonna hit your head back there. Ya must have been sittin' just right."

I cleared my throat. "All right. For those of us who are mentally challenged, would either of you care to elaborate on just what it is I'm missing here?"

Lou nodded. "Both you and the assassin were wounded when my buddy Baker hit ya. Both of ya left a fair amount of blood in the same car yesterday. Hair and fingerprints are one thing, blood is somethin' else."

"So, the fact that my blood was there gives credibility to my story about being chased?"

"Exactly. It puts both you and the assassin in the same place at the same time. And then there're the guns we found on him and in a rental car he had parked near my office. Ballistics is workin' on that. I'm sure one of them will match with the slugs found in those four officers that were killed. If this plays out the way I think it will, we'll have shut down a genuine killer. Many lives will have been spared. When the dust finally settles on this one, a lotta people are goin' ta owe ya an apology, kid."

We took an opportunity to share with Lou what had happened to Kelly and me at the library and the success I'd had in eluding the assassin in the mall. When I'd finished, he was nodding his head. "Now it's making some sense."

"What are you talking about?" I asked Lou.

"Well, ya knew I was toying with the idea of drawin' him out."

Both Kelly and I nodded.

"Well, when I finally decided to put out the bait usin' the Internet, I had a response in less than twenty minutes. He wanted ta meet with me immediately."

"Is that rare?" I asked.

"Rare? It's unheard of, kid. It usually takes days, weeks before ya get a nibble. I had just got off the phone with Baker when a few minutes later, the assassin's standin' at my door. Then Kelly called. It all happened so fast."

"So how do you explain the speed with which he contacted you?" Kelly asked.

Lou was silent for some time before he finally cleared his throat and attempted an answer. "I told yous how the Red Mafia has connections in cyberspace. Well, what if this guy had associates keepin' a lookout for anyone in our area showing a sudden interest in the vodka scam. Key articles can be tagged, I'm told—hits and addresses recorded. Mebbe he coulda done it himself."

I nodded. "You're saying he was on to us that first day we were in your office, on the computer?"

"Mmm, probably. Later he coulda been casing the place and keepin' an eye out for ya."

That explained my sense of unease the evening we visited Lou just after ten o'clock. "Which is how he'd been able to follow us around after our second visit with you and then to the library."

Lou nodded. "You were lucky he wasn't desperate, kid. He was probably outside yer hotel all night."

"So why not take me out right there and get it over with?" I asked.

Lou contemplated the question for a few seconds, rubbing the side of his thick index finger over his upper lip before finally throwing out an answer. "Well, there were security cameras in the parkin' lot. More and more business owners are puttin' them in ya know, but . . . I think you have Kelly to thank for that one."

"What do you mean?" she asked.

A humorless grin played at the edges of Lou's mouth. "Just the fact Kelly was involved probably put a big wrench in his plan. If he killed you right then and there, he'd then have to deal with Kelly—who's death would open up an entirely new can o' worms. The fact he'd taken yous both from my office tells me he musta come up with somethin'. At the hotel he just wasn't ready yet. Naw, my guess is he waited until mornin' for the chance ta pull ya away from the library and Kelly, and then take ya somewhere and take care of ya discreetly—makin' it look drug related again somehow. I dunno. I told yous before, it's all a kinda big game ta them."

Kelly was nodding her head. "Presentation is everything."

Lou nodded. "And when Jason took off the way he did, our killer got fed up," finished Lou.

I ignored both of their comments. "But how had he managed to track me down to that first hotel I was shot at?"

"I dunno. He'd managed to keep up with ya somehow. These guys *are* professionals."

"Excuse me. Lou Marino?" A flight attendant with a million-dollar smile was standing in the aisle, leaning toward him.

"Yeah, sweetie. That's me."

"Sir, you have an emergency call coming in over the plane's radio."

Lou looked surprised. "For me?"

"That's right."

"But I'm not allowed into the cockpit am I? 9-11 took care of that."

"The flight attendant flashed another smile. "If you'll just follow me to the rear galley you can speak with the captain via the intercom. He can relay the conversation back and forth between you and the person on the ground."

"Not compromisin' the flight deck security. Smart."

Lou looked at each one of us in turn. His eyes settled on me. "This must be pretty serious for the boys ta be callin' me up here. I'll be right back."

Kelly stood to allow Lou the chance to squeeze himself out of the cramped airline seating. My eyes followed him as he lumbered down the aisle until he finally disappeared behind the heavy curtain covering the rear galley.

"You were very lucky, Jason, sleeping in the car the way you did back there," Kelly whispered when she'd returned to her seat. "*Someone* was watching over you."

"Yeah, I guess so," I whispered back.

A mutual silenced followed.

"I guess your intuition was right after all," I finally said, my voice no longer a whisper but taking on a more conversational tone.

"What do you mean?" she asked, her eyes staring at the back of the seat directly in front of her.

"The phonebook you opened back at the hotel. Lou's really come through for us after all."

"Hmm? Oh, yeah. He has. Just goes to show you can't judge a book by its cover."

"Yeah, I guess you're right." Kelly continued staring at the back of the seat in front of her; she looked distant.

"Hey, Kelly." She blinked a few times before finally focusing on my face. I reached out and held her hand. "When we get this straightened out, I hope you know it's your turn next."

She looked confused, but grinned ever so slightly. "What are you talking about, Jason?"

"That review committee you were telling me about. After they learn why you missed your appointment, surely they'll reschedule."

The small grin on her face quickly evaporated.

"No, Jason. I . . . I told you. They're a cold group. It's cut and dried. Either you show or you wait. There's never been an exception."

"Never?"

"Not according to the dean, the records department, and the professors in the department. I talked to them myself before heading down here."

"But surely if Lou, the police, and I walked into the office they'd—"

"Tell you to turn around and walk back out. Business is business, Jason. It's the letter of the law with them."

Before I could utter another protest I heard Lou returning. He looked angry. When he dropped into his seat, he began rubbing his eyes with the heels of his hands.

"What is it, Lou? Who was that?"

"Huh? Oh, nobody. Don't worry about it, kid."

Kelly had sat back down as well. "Lou. You said yourself it would've had to be pretty important for them to contact you up here. Who was it, Lou? What's going on?"

Lou pressed his lips together and looked hard into my eyes. "Our assassin's gone."

"What?" we both yelped.

Lou shrugged, looking at both of us in turn. "They only posted one officer in front of his door. That officer was found an hour ago with his throat slit. He'd been stuffed in a closet. But that's not all."

"What do you mean?" asked Kelly.

"A car's also been reported stolen."

"So he's loose again?" I muttered.

"That's right, kid. He's loose."

CHAPTER 27

The entire afternoon was spent at police headquarters in Denver. Both Kelly and I met with several officers and investigators. Thanks to Lou, who stuck by our side, we had someone there to guide us all the way. I must have told my story three times from beginning to end. Each time I did, I left my listeners scratching their heads. Lou later explained just what those reactions were all about. They weren't a product of my being a school teacher caught up in all of this. Nor did the reactions stem from the fact that I was involved simply because my name had been pulled from thin air. What fascinated all who would listen was the inescapable fact that I had lived to tell about it.

After recovering my mountain bike, tent, and daypack, several officers spent the afternoon verifying every move I'd claimed to have made. The more my story panned out, the more relaxed those around us became. I felt as if a tremendous weight was gradually being dismantled and lifted piece by piece from my shoulders.

Just as importantly, those I made eye contact with began to look at me as if I really was a member of the human race again. I was beginning to believe I would soon have my life back.

"Look, kid. Why don't ya call the folks. I know they'd love to hear from ya."

I smiled at Lou, appreciating his concern. "The police tell me they've already been told what's happened. With our assassin running loose, I'd just as soon lay low like Detective Lowery suggests. He says it'll only be a matter of days before they catch him. My parents will understand."

"Yeah. Sure." Lou looked skeptical, and I wasn't quite sure what he seemed to be having doubts about—my parents' reaction to all of this or the idea that the police were going to catch the assassin. "Well, yer in good hands now. Do what ya think is best, kid, and be careful."

When he stood up and offered me his hand, all I could do was grin.

"Come on, kid. Don't leave me hangin' here."

I stood and we shook hands. "I don't know how to thank you," I said.

The short, burly man laughed and gave me one of his knowing grins. "Well, I'm sure you'll find a way. Especially after ya get my bill."

I laughed, though my expression changed suddenly when I realized he hadn't let go of my hand.

"Thanks," said Lou, softly. "You reminded me of just why I went into this kind of work in the first place. It felt . . . good . . . workin' on this one."

"You're the best," I replied, touched by the genuine sincerity I saw in his eyes and felt in his grip.

When Lou finally let go of my hand, he turned slightly to face Kelly. She rose from her chair, towering a few inches above him. The sight was almost ridiculous.

"Well, little darlin', with you it has been a pleasure. I wasn't sure when we first met if we'd ever get along."

Kelly leaned down and kissed him on the cheek. I could hear her whisper a thank-you into Lou's ear. When she pulled away, the sloppy, rough-around-the-edges investigator was blushing.

We all laughed at that.

"Well, don't thank me yet," replied Lou with a grin, wiping his eyes. He threw me a quick wink and headed out the door.

"And just what does he mean by that?" asked Kelly.

"You got me," I replied, grinning.

We'd just returned to our seats when Detective Lowery, a thin, grim-faced man, returned. "All right, I think we've got what we need. I appreciate your patience with all of this. We've made arrangements with a few hotels in the area."

"Hotels?" I asked.

"It's just a precaution. For the next few days we're going to give you two a place to stay. You'll be under guard until we either catch this assassin or we're sure he's hightailed it for someplace out-of-state. Doctors tell me he'll probably be heading to a hospital first."

"What do you mean, Detective," Kelly queried.

"Well, it's just that without medical care he's going to be in a lot of pain. Plus the risk of infection is high. He had a pretty bad concussion after the crash, not to mention one beauty of a gash they had to stitch up. We've alerted all local and regional hospitals and emergency care centers to be on the lookout for him. It really shouldn't be long until we hear something."

I nodded slowly. "I see."

Detective Lowery then opened the door of his office and nodded to two plainclothes officers who entered. They must have been standing just outside his door the entire time. One reminded me of the actor Tommy Lee Jones, the other looked more like my Uncle Lee—tall, thin, and angular. "This is Officer Duncan and Officer Ricks. They'll be covering your back tonight."

I nodded—out of habit—in response to the detective's words, though I was having trouble accepting all of them. Just when I thought I was free, both of us were now headed back to an empty hotel room.

"And this is just for a few days?" I finally asked.

"Yeah. I'm telling you, the guy's going to need help. He's wounded *and* beaten. I really don't think you have anything to worry about. You should be back in the classroom by next week I would imagine."

All Kelly and I could do was thank him.

* * *

The first place we stopped, once we'd left headquarters, was a restaurant. I'd been told my bank accounts had been unfrozen, and I very much wanted to treat Kelly—for a change—to a first-class meal. The two officers assigned as our protection sat at separate tables in the restaurant, which allowed us some privacy.

Both Kelly and I were exhausted and hardly spoke to one another the entire meal. I wondered just where our relationship was headed. Deep in my heart, I didn't want us to drift apart again. I was hoping Kelly felt the same way.

Later that evening I pulled the nondescript car we'd been given into the parking lot of what I sensed would be the first in a long line of hotels. The officers assigned to us hung back and parked across the street. They'd given us our hotel keys after dinner and must have felt they were parked at the perfect vantage point.

It had been a clear night when I'd stepped out of the car with Kelly earlier that evening, but it smelled like rain was on its way again.

At least I'll be in a warm hotel room, I thought to myself. *Dry and with a bed to sleep in.* I involuntarily shivered at the thought of struggling for warmth on a distant hillside in Golden. No, I wasn't about to complain.

We'd been given separate but adjoining rooms on the second floor of an older, out-of-the-way hotel. The hotel's front door was the only way into each room. I leaned against the wrought iron railing that ran along the edge of the second level. I was still holding Kelly's hand.

"I wish this was your actual front door, Kelly."

"I know. But, hey, once again you've shown me a very . . . interesting time."

I appreciated her good-natured attitude with all of this, but I could see that she, like me, wanted it all to end.

"Well, I hope I can soon take you on a really boring date."

Kelly smiled and stepped in close. "I'd love that. Good night, Jason."

We kissed each other good night.

When Kelly closed the door to her room, an odd uneasiness crept over me. But when I glanced once more over my shoulder and saw the car with the two officers in the distance, I immediately chalked it up to fatigue. *They'll watch over us,* I thought. And for the first time in a long time I had every intention of getting a fantastic night's rest. I hoped Kelly would do the same.

After shutting the door, I stood there a moment, grateful for the clean, warm room. I walked over to the side of the bed and sat down. It was quiet—too quiet. And then it dawned on me that for the past week I'd been sharing almost all of my waking time with Kelly. And, despite the fact we had spent our nights apart, I was already missing her voice and company—now more than ever. I glanced at the door that joined our two rooms and wondered if she was feeling the same way.

I slipped out of my shoes, stood, and pattered to the bathroom. After washing my face several times, I finally looked at my reflection in the mirror. Suddenly I wanted a razor. I don't know how effective a disguise my beard had been, but I was ready to get rid of it. When I slept, I sometimes felt like I had a wool sock pasted to each side of my face. I knew several guys with beards and couldn't help wondering how they could stand it.

I pulled a towel from the rack above the toilet and was in the process of drying off my face when I heard a gentle knock coming from the adjoining room. My grin was not only wide but also instantaneous. My guess was that she, like me, missed being together and wanted to say good night one more time.

I tossed the towel aside and walked to the door. Two individual deadbolt locks gave each occupant control of the door. The gentle knock came again. "Yes?" I called out.

"Can we talk?"

I unbolted the door and heard Kelly doing the same on her side. I opened it. Sure enough, it was Kelly.

But a leather-clad arm had seized her neck, and the muzzle of an automatic pistol almost seemed to be attached to the side of her head.

CHAPTER 28

The man standing behind Kelly had clearly met up with hard times. He still wore the black leather jacket, though his fine silk shirt and slacks were rumpled and stained. Sweat streamed from his bald head, the large blood-stained bandage on his forehead barely clinging to his skin. His eyes held the viciousness of an attack dog, his mouth the ugly sneer.

"Try anything, *Musor,* and she dies."

A hundred questions flitted through my mind. How did he know we were here? How had he slipped by the two officers below, and where were they? Did they know what was happening? Had he killed them first? Were there more with him?"

"Back up, *Musor.*" He dug the end of the pistol into the side of Kelly's head. She cried out, but only for a second.

I backed up toward the bed, nearly falling over it when my legs banged against it. He kicked the door shut and, keeping Kelly's neck in the crook of his arm, forced her to secure it. When he kept advancing, I moved around the bed and stopped only when he stopped. We were now well into the room.

"Look, we both know I'm not the person you say I am. Why don't—"

"Shut up, *Musor!* You are who I say you are." His eyes looked droopy, and I was convinced he was on the verge of collapse.

"Fine. But she has nothing to do . . ."

My voice trailed off when I noticed him canting his head to one side and smelling Kelly's hair. "Maybe not, but I know many that wouldn't mind involving her in something. Know what I mean?"

My eyes went from the gun to Kelly's panic-stricken face and then back again. My blood began to boil at his taunt, and I mentally struggled for a way to overpower him. "She's got nothing to do with—"

"I say she does!" he yelled, cutting me off.

The room was silent for several seconds while both of us stood there eyeing each other. Kelly's eyes were now closed as she struggled for air, her lips moving ever so slightly in what I knew had to be a prayer.

"I give you my word that I'll go with you. Just . . . just let her go."

Kelly's eyes opened wide.

The assassin's unexpected reaction surprised me. He started to laugh. It was low and guttural and seemed to emerge from deep within his gut, crawling—slithering—slowly out of his mouth.

"I said I'll go with you." I made sure to enunciate each word clearly. "Now let her go."

"No, *Musor*. I make that mistake before. Not this time. I will not take you with me." He pulled the gun from Kelly's temple and pointed it directly at me. "You will die . . . here."

I could see his trigger finger begin to contract and I knew it was over.

With my eyes wide open, I waited, statuelike, for him to pull the trigger. My only consolation was that I'd die quickly.

"No!" Kelly screamed as she grabbed the man's arm, swinging it away from me. He fired and the shot took out a small lamp on the nightstand next to the bed.

I suddenly found myself lunging, almost out of instinct, for his arm, grabbing the gun with both hands before he had a chance to use it on Kelly.

Kelly had broken free from the man's grip and run for the door. I heard her fling it open.

My focus, however, was not on Kelly, but on my two hands that were grasping the demon's gun hand. Using his other hand, he began to claw at my face.

I backed him up against a long, low six-drawer dresser, which threw him off balance. Putting most of my weight on top of him, I pinned him to the wall. With my eyes squeezed shut in a feeble attempt to protect them from his clawing hand, I began pounding his gun hand against the wall behind him. The third hit broke through the drywall, but I kept slamming his hand against the hole I'd just made.

Suddenly, I felt something crack within my hands. The adrenaline rush I was experiencing confused my thinking. At first I thought the cracking had been made from the firearm itself. When the assassin's grip slackened and the gun fell through the hole in the drywall, I knew I'd broken his hand.

Instead of backing down from the agony I knew he was experiencing, this latest injury seemed only to enrage him even more. More animal than human, he lunged forward, pushing himself off the dresser with his elbows, unexpectedly battering my gut and sending me flying.

I clipped the edge of the bed before finally slamming flat on my back on the floor.

He landed on top of me, his hands now going for my throat.

My own hands flew to his face. My first punch caught him on the jaw, having as much effect as a baby caressing a balloon. His head shifted with my second swing, and, rather than connecting with his jaw, my fist gouged the blood-soaked bandage on his forehead instead. The gauze fell from his head, and his hand let go of my neck and flew upward.

Inadvertently, but propitiously for me, I'd reopened the large gash on his forehead. Torn and pulled stitches disappeared instantly in a deluge of blood that streamed into his right eye. I rolled and slipped out from beneath him. I saw that the room's door had closed on its own, and I struggled to get back on my feet, catching a glimpse of the assassin in the process. His mouth was again twisted into a mad-dog snarl, and his left eye was also blood-covered. He lunged again, but by this time I'd opened the door and there was nothing behind me.

As he rammed into me, we flew through the open doorway. I nearly blacked out when my back slammed into the old wrought iron railing just beyond the door. My legs were spaghetti-limp, and in that brief, horrifying moment I realized we had not only bent the railing but were now tumbling over the top of it!

I felt completely weightless as both our bodies tumbled helplessly through the air. I couldn't tell if I was falling up or down.

We landed with a sickening thud, not unlike the sound of a gunny sack full of large fruits.

Slowly, I opened my eyes. We'd fallen from the second level. Miraculously, when we'd plunged over the railing, I'd landed on top of the assassin. His eyes stared blankly into the night sky. I carefully rolled myself off his broken body. My shoulder and right knee sent horrendous shock waves of pain through my body.

I could hear running footfalls coming from somewhere, and then felt a pair of hands caressing either side of my face. I tried to swat the hands away, convinced the assassin had somehow managed a final attack. But a calming, familiar, soothing voice followed their second touch.

"Lie still, Jason. Just lie still."

It was Kelly! But from the tears in her eyes and the look on her face, I figured I was in pretty bad shape.

I could see the pant legs of others brush by me—some in jeans, others in uniform. I assumed they were police officers, though my eyes weren't focusing on anything for very long.

"Don't move, Jason!" someone shouted again. It was a deep voice that I was sure belonged to Officer Duncan. *Or was it Ricks?* I wondered futilely.

But it wasn't his curt command that kept me lying motionless on the ground. It was the feel of those two soft hands on either side of my face.

I closed my eyes, taking comfort in what their touch meant. Kelly was alive and safe.

Then I lost consciousness.

CHAPTER 29

I suppose I'll never forget the last image I had of the assassin. I regained consciousness just before being loaded into an ambulance. Amid a sea of individuals in varying types of emergency uniforms, and under a dizzying array of flashing lights, I caught a glimpse of his still body. He lay several feet away, exactly where we had landed. A white sheet of some kind covered his crushed form, and I thought I saw a small trail of blood slithering along the blacktop, dripping into a storm drain only a few feet away. Despite this evidence of his death, I expected at any moment to see him rise. To look at me. To draw a gun of some kind and take me out once and for all. But of course that was impossible now. He was dead. And even though the sheet covered his face, I suppose I will forever see his sightless eyes staring up at me after I'd landed on top of him.

But I had beaten him.

The amateur school teacher had succeeded in quite literally *crushing* the mafia grandmaster.

I was treated and released from St. Luke's Medical Center, Kelly at my side the entire time. I'd suffered only a sprained knee and shoulder, plus multiple bruises to my legs, arms, and right hand. I was thankful just to be alive. With the assassin dead, my parents and siblings wasted little time getting to me at the hospital. It was a tearful reunion with my father's pride kicked clear into overdrive. He insisted on holding a press conference then and there so that he could "rub the media's nose" in what Kelly and I had just been through. It took all of us to calm him down.

I was just grateful to see both of my parents so happy again.

Kelly and I were then escorted back to police headquarters where we once again bumped into Lou. He had heard about my accident over his police scanner at home and wanted to see how we were doing with his own eyes. Before he left, I pulled him aside and asked him if I should still consider my life in danger. Would the Red Mafia seek retribution for the assassin's death? His answer surprised me.

"Naw. This has gotten too much attention as it is. And tomarra, when the press gets holda this, forget about it. The way I see it, Jason, they had a power-hungry soldier on their hands that went rogue. Higher-ups'll want all of this to blow over, believe me. They know the importance of blendin' in, especially when so many in this country don't want to admit there's a problem with the Red Mafia in the first place. I'll tell ya one thing, though," he said, his voice dropping to a whisper, "the police are gonna have their hands full tryin' to figure out who leaked the information concernin' yer hotel rooms. I'm telling ya, these mobsters have infiltrated everythin'. This might just be the sort of wake-up call this country needs."

* * *

A week after my spill over the hotel railing, Kelly and I flew back to New Mexico to retrieve Mr. Shepard's Saturn. On the drive home we talked for some time about all we'd been through and what a good team we'd made when things got rough.

"Yes, sir. I'll tell you, we were a regular Bonnie and Clyde."

Kelly laughed and reached over to adjust the air conditioner. "They were bad guys, Jason."

I reached down along the side of my bucket seat and adjusted it to a more upright position. "Okay. How about Batman and Robin?"

Kelly looked at me, raising a single eyebrow.

"All right. How about Bogart and Bacall?"

"Jason, I think you should—"

"Burns and Allen?" I interrupted.

This stopped her.

"Who?" she asked.

I laughed, which only got Kelly laughing.

When we'd settled down, Kelly reached over and took hold of my hand. "How about Jason and Kelly?"

I placed my other hand on top of hers and grinned. "That has a certain ring to it."

I glanced out the Saturn's windshield noting the long, seemingly endless highway in front of us. The view was just as empty and barren as I remembered from the first time we'd passed through. But this time we were safe and free to enjoy one another's company without any fear of being pulled over by police or hunted down by a rogue assassin.

My eye suddenly fixed itself on a mile marker that was coming up. I suppose in hindsight I should have had Kelly pull over—or at least waited until I could take her someplace special. But after what we had been through together, a borrowed car in the middle of nowhere felt just right.

Mile marker 224 flashed past.

"Kelly?"

"Yes."

"Will you marry me?"

Startled, Kelly inadvertently turned the steering wheel to the left, but quickly righted it when she realized what she'd done. She then checked her rearview mirror and signaled as she pulled the car over. When the car had come to a complete stop, she threw it into park.

"Jason L. Harrington, do you know how dangerous that was? You could have killed us both with that little stunt!"

I couldn't help but smile. "I would have thought you were used to that kind of danger by now."

Kelly shook her head and broke into a smile.

Just then a semi passed, our small car jolting as it flew on by.

"We're probably safer on the road than off it," I teased. "Perhaps you'd better answer quickly so we can get back on the highway."

Kelly leaned over and our lips met. It wasn't until another semi had passed us that she finally pulled back.

I looked into her eyes, so grateful to have found her once again. "Is that a yes?"

A mischievous glint flashed in Kelly's eyes and she sat back and made a show of adjusting the rearview mirror.

"Is that a yes?" I asked again, throwing her a sidelong glance in the process.

She put the car back into gear and signaled, calmly looking over her left shoulder to make sure it was clear before finally pulling back onto the highway.

"Kelly?"

She looked down at the speedometer and waited with her finger resting over the cruise-control button on the steering wheel. It wasn't until she'd pushed it that she sat back and finally looked over at me. "I'll let you know when we reach the next gas station."

I looked out the windshield and couldn't see even a tree for as far as the eye could see. "You've got to be kidding."

It was then we both burst into laughter.

* * *

In two months, three days, and four and a half hours, I will no longer be coming home to an empty apartment.

Perhaps the greatest surprise to come out of all of this was a letter Kelly received from the university that offered her the opportunity to make up the appointment she'd missed. Both of us found their change of heart incredible—too incredible. Though Lou denied it, I knew he had something to do with it. I cringed to think of what dirt he'd have to have dug up on the committee members to use as leverage, but I loved the idea that the letter of the law might have been used against them for a change.

Her appointment is in a week and I know she'll do an outstanding job. The university could use more people like Kelly. Heart counts for something. More people need to learn that.

As for myself, I'm headed back to work the day after tomorrow. It feels good having my life back, and I know I'll never look at a stack of ungraded essays the same way again.

I've also purchased a new 72-hour kit. It's a deluxe model.

Of course, I still find myself waking up at night, disturbed by all I've been through. What makes it bearable, though, is Lou's take on the whole thing. The way he sees it, Kelly and I are responsible for the death of a vicious and dangerous man. The tattoos law enforcement authorities discovered on the assassin's body revealed a man anxious to climb the ladder of success within a corrupt organization and willing to do so at any cost. He was a ruthless killer and, if left alone, he would have killed again.

Kelly brought up Chaos Theory once again. Specifically, she wondered if everything we'd been through, the chaos we'd both experienced firsthand, was all a great design to help us get back together—to find each other once again. For a time our lives seemed to have completely fallen apart, indeed plunged into chaos. And yet everything has worked out somehow as if we were in fact doing what we'd been expected to do. I suppose Kelly summed it up best last night at dinner.

"Order or chaos," she said. "It's all the same when you trust in the Lord."

And you know something?

She's absolutely right.

About the Author

Jeff graduated from Utah State University with a degree in elementary education and has been involved in a variety of teaching and mentoring experiences. Currently he teaches junior high in Terreton, Idaho. He is an avid reader who enjoys learning from books, as well as from people. Jeff and his wife Kara are the parents of four children and live in Rexburg, Idaho.

Jeff believes literature should enlighten and edify. As Jeff puts it: "A biographer commented on one of my favorite authors. He said of the man, 'He knew obscenity for the comparative triviality which it is, and his work was always free from the defect which reduces so much of modern fiction to a diseased sterility. He was neither under the necessity of asserting, nor the folly of supposing, that the lowest gutter gives the broadest view.' I strongly believe this to be true, and I'm grateful for those publishers out there striving to produce uplifting and inspiring material."

If you would like to be updated on Jeff's newest releases or to correspond with him, please send an email to info@covenant-lds.com. You may also write to him in care of Covenant Communications, P.O. Box 416, American Fork, UT 84003-0416.